T0385289

Show Me Where It Hurts

Claire Gleeson is from Dublin, where she lives with her young family and works as a GP. Her short stories have been short- and long-listed for numerous prizes. In 2021 she was awarded a Words Ireland literary mentorship while she worked on the first draft of *Show Me Where It Hurts*, which went on to be a runner-up at the Irish Writers' Centre Novel Fair 2023.

Show Me Where It Hurts

Claire Gleeson

Sceptre

First published in Great Britain in 2025 by Sceptre
An imprint of Hodder & Stoughton Limited
An Hachette UK company

1

The authorised representative in the EEA is Hachette Ireland, 8 Castlecourt
Centre, Dublin 15, D15 XTP3, Ireland (email: info@hbgi.ie)

Copyright © Claire Gleeson 2025

The right of Claire Gleeson to be identified as the Author of the Work has been
asserted by her in accordance with the Copyright, Designs and Patents Act 1988.

All rights reserved. No part of this publication may be reproduced, stored in a
retrieval system, or transmitted, in any form or by any means without the prior
written permission of the publisher, nor be otherwise circulated in any form
of binding or cover other than that in which it is published and without
a similar condition being imposed on the subsequent purchaser.

All characters in this publication are fictitious and any resemblance to real persons,
living or dead, is purely coincidental.

A CIP catalogue record for this title is available from the British Library

Hardback ISBN 9781399734721
Trade Paperback ISBN 9781399734738
ebook ISBN 9781399734752

Typeset in Sabon MT by Manipal Technologies Limited

Printed and bound in Great Britain by Clays Ltd, Elcograf S.p.A.

Hodder & Stoughton policy is to use papers that are natural, renewable
and recyclable products and made from wood grown in sustainable forests.
The logging and manufacturing processes are expected to conform
to the environmental regulations of the country of origin.

Hodder & Stoughton Limited
Carmelite House
50 Victoria Embankment
London EC4Y 0DZ

www.sceptrebooks.co.uk

For my parents

Something Wild and Terrible

'Are they asleep?'

His voice is a jolt in the car. Rachel realises that she has been dozing, her brain depleted by the afternoon with Tom's parents; the languor brought on by food that is too heavy, and conversation that is almost painfully light.

She turns her head to peer into the darkness of the back seat. Yes, they are asleep, both of them in synchronicity for once; their heads tilted towards each other, one blond and glossy, the other dark and coarse, unruly like her own. She doesn't know where the flaxen hair of their eldest came from, for Tom too is dark, his hair a deep, autumnal brown. Though indeed her mother has often told her that she herself was fair as a baby. It is just short of an hour, this drive back from his parents' place up in the Wicklow mountains, but they are worn out by the afternoon of unceasing attention and the rafts of sugar, and Rachel wonders if there is any chance of being able to lift them straight from the car to their beds and avoiding for once the night-time story, the endless questions.

'Your dad looks better.' She turns back around in her seat. She has said it to reassure, and it is true that Joe had seemed a little brighter, his colour normal again for the first time since the pneumonia at Christmas. But there is a new frailness there, too, that Rachel thinks will probably never leave him.

Tom shrugs, but does not answer. His father's illness had shaken him badly; he had been convinced that Joe would die, that the panicked ambulance ride on Christmas Eve would turn out to be his final journey. Tom had spent most of the day sitting in A&E with his mother, while Rachel peeled spuds at home and boiled the ham and tried to keep the children going with Christmas films and carefully rationed chocolate coins. It had been exhausting.

She gazes out the window. They are already past the last of the three little villages that mark the route from his parents' home, and into the quiet stretch of country road before they hit the motorway. To the left, the ground drops away sharply, down to a deep ravine filled with trees; to the right, somewhere in the distance, is the sea. It is nearly dark now, the twilight that had surrounded them as they said goodbye in the garden of the bungalow sinking rapidly into night.

'They're definitely asleep?'

She glances at him, wondering; checks the back seat again. 'Yes. I told you. They're conked out.'

There is a pause then, a gap; six seconds, maybe seven. An eternity.

'I'm sorry.' And now his voice is not the same, it is something wild and terrible, and she whips her head around to look at him in alarm, but already he has pressed his foot to the floor and the car is speeding up. Up, up, up it goes to a stupid speed for this narrow road, and now he is wrenching the wheel and the car is flying – it is so quick, the whole thing – and all at once the sound of the car changes and the road under them is suddenly gone, the car riding on air now, but the air is nothing, it is the absence of everything, and the only way is down, down to where the earth is dark and silent and ready to embrace them all.

And then there is only black.

AFTER

Three Weeks

You Could Be Anyone

There are spaces everywhere. By the door, where their coats used to hang; on the shoe rack under the shadow of the stairs. When the newspapers were pushing for a picture, somebody – Rachel does not know who, her sister perhaps – must have taken down the smaller canvas from the set in the living room, because where it used to hang there is only space now, and a darker square of the greenish paint, unbleached by the sun.

Their bedrooms are untouched. Nobody has dared to enter there, to pick their way through the litter of Lego bricks and dolls' clothing to open the curtains. Even when her mother comes, daily still, to make soup that will go uneaten, to stand fretfully in the kitchen, wringing the tea towel between her hands – even she has not dared to touch the bedrooms. Rachel is the only one who goes in there. In her daughter's room she stands in the centre of the rug and gazes first at the bed with its pile of soft toys, then at the line of little dresses hanging in the wardrobe. She checks to see that her smell is still there.

She has taken to sleeping in her son's bed. It is too small, of course; it is only a toddler bed, the largest the boxroom could hold. They had talked about converting the attic someday, about getting a third proper bedroom and another bathroom perhaps; somewhere there are pencil sketches with angles and dimensions written in Tom's careful hand. Rachel doesn't remember their son ever sleeping a full night in this bed; invariably he would arrive in their room at three, four o'clock in the morning, and clamber into the bed beside her. Often Rachel would not even rouse but would find him there when she woke the next morning, his stubby legs flung across hers, her arm dead from the weight of him. But still the pillow on this too-small bed smells of him, and now she will never wash it.

Not that she really sleeps anyway, and never at night. She goes through the motions – switching off the lights downstairs, exchanging her clothes for pyjamas, brushing her teeth while she stares into the bathroom mirror as if at a stranger. But sleep refuses to come, no matter how long she lies curled up in the little bed, and eventually she gets up again and wanders ghost-like through the empty rooms of the house. Her tour is marked by pilot lights – the red dot of the television on standby, the green of the wireless router, the orange glow from the socket where the fridge plugs in. The light for the alarm system, which she rarely bothers to set any more, there being nothing left to protect – this light too winks at her as she prowls the house. When she gets cold enough she huddles into a corner of the couch, drawing a blanket over her, and waits for the first light to streak the sky; sometimes she will wake with a start and realise that she has been dozing, finally, her mouth furry with sleep. And then it is morning, and it all starts all over again, and oh God, this is torture, she cannot endure it.

~

Her mother comes every day. Rachel resents the intrusion, and sighs with frustration when she hears the click of the garden gate and her mother's slow footsteps on the gravel path; and yet if she is late, ever, if she has not arrived by the time Rachel has dressed and poured her second cup of coffee, she finds herself reaching for her phone to call her and ask querulously the reason for the delay.

Her father will not cross the threshold. Even when they brought her home that first day, the day after the funeral – her mother in tears that Rachel was coming back here at all, that she would not stay with them permanently, move back into her childhood bedroom and let them all pretend that none of this had happened – even then her father had stopped short at the end of the path, and shaken his head silently, and turned around to go back to the car. He cannot bear to see the places where the children used to be. Rachel knows this, and this too she resents, because she herself cannot bear it either, and yet she must.

Her mother has her own key, but she always rings the doorbell and waits to be let in. She hands Rachel a stack of envelopes.

'I met your postman outside, he gave me these.'

Rachel tosses the pile onto the hall stand without looking at it. 'He shouldn't really do that. You could be anyone.' And the pleasure she takes in the wounded look on her mother's face is cruel, and cruelty is not like her, and yet she cannot help herself.

'Well. Anyway.' Her mother takes off her coat, and hangs it carefully on the rack, and glances into the hall mirror. She is a good-looking woman – 'for my age', she will caveat, whenever anyone offers this compliment, and Rachel always wants to shake her. She lifts a hand now, smoothing a strand of hair back from her forehead, and then seems to remember herself, and drops her hand quickly as if she has been caught at something frivolous. Rachel turns away and wanders back into the living room. Her mother doesn't follow; instead she goes to the kitchen and begins to wash dishes, although precious few have collected since she washed them the day before. But it is part of the ritual, the one they have established between them over the last few weeks. Soon she will flick the switch on the kettle, and make some toast, and Rachel will come into the kitchen and sit on one of the high stools and accept a single slice, cut into four as if for a child. There will be an attempt at conversation.

'It's getting milder out.'

'I still think it's freezing.' Rachel grips the mug with both hands, as if to prove her point. 'I can't get warm at all.'

'You should try and open the windows every day, though. Just for a few minutes, even.' Her mother has always been a great believer in the healing qualities of fresh air.

'Yeah, OK.' She tries not to sigh. She is reminded of her own teenage years, even the mildest parental interaction somehow an intolerable imposition.

'Has Bernie been on to you?' Margaret's tone is casual, practised even, but there is a slight hitch in her breath before she speaks.

'She phones, most days. I don't answer.'

Rachel says this with a challenge in her voice, and barely waits for her mother's silence in response.

'What? You think I should be making her feel better?'

'No. Of course not. Just – well, it's very hard for her too.'

'I'm aware of that, thank you.'

Her mother's eyes fill with tears; nothing she says will ever be right.

~

After lunch – she does not eat any lunch, but she sits and sips tea at the kitchen table while her mother eats a sandwich in small, tidy bites – Rachel goes to lie down for an hour. She can tolerate her own bedroom by day, just about; the ghosts are fewer then. She pulls back the duvet and lies down. She has not changed the bedding since, and it smells musty and unwashed; yet there is some reluctance in her to strip the sheet, to wrestle the pillows from the cases with their faint stains of saliva.

She cannot lie on her left side; it is still red and tender to the touch, the skin only starting now to grow back where it was scraped away by the broken window. So she must face the other way, and stare at the empty space where her husband used to sleep. She fancies she can see some sign of him, a dent in the mattress where he used to lie; but when she stretches out her hand and runs it over the spot, it does not feel in any way remarkable. She dozes like that, her hand adrift in Tom's empty space.

~

From downstairs, her mother's voice comes low and fretful.

'She's asleep now, I think. No, barely anything. She's looking very thin.'

A pause, and then her voice is higher, defensive.

'Well, I know that, but what can I do?'

Rachel stands just out of sight at the top of the stairs; a child again, eavesdropping on adult things.

'No. No, I know. We just have to give it time, Frank. All right. All right.'

There is no goodbye, just a soft sigh as her mother closes the cover on her phone again, and Rachel steps back into the shadows.

~

Margaret leaves at five, having offered to spend the night and been refused, but Rachel hugs her for a long time before she leaves, and when she has shut the door behind her she stands in

7

the hall for another long time, listening to the new silence of the house and wondering why it is so cold, even with the heating on. She goes to the kitchen and stares at the meal her mother has left her, and then she opens the fridge and takes out a piece of cheese and returns to the living room. The blinds are already closed, and now she pulls the curtains across and curls herself into the corner of the couch. The night ahead of her seems very long, and yet she cannot endure company; even the few hours with her mother seem to have sucked any remaining energy out of her.

She stares at the bookcase opposite, the untidy pile of cards stacked on one of its higher shelves. There have been so many cards, both the ones pushed into her reluctant hands at the funeral, and the trickle of them dropping through the letter-box each day since. She hasn't known what to do with them; it seems odd, not to arrange them on the mantelpiece in a decorative flourish as she has done with all the other cards that have arrived at the house over the years, the ones featuring baby feet and birthday balloons and snowy landscapes. But these ones, surely, are not for display. She hasn't even read most of them properly, her swollen eyes refusing to land on names that should be familiar but somehow are not.

There is a step on the path outside. Rachel waits, hoping it is some leaflet-dropper ignoring the *No Junk Mail* sign, as they always seem to do. But then the doorbell rings, and her heart seems to thunder in her chest, and she sinks further into the couch and pulls a blanket over herself as if she can somehow become invisible. The bell rings again, and then a thin, reedy voice is saying her name.

'Rachel? It's only me, love, it's Bernie. Can I come in?'

The sickness crashes over her, and she is afraid for a moment that she will vomit there where she sits. She breathes deeply, through her nose, and waits for the feeling to subside. Outside,

8

she hears her mother-in-law's feet on the gravel, and then there is a rap on the window, only feet from where she sits on the couch, and she has to stifle a scream. She is afraid even to breathe now, for fear that she will be heard. She waits, and waits, and finally she hears the heavy steps going back down the path, and only then does Rachel sit up, and push the curtain aside, and slip her hand between two of the wooden blinds so she can peer out into the dusk. Her mother-in-law is sitting back into the driver's seat of her car; she closes the door, catching the end of her long coat in it, and has to open it again. She sits for a long minute, looking down into her lap, and then she gives one final glance towards the house, and drives away.

BEFORE

Ten Years

All Things Soft

'My friend here thinks you're stunning.' He is short and compact, this guy, with reddish hair and a port-wine stain on one
cheek, and as he leans in to Rachel's ear she can feel the heat of
the nightclub coming off him. The friend, around whose neck
his arm is thrown, is taller and dark-haired, and is blushing.

Rachel takes another sip of her drink, bouncing on her toes. She
wonders if he is a Garda, or a teacher, the usual Saturday-night
clientele of this place; he doesn't look like another nurse, and there
are so few male ones that she tends to know them all anyway.

'Now, I'm going to leave ye to it. You're welcome, buddy.'
The red-haired guy slaps the taller one on the back and disappears into the crowd again. Rachel can see that the back of his
shirt is damp with sweat.

'Sorry about him.' He has to stoop to get close enough to her
ear to be heard. There is something old-fashioned – gentlemanly,
even – about the motion, and Rachel is immediately interested.

'No problem.' She stirs the remaining pieces of ice with her
straw, watching their rapid melt into the faint pink dregs of her
cocktail.

'I do think you're stunning, to be fair. Can I get you another
drink?'

They talk all night, going outside the club to the smoking bit
behind, where at least you can chat without having to repeat

every other word. It is a wet night and there aren't many smokers out, but they lean in under the galvanised sheet that is serving as a roof of sorts, and as it gets colder he takes off his jacket and drapes it over her shoulders. The smell coming off it is the smell of him – sweat, and beer, and something else deep and earthy.

He is not a nurse, and not a teacher or a Garda either; instead he is an architect, just finished his postgraduate exams and working at a big commercial firm in town. But his long-term plan is to open his own business with a friend, a guy named Gavin from his course who is working in London now but has grand designs of his own, and the money to put behind them.

'Johnny's a teacher, though.' He nods back towards the club, dark and heaving.

'Your friend with the—?' She lifts her hand to brush her cheek, and then drops it, mortified.

But he is laughing.

'Yeah. We were at school together. He drags me here sometimes.'

'Well. I'm glad he did.' And then they are kissing in the drizzle and the pall of other people's smoke, and she knows at once that this is different from anything that has gone before.

~

He surprises her constantly; the fact that he surprises her is in itself unexpected, because at twenty-two she has by now had a succession of boyfriends who all seemed cut from the same mass-produced, slightly shiny cloth. An initial deluge of charm, mainly in the form of liberal quantities of drink being pressed on her as they huddled in corners of the same half-dozen bars and clubs around Stephen's Green. A period then of relative tranquillity, her predominant emotion, were she to admit it to herself, more satisfaction with the idea of being in a relationship than excitement about the reality of it. And then the inevitable slow waning of manners, of effort, on both their parts. She could not, with any truthfulness, say that she had ever lost her heart.

Tom is different.

Their first date together – the club didn't count, not officially, although he had walked her to the taxi rank and stood there with his hands in his pockets and that great slow smile on his face as she was carried away – she meets him in the Phoenix Park, at the bottom of the Pope's Cross. It is ten in the morning, a warm day in June, and that smell is in the air for the first time this year – the fresh, grassy smell of summer in Dublin. He is waiting there when she arrives, and he gives a funny little half-bow, and laughs at himself as he does. She laughs too, it is impossible not to; the frankness of his eyes, their blue endless depths.

Together they walk the Fifteen Acres, and back around by the Ambassador's Residence and past the cricket grounds. They walk for miles. At the Magazine Fort they stop and Tom produces from his backpack two bottles of beer, and half-baguettes wrapped up in foil, and crisps. They sit with their backs to the rough stone of the wall.

'Did you come here a lot as a kid? It feels like we're recreating some childhood odyssey.' The crisps are sticking between her teeth, but she resists the urge to poke them out with a finger; *not yet, not yet.*

He snorts. 'No. I grew up in the country, in Wicklow. But long walks up the mountain in the rain, yeah – lots of those in my early days.'

'That sounds nice. Very wholesome, John-Boy.' She sips her beer. She doesn't like beer, not really, but she likes the image of herself she can picture, with the bottle to her lips; a cool girl. 'Do you have a big family?'

'No, there was only me. And my parents, obviously. But no siblings or anything.'

'I've a sister, just.'

He plays with her fingers, studiedly casual. 'What's she like? Is she older or younger than you?'

'She's younger, only by a year or so.' Rachel can feel the callus at the base of his ring finger, and the sharp scratch of a nail that has been torn roughly off. 'She's grand, most of the time. She's much prettier than me, I'd better put that out there from the start. In case you want me to introduce you, like.'

He pauses before he answers, and she can feel the smile in his voice when he does. 'I'm all right, actually.'

Rachel leans into him, lets her head rest on his shoulder. She feels him still, and then exhale deeply, and the press of his nose against her hair. She has kicked off her runners, and she sees now there is a hole in the toe of her sock. Through it one toenail is visible, pink and badly chipped.

'So where do you live now? You don't come in from Wicklow?'

'God, no. No, I moved up for college, I never went back. I've a flat with Johnny in Ranelagh.'

'Is it very fancy? What with you being an architect and all.'

He laughs; she loves the throaty bubble of his laugh, and the fact that she is able to draw it from him.

'It's about as fancy as you'd imagine a two-bedroom hovel with two blokes in it would be. But we got the literal mould in the bathroom sorted last year, so that's something. What about you? You're in Phibsboro.'

'Yeah. With my friend Helen, we were at school together.'

'Is she a nurse as well?'

'No. No, she did a business degree. She works for – God, I can never remember the name of them. It's some crowd off

13

Marlboro Street, they do IT stuff for the banks. I don't really understand what Helen does there, exactly, but she definitely makes more than I do.'

'But you have that spiritual reward of knowing you're saving lives every day. That's priceless, that is.'

'My landlord doesn't accept spiritual reward for the rent, unfortunately. I did ask.'

That is when he kisses her, turning her face up to his with a jerk that is almost rough in its suddenness, but when his lips meet hers they are not rough at all, they are green moss, butter, and light, and all things soft. Her fingers find the back of his head and she pulls him to her. They kiss in the long grass for what feels like hours, and when he pulls back finally his face is flushed and the look in his eyes makes her feel more powerful than she has ever felt before.

～

Other surprises – he speaks fairly fluent Spanish, the result of an Erasmus year spent wandering among Barcelona's turrets and spires at the International University of Catalonia. He has never drunk red wine. When he was seven he inadvertently saw the first half of a seventies horror film after his father fell asleep in front of the TV, and it scared him so much that he refused to watch television – any television – for more than six months. This last one Rachel finds the hardest to believe; she herself feels she was partially raised by children's TV, a sort of easy-going third parent in the corner of the living room. Although when she has children herself she will be rather strict about it, she thinks now.

～

Unwise, she confides in her mother long before she should, and then there is no going back; each subsequent conversation is brimful of pointed questions, knowing looks and what Rachel supposes is meant to be the mildest sort of innuendo. She is dying to meet him, of course, Margaret, but this Rachel resists as long as possible. But she does relent and show her a photograph, on the little digital camera that had been her Christmas present; Tom, tall and dark and silly-faced, standing ramrod straight amongst the sand dunes at Dollymount. His hair is lifted by the breeze.

'Oh now.' Margaret puts on her glasses to peer at the little screen. 'He's very good-looking, isn't he, Rachel?' The surprise in her voice could almost be taken as an insult, if you were looking for it.

'He's all right, I suppose.'

'Oh, he's lovely.' She is purring like a cat. Rachel cannot help but feel a little smug.

The glasses come off again, and Margaret looks at her daughter.

'Is he the one, do you think?'

'Jesus, Mam. Would you stop?' She hears her father's step on the stairs and takes the camera back quickly, unable for any more of this.

~

But *yes*, is what she would have said, if she were able to be honest. *Yes, yes, he is the one.* She is not sure if she believes in any of it – soul mates, destiny, the one true love. Yet despite this she knows that, for her, Tom is it.

AFTER

Six Weeks

Only a Madwoman

She has waited until nine o'clock to go, and surely this is late enough, there will be nobody to see her. Only a madwoman would be out grocery shopping at this time of night, and on a Sunday too. Still, she sits for a long minute after she has parked, looking at all the other cars – too many of them, what on earth are they doing here at this hour? – and making sure that there is none she recognises. It has started to rain, and she is grateful for the excuse to pull up the hood of her raincoat before getting out of the car, and to scurry quickly across to the big doors. A hot blast of air greets her as she steps through them, and then she is inside, and she starts to breathe a little easier.

She has forgotten the bags, she realises straight away, and she has to stop herself from turning and darting back to the car. She steels herself. She needs to do this – she is out of milk, for a start, and she cannot keep calling her mother to rescue her every time the well runs dry. Besides, she thinks she will probably lose her mind entirely if she spends another day without setting foot out of the house. She takes a basket and pulls down her hood, sodden now, and pushes the wet strands of hair back from her face. Milk, and coffee, and sliced meat of some sort; that will be enough, for today. No need to push it.

Nothing in the familiar shop has changed, and yet she finds it difficult to orientate herself, and must read the signs swaying

16

high above the shelves in order to work out where she needs to go. It is a bit further from the house, this supermarket, but she has been coming here regularly for six months now, ever since they stopped being able to go to the nearer place – ever since that nightmarish, unreal weekend when she had knelt in the cereal aisle beside a sobbing Tom while her children stared wide-eyed from the trolley. No, this place is not that one, although once inside they all feel the same really, the familiar brands and the piped music, and she has never again been able to fully relax in any of them.

At least it is not, in truth, very busy, despite all the cars outside, which she realises now are probably for the cinema next door. She gets the coffee pods, and a box of tea as well, and remembers then that she is almost out of bread, and goes to find that too. She passes the aisle with all the drink, and wonders whether to pick up a bottle of wine, but decides against it in the end. She has not had a drink since it happened; it feels like a road that might prove far too easy to go down.

In the mirrored end of a freezer cabinet she catches sight of a woman, pale and large-eyed and haggard, her posture hunched and wary, like an animal that has been hurt. It is with a lurch of her stomach that she recognises herself, and turns quickly away. She realises she has been avoiding mirrors for weeks.

It is while she is standing in front of the open fridges, trying to remember today's date as she stares stupidly at the packets of ham, that she becomes aware of somebody at the edge of her vision. She ignores them at first until she realises, her mouth suddenly dry, that whoever it is has not moved in some moments. Only then does Rachel turn and face the woman, who is standing six feet away and raising one hand slowly to her cheek.

'You're that poor lady.'

Rachel is frozen, her heart a silent, thundering train that at any moment will come tearing out of her chest. The woman's hand is still at her face, and she closes her eyes and shakes her head silently as if there are no words for what she wants to say. She is older than Rachel, though younger than her mother; fifty-five, maybe, or a good sixty, and the bottom few inches of her trousers are dark with rain.

'I remember you from the news. Those poor little children.' She blesses herself, her eyes closing for a fraction of a second.

Rachel finds that she is shaking, and she puts one hand on the edge of the fridge to steady herself. There is nobody else in sight. She wonders how long she is expected to stay here, an audience to this stranger's vicarious flirt with grief.

'Those poor, poor children.' The woman is shaking her head again; she seems almost to be talking to herself. Everything she says is slow and heavy, as if laden with profundity.

Rachel clears her throat, looking to the shelves of cooked meat and sausages for inspiration. She is glad there is nobody else around; aside from anything else it is supremely embarrassing, this, and she finds herself angry that she has been drawn into it against her will.

The woman bends, finally, to pick up her basket from the floor. As she rises again – all her movements too are slow, as if she is affording them the appropriate gravitas – she nods to where Rachel's hand is resting on the shelf.

'You're still wearing those. God almighty. I would have thrown them in his face.'

Rachel follows her gaze to see what she is talking about. She sees them then, as if for the first time – the slim platinum band with the two small diamonds; the slightly wider, unadorned one in its shadow. They are beautiful, her rings.

The woman leans over and pats Rachel's arm in a way that is probably meant to be consoling.

'I'd take them off, if I were you. Might give people the wrong idea, after everything.'

Rachel wonders what, exactly, the 'wrong idea' might be in this scenario. She is angry with herself, and with the woman, for the sudden shame that fills her now. She has never been somebody who sets much store by symbols, or ascribes meaning to objects beyond their practical or aesthetic use. Beautiful things she will keep, yes, but not the ones that are merely sentimental; after the obligatory day or two of admiration she used to, quite happily, direct all of her children's artwork quietly to the recycling bin. The rings have never burdened her beyond their paltry weight in metal.

She had, quite simply, forgotten she was wearing them.

She opens her mouth, finally, to speak, although she has no sense of what words might be about to emerge. She feels dangerous, unleashed.

'Excuse me.' A man leans politely between them, tall and young and dark; thin white cords run from his ears to vanish into the depths of his duffel coat. He takes a packet of cooked chicken from the shelf and steps back again, his smile apologetic.

Very slowly, as if she is afraid any sudden movement will precipitate some greater emotional crisis in this blight of a woman, Rachel bends her knees and places her basket carefully on the floor. Then she turns around and walks quickly to the checkouts, and straight through them, and out the door.

BEFORE

Nine Years

An Ordinary Room

Tom's parents are older than her own. Tom has shown her a picture, and although the word 'elderly' would not truly apply, still there is something almost generationally different about them compared with her own mother, who at barely sixty still jogs a three-mile circuit most mornings. Rachel knows that they are sixty-eight and seventy-three respectively, for she has asked Tom questions with the doggedness of someone compiling a dossier, until eventually he had laughed at her.

'You don't need to be nervous. They're grand, the pair of them.'

'I'm not nervous.' Rachel bristled, offended only because it was true.

'Fair enough, so.' He didn't even attempt to make it sound like he believed her.

They were in bed, in Tom's flat this time, Johnny's absence for the weekend giving Rachel an unusual sense of freedom. She revelled in walking to the bathroom in just her underwear, in slipping on a T-shirt of Tom's to investigate the fridge for breakfast possibilities. Now she rolled over and butted his shoulder with her head.

'I just want them to like me. It's not a crime.'

'God, of course they'll like you. I'm not worried about that in the slightest.' He crushed her to him, his big hands roaming.

'I'm more concerned about them doing something massively embarrassing. They've got form for it.'

'Well, that I can probably handle.'

Now in the car, a nervous gnawing in the pit of her stomach as the dual carriageway gives way to countryside, Rachel does the maths; Tom is several years older than she, and yet even so they must have been old for new parents, pushing forty when he was born. She wonders what they are thinking, imagining them looking out the window for Tom's car to appear at the turn of the road; if they are secretly waiting to compare her to some previous girlfriend of Tom's they had grown attached to, and find her wanting. She knows there have been other girlfriends, although none, in the retelling, who merited more than a brief mention, a placemarker in the chronology of Tom's life. She had not asked for more details.

At last Tom turns the car into a long and steep driveway, crunching over the gravel to pull in beside a faded blue Volvo. Rachel steps out of the car, her stomach roiling gently as it always does on country roads. The door of the bungalow opens, and Tom's mother comes out, taking the step with the careful gait of one who knows that a stumble could be catastrophic. Behind her is a tall, slightly stooped man who stands with hands in pockets and a reluctant smile – Tom's smile – spreading on his face.

'There you are, love.' Tom's mother holds both hands up to him, the delight all over her face.

Tom stoops to kiss her. She turns then and takes Rachel's hand in both her own.

'And this is Rachel. It's lovely to meet you, finally, Rachel. Come in, come in. I've the kettle on.'

~

Oh, but they are kind, and so very welcoming. They love that she is a nurse; his mother uses the phrase 'angels on this earth' unironically, and Rachel has to stop an unforgivable snigger from escaping. Rachel can tell she is just the sort of girl they had hoped Tom would bring home one day. She hopes that this is not off-putting for him, that seeing herself through his parents' eyes does not awaken in him some adolescent yen for rebellion. But no, today he seems happy, proud of her even, his arm snaking around her shoulders as they sit in the slightly gloomy living room of the bungalow and drink tea. His father keeps half an eye on the hurling on the silenced television in the corner, the ball almost invisible against a cloudless sky.

The dinner produced by his mother (*Call me Bernie, Rachel, won't you?*) is monstrous, the plates piled high with steaming vegetables and great slabs of meat, but Rachel has never had any trouble putting away good food. And she can see that this, too, pleases them, another check mark on the invisible list; Joe even stirs himself to an admiring 'Good girl yourself' when she accepts the offer of another roast potato. After dinner there is an apple tart, and more tea – she would like coffee, but it does not seem to be on the menu – and then Bernie suggests that she show Rachel the garden, of which she is clearly proud. And it deserves pride, that garden; it is huge, meandering way back up the hillside, and filled with heathers and hydrangea bushes. As they walk Bernie takes her arm, and squeezes it for emphasis from time to time.

'Would your parents have much of a garden, now? Up in Dublin?'

'Not like this,' Rachel answers, and can see that this has gratified her.

'Ah well, sure. It's different, isn't it? And it's nice to be close to things, all the same.' Bernie's speech is full of these half-finished thoughts, as if she and Rachel have a common shorthand stretching back years. It is flattering, if sometimes unintelligible.

'Have you always lived here?'

'We had a smaller house in the village, when we were first married. This one came up, then, when Tom was three or four. It was great for him, all the space to run around.'

'Oh, it must have been.'

'We thought we'd have more children, of course.' She says this almost apologetically, then gives a little laugh. 'Back at the beginning. But, sure. What will be will be, as they say.'

Rachel is not sure what to reply to this. They walk on. At the end of the garden is a fence of black wire, almost invisible among the bushes. Beyond it the mountainside stretches up and up, wilder now, the brightly coloured curation giving way to a patchwork of muted greens. Somewhere she can hear the gentle music of a stream, although she cannot see it.

'It's harder when they're teenagers, of course. They're a bit cut off from things, up here, always wanting lifts into Dublin. Though he'd friends in the village, of course, Tom, he always had lots of friends.'

Rachel smiles. 'I'm sure he did.' She is receiving each of these fragments of information like tiny gifts, storing them carefully away to be mulled over later in solitude. The luxury of seeing him through his mother's eyes.

'Still, it's great for them, growing up in the country. You'd be a city girl, now, you wouldn't know what I mean, but I tell you now – you can't beat this sort of a place for kids.'

Rachel considers taking this remark for the criticism – or even warning – it could be read as, but decides against it. Already she can tell that Bernie simply lacks the filter that she finds so tiresome in her own mother, every sentence carefully selected and parsed before emerging, bowed under the weight of its own expectation, from her lipsticked mouth. No, Bernie will be an easy ally.

Rachel breathes in deep lungfuls of the mountain air, and imagines small children running ahead of them.

~

Back in the kitchen, the kettle is on the boil again. Never has she drunk so much tea in one afternoon; she is afraid she will have to ask Tom to pull over at the side of the road on the way home. She sips at her cup while Bernie and Joe list off for Tom's benefit the people from the locality who have suffered illness, or – most newsworthy of all – death, since his last visit.

Rachel excuses herself to go to the bathroom, which is at the other end of the wide, shallow house. Tom's mother escorts her there in lieu of giving directions, but thankfully she does not linger outside, and soon Rachel can hear the hum of conversation from the kitchen again. Rachel sits for a moment longer than she needs to. It is a lot, this, for all that it is going well, and she feels physically drained.

On the way back to the kitchen she glances for a moment through the half-open door of a bedroom. The walls are painted in a pale blue, and she knows immediately that this is Tom's room. There is just space to slip her head through the gap without opening the door any further – this feels vitally important, although she cannot say why – and she stands for just a moment to take in the small single bed, the chequered duvet, the football posters on the wall. There is a scouting bandana dangling from a nail on the wall by the window, and two model aeroplanes hang suspended in perpetual flight from the ceiling. Through the small window she can see a square of mountainside dotted with bushes of yellow gorse, and there too is the stream, the

24

one she had been able to hear earlier. Tom's view, the one he must have grown up with; the small patch of sky he would have woken up to each morning, and watched fade into darkness as night dropped over the mountain.

That is all; it is an ordinary room, containing nothing she could not have imagined, and yet somehow she feels she knows Tom now so much better than before.

She gets back to the kitchen in time to hear that that's all the Conway brothers dead, now, and would you ever have believed that Jimmy would be the last one to hang on?

~

When it is time to leave, laden with leftovers and a second apple tart that has not even been cut, Tom's mother pulls her close, and for a moment her hand rests on the back of Rachel's hair. It is curiously intimate, this gesture, and Rachel has to suppress the sudden urge to pull away. Bernie's voice is very soft, and clearly intended only for her ears.

'God bless you, now. We were waiting for someone like you to come along.'

There is no time for a reply, even if she could muster one, as Tom is pulling her away, and she manages only to wave and to shout incoherent thanks for the food, the bottomless tea, the effusiveness of the welcome. Rachel wonders if Bernie's remark is something she will relay to Tom on the way home, and they will laugh about in the safety of the car, but she thinks, on reflection, not; it would seem disloyal, somehow. And already she likes the idea of a relationship with Tom's mother, however slender, that is outside of what she has with Tom.

It makes her feel, as ludicrously premature as it is, like one of the family.

AFTER

Two Months

Slipping Away

It's not the family liaison officer this time, the nice woman with the peroxide hair and the world-weary expression. Rachel had always found it soothing, her attitude of total acceptance that the world is an awful place in which nightmarish things frequently happen; she was someone who had clearly made her peace with that. Rachel thinks she might have committed physical violence had she been forced to contend with a cheerier type, or a solemn one who offered platitudes.

Anyway, it wasn't the FLO who had phoned the day before, and it isn't she who stands now on Rachel's doorstep, waiting to be asked inside. Instead it is the older detective – Rachel cannot remember his rank, if indeed she ever knew it, but he is senior enough; she could tell it from the way he spoke to the other Gardaí that night at the hospital, and the slow, deliberate way he made notes in a tiny yellow book.

'Sorry, come in, come in. It's a rotten day.' She stands back to let the bulk of him pass her; he is a big man, heavy in the way her father is, all gut and bristle. His movements are gentle, though, and unhurried. He waits in the hall for her to close the front door against the rain, and to lead him into the living room, where she has made some attempt at hospitality; a plate of chocolate digestives, a cafetière. It is all a bit grim.

He takes the armchair by the fire; Tom's chair, she thinks automatically, although she does not say it. He is too big for it, and the sight of him trying to settle himself comfortably between the two arms might have been comical, were it not for the fact that Rachel can't look at him without remembering the first time they met. The single room off the A&E corridor; the way he had waited for her parents to sit, one on either side of her trolley, and for her mother to take her hand before he spoke. The impenetrability of what he was telling her, although his words were clear and unencumbered by euphemism. *Both of them?* she remembers asking, her voice incredulous and shrill. *Both of them?*

He smiles now as he looks at her, and accepts a biscuit from the plate, and says he will take his coffee black.

'I won't ask how you are. I'm sure you're sick of that question.'

This brings the ghost of a smile to her lips. 'I never know what to say.'

'I wanted to have a chat, just to fill you in on where we are now. With your husband's case.'

She flinches at the word 'husband'. She cannot help herself; even to accept its utterance seems disloyal.

'You haven't seen Tom, yourself, since the accident?'

Rachel shakes her head mutely, and he goes on. 'We got the report from the independent psychiatrist last week. I can't show it to you at present, but I can give you an idea of the main points, if you'd like me to?'

She nods, wordless still, and he gazes out the window for a few seconds before continuing. The rain has obscured any view.

'They feel – with a fair degree of certainty, I think – that Tom was severely depressed at the time of the incident. Depressed to the point of psychosis, where he had lost touch with reality.

When he was first interviewed, when he was well enough – it was within a couple of days – he still believed that in killing the children he had saved them from a terrible fate.'

'Wh—?' The voice that first emerges is only a croak, and she has to clear her throat and try again. 'What fate?'

The detective frowns. 'That's never been fully clear. He has talked a lot about financial problems; apparently he feared becoming bankrupt, that you would lose this house. The shame of that seemed to be – well, something he couldn't contemplate living with.'

Rachel shakes her head impatiently. 'That was all sorted now, he'd got a decent job. And the house was never in danger, anyway.'

'I understand that.' He nods once, then shrugs his bulky shoulders. 'These were not rational beliefs, Rachel. The crucial thing is that he believed that they were. His only regret was that – well, that he hadn't completed the job, as he saw it.'

She thinks she is going to be sick; she looks around for a bin or a bag, anything that she could use to catch it, but there is nothing handy. She presses her wrist to her mouth.

'This is hard. I'm sorry.' His voice is very kind.

'It's OK.' The sickness passes, and she resettles herself on the couch, and nods at him to continue. 'Go on, please. I'm all right.'

He takes a long drink from his mug before speaking again. 'In layman's terms, I suppose you'd say he wasn't in his right mind. He didn't understand that what he was doing was wrong. Based on this, the DPP feels that an insanity defence is likely.'

'Insanity.' She stops. The word is so ludicrous, so antiquated; so *unprofessional*, she thinks, it is a word that would have her fired on the spot if she were ever to use it about a patient. Insanity. *He is insane. I am going insane.*

The detective nods slowly.

'What that means is, if the defence is accepted, he'll be found not guilty, and committed to psychiatric care. Indefinitely.'

'At the same place he's in now?' An image of it flashes into her mind from a documentary she saw years ago – the long gloomy corridors, the high walls obscuring it from the city.

'Yes. They think the trial will be early next year, most likely.'

'Will I have to go? To give evidence, like?'

'I don't know at this stage. It's possible. That won't be easy, I know.'

Rachel can't imagine it, standing up in some oak-panelled courtroom and talking about her children. Saying their names out loud. She shakes it from her head; there is something else she wants to know.

'Have you seen Tom? Recently, I mean. Do you know how he is?'

'No, we completed our interviews early on. It's out of our hands really, now. I just – I wanted to make sure you knew what was going on.' He shrugs again. 'Families can get a bit – lost, in this kind of thing.'

'You're very good. I appreciate it.' And she means it; she is touched, this big, awkward man sitting in her living room on what is possibly his day off, trying to ensure that some bit of this is made easier for her than it might otherwise be. It is not his fault that nothing could make it easier.

'Well. Thank you for the—' He gestures with the coffee mug, and stretches to place it on the mantelpiece behind him. They both stand, he using the narrow arms of the chair to lever himself up.

'If you have any questions – at any stage – you have my number.'

'I do. Thank you.' She presses her fingers to his forearm fleetingly, then is embarrassed, and turns away to lead him back to the front door. The rain has abated, but there is a steady drip as water falls from the portico over the door, from the tree that reaches almost to her daughter's bedroom window.

He turns on the doorstep to take his leave, and suddenly Rachel does not want him to go. The house is so empty.

'Does this mean I'm supposed to forgive him? If he didn't know what he was doing. Am I meant to forgive him?'

He pauses; he looks at her, and his eyes are suddenly a father's eyes, and full of pity.

'I don't think you're supposed to do anything. If you think it would help you to forgive him . . . I don't know. But if you need permission to hate him, you have it. You have mine, anyway, for whatever that's worth.'

He nods again, and tips a non-existent hat, and walks down the path. Rachel waits, holding the door open, until he is out of sight. She does not know if she hates Tom. She does not know if she would need permission for that. Still, it feels better to have been given it.

~

Later she goes to the bedroom and sits restless on Tom's side of the bed, staring at his bedside table. There is nowhere else to search for clues to him, that is the problem. The police took everything, that first night after talking to her at the hospital, after it became clear what Tom had done; even before she came home they had been here, poking through the minutiae of their lives together, packing Tom's laptop into a see-through bag and taking it off for forensic analysis. His phone is gone too, of course, taken from the wreckage of the car that night. So what is she looking for here? She thinks it unlikely she will suddenly chance upon a letter from her husband explaining everything to her.

The table is dark wood, with two deep drawers. She opens the top one; earphones, an old pair of glasses, some aftershave he had been given by his mother one Christmas and never opened. A box of condoms, nearly full; they had been using condoms since their son was born, Rachel reluctant to go back on the pill. There had been discussions about having a third baby; sometime last spring she remembers a few nights of earnest chats about it, she pushing to round off their family in the way she had always pictured it, and Tom displaying a resistance that surprised her at the time. He the typical only child who had always wanted a big crew. They had agreed to shelve the discussion for the moment, although it had kept playing on Rachel's mind, and she had put off starting any more long-term method of contraception in the hope that he would become more receptive to the idea. And then, somehow, without her really noticing, they had stopped having sex at all, and the whole thing had become moot.

The second drawer opens stiffly, as if unused to the movement. There are more odds and ends in it – mainly papers inherited from Tom's defunct architectural firm, loose spreadsheets and pages from business plans that have somehow escaped the stack of box files now relegated to the attic. Half-heartedly she lifts the pile and sees beneath it a small, green, leather-bound book, its cover mottled and held closed with a thin strip of black elastic. Rachel's breath catches in her chest. She knows with a sickening certainty that this will be it – the missing piece of the puzzle, somehow overlooked by the Gardaí with their latex gloves and their inquisitive fingers, which will open the mysteries of Tom's mind to her. Her fingers are trembling and slightly damp as she reaches into the drawer to lift it, and in her haste she drops it once before she manages to lift it to her lap and open the cover.

31

The notebook is blank. Its spine is unbroken, its pages slightly stuck together as if they have never been turned.

Rachel slams the drawer shut hard enough that the little wooden knob, slightly loose for years, falls off and lands silently on the carpet.

~

Her phone rings later as she sits in front of the television, finishing off the chocolate biscuits in lieu of dinner. She is expecting her mother, who still calls every evening, but the name on the screen is instead Helen's, and she sits up straighter to look at it. The picture is of the two of them on Helen's wedding day, Rachel's head on Helen's bare shoulder. As she stares at the screen the ringing stops, and the picture fades again to black.

She waits ten minutes before sending a text.

Sorry I missed you there, was just in the shower.

With someone like her mother this would be a dangerous tactic, inviting an immediate call back – *I thought it would be quicker to ring you* is how Margaret opens most conversations – but Helen is of Rachel's own generation, and she knows the etiquette. Her reply comes a few minutes later.

No problem. Just wanted to see how you were.

Rachel's thumbs hover over her phone. She does not know what to say to Helen, so eventually she puts it down and goes to make another cup of tea. When she sits down again the credits are rolling on the TV.

I'm all right. Had the detective here today.

Really?! Any news?

Not a whole lot. Just that it'll be an insanity plea. But we kind of knew that anyway. She cannot bring herself to type Tom's name.

This message, read, goes unanswered for a few minutes. Rachel has put the phone down by the time it chimes again.

I don't know how you're putting one foot in front of the other at the moment. I really don't.

Rachel never knows how to respond to sentiments like these. They come often – in sympathy cards, in the tilted heads of neighbours who spot her from their driveways, in the silent beats that scatter the desultory conversations with her mother. *How can you go on?* She hears different things, depending on who is speaking and the kind of day it has been – awe, and curiosity, and there is of course judgement in it too, as there is judgement in so many of the things people say to her, though they would all deny it. *If it were me . . .* She does not blame them, exactly, although the question makes her uncomfortable. She would wonder too. How *can* she go on? It is impossible, surely.

Anyway. Any news with you?

This time it is Helen's reply which is a long time in coming, and when it does finally arrive Rachel feels she can see, like some modern-day palimpsest, the ghosts of all the messages Helen has written and then erased before settling on this one.

Another cycle this month. No joy.

Rachel stares at these six words, a shorthand she under-stands well but resists interpreting. She has been there, even if just at the end of the phone, for all of the previous joyless, doctor-orchestrated cycles; she has commiserated and cried with her friend, she has sent flowers and cards and gin, and once, the one time it stuck, she had driven Helen to the hos-pital with a miscarriage that was viscerally brutal and cruelly late. She had sat with her while she wept over the phone to her husband Neil, pacing furiously around his bedroom in a business hotel in Berlin; sat there holding Helen's hand while her own perfect daughter slept peacefully at home, and her

33

as-yet-unknown son rolled in gentle aquatic movements under her maternity top.

But she cannot be there for Helen this time. It is too much.

She does not reply to this last message, because she cannot think of anything to say, and eventually enough time has passed that it is too late. She turns the volume down on her phone, and switches off the television, and pulls a blanket over herself in the room that has grown suddenly cold.

She feels like everything is slipping away; but no, that is not correct – everything has already slipped away, surely. No, now it is she who is slipping, gathering speed, and that sound she can hear when she closes her eyes tight in the darkness of her living room is the scrape of her fingernails, trying desperately to cling on.

BEFORE

Six Years

Just What You Wanted

They get married on a Friday – it is cheaper on a Friday, not as cheap as a Thursday but you save a bit, and it's easier for people to get the day off work. It is a big wedding, very Irish, with cousins spilling out of every corner and several guests that Rachel is fairly sure neither she nor Tom could name with any confidence. But it's a great day, all the same. Her mother is in her element, a confection in pale lemon taffeta; her face is suspiciously unlined, and although she swears that this is the result of sensible amounts of sleep and an attention to hydration, Rachel suspects that something more pharmaceutical has played a part. She does not ask. Her father relaxes visibly once the formalities of the day are done with, and sits for long hours with various relatives he has not seen in years.

Bernie and Joe are almost unrecognisable. Rachel acknowledges with some small shame the unkind part of herself that would not have thought it possible, that Bernie with her house shoes and her sensible cardigans could approach this level of glamour. But here she is in a long fitted dress, the colour of summer skies, that drapes elegantly in all the right places; a matching jacket that could only be described as chic. Rachel wonders who helped her to pick it out; she has no daughter, Bernie, no practical twenty-something who would lead her to the correct shops and convince her to spend more money

35

than she had ever considered on the blue that brought out the colour of her eyes. She had not asked Rachel for help, in any case.

Sometime after two in the morning – the DJ is still packing up, and the staff have begun to sweep, and scattered around the room are little groups with ties undone and shoes kicked off and feet up on chairs – Rebecca comes to find her. Rebecca, who six weeks before the wedding had decided to invest in a large tattoo running the length of her upper arm, its border neatly edged by the silky strap of her bridesmaid's dress. Their mother had been horrified, Rachel tight-lipped and silent; Tom had, she suspects, found the whole thing hilarious. It would not have been deliberate on Rebecca's part, that is the thing; she is unthinking, yes, but she is never vindictive, and nor would she have had any thoughts of stealing her sister's thunder. It would have just – like so many of Rebecca's whims and fancies – seemed like a good idea at the time.

But in any case it is all forgotten now, and here is Rebecca, fair as a Viking queen, flushed and doe-eyed, her feet – strikingly wide and flat, those feet – bare and tipped with pink. She is drunk, or more than drunk, but Rachel does not ask; the hour and the emotion of the day have made her forgiving, and it doesn't really matter what Rebecca and her current boyfriend, a Kiwi musician named Doug who will not last, have been getting up to in the bathroom.

'Rachel! I've been looking for you.' She stretches a hand to stroke her sister's hair, wisping loose now from the artful chignon with its hundreds of pins.

Rachel brushes her fingers away. 'You all right?'

'I'm great.' She hugs herself, the sharp angles of her elbows somehow childlike. 'It's been such a good day, hasn't it? I'm so fucking happy for you.'

'I'm pretty happy for myself.'

'And Tom. Tommy Boy.' Rebecca slips one arm around her shoulders and leans her head against Rachel's. They are exactly the same height. They look up towards the platform where the band had earlier played. Tom is sitting on the edge of it, his shirt sleeves rolled up, a bottle of beer clasped in his hands. He is looking down at the floor as Johnny Dolan, always expansive when drunk, talks above his head. There is a small, tight smile on his lips.

Rebecca tilts her head. 'He looks a bit like a better-looking Prince Charles, do you not think? When he was young, I mean. It's the wavy hair.'

'Jesus, don't let anyone hear you say that. Some of those Cavan cousins look like they could be roadies for the Wolfe Tones.'

Rebecca laughs; a fraction too loudly, and from the corner of her eye Rachel sees heads turning, and then away again. 'Ah, no. I'm only messing. We're mates now, me and Tom. I wasn't sure, at first; he seemed a bit – you know.' She waves one hand in the air, as if for clarity. 'But I love him now. I really do love him, Rach.'

Rachel decides not to parse the varied elements of this speech. It is enough that her family has welcomed Tom into the fold; that her father will solicit his opinion about the merits of petrol over electric garden tools, that her mother has stopped asking him if he will have tea or coffee, but instead simply presents him with the steaming cup. That Rebecca herself makes free with her jokes, often of a kind that Tom does not quite get, but appreciates nonetheless for what they confirm – that he is one of them now.

'It's just what you wanted, isn't it? All this.' She gestures vaguely around the room.

Rachel nods, believing it. She looks at her sister – troubled, high, frenetic, beautiful – and feels her own good fortune like

37

something tangible, a small and solid rock at the very core of her.

~

Afterwards they go to Italy for a fortnight. A week in Rome first, where they do all the things you're meant to do when you visit Rome, and take photographs of each other standing outside the Colosseum and throwing coins into the Trevi Fountain. They stay in a small hotel in one of the central squares; there is a tiny, dark reception from where a narrow staircase leads up to a room that gleams with polished wood and distant Mediterranean sunlight. In the evenings they eat their body weight in pasta and *gelato*, and wander through the narrow streets near the Vatican where the shop fronts are filled with mannequins dressed in the sober black and white of the religious orders. It is, Rachel thinks, like a scene from a sketch show.

'Is this for real? Do you think the Vatican lads come here on their days off and try on a load of different black robes and ask their mates what they think?' Tom poses before an invisible mirror, narrowing his eyes and jutting out one hip.

'Shh!' Rachel is laughing, but half fearful too, looking around anxiously for disapproving glances. She has been struck, this week, by the matter-of-fact evidence of devotion in everyday life here. Ireland has nothing on this place, really, for all its talk.

Tom grabs her by the waist, pushes her against the narrow strip of wall between the shops. She is wearing a pink and white sundress with a halter neck, and the brick is cool against her bare back.

'Maybe we should bring home one of the nun outfits, what do you think?'

38

For the second week they have booked an apartment in a villa in the Tuscan hills; they arrive late at night, having got badly lost in the rental car and despaired of ever finding the place. Tom is tense and sweaty with frustration and the heat, and Rachel is trying desperately to decipher the map in the weak glow of the car's internal light; there seems to be no mobile signal up this high. There are no streetlights either, and she finds being on the wrong side of the road disorientating, vertiginous almost, and closes her eyes whenever they are passed by another car.

At last they see it, looming out of the darkness, the big white sign with *Agriturismo* in block letters. Rachel shrieks and points excitedly, but Tom is already turning the car in through the wooden gates and along a narrow, unpaved track. He turns to her and squeezes her bare knee, his eyes clear again, his smile a broad beam.

It has been worth getting lost for.

'Apartment' is the wrong word for it; it is one half of the ground floor of a beautiful stone house with tiled floors and roughly plastered walls. The furniture is minimal – the bed *matrimoniale*, the small dining table with unmatched chairs; a long, low couch in the sitting room. The owner, who has been waiting for them all afternoon, shows them the patio at the back and the bathroom with the mosaic tiles, and how to work the shower. They eat most of the food they have bought along the way, and fall into bed.

In the morning Rachel wakes first, bathing in the utter silence of the place. The day is still cool when she steps outside, but the clarity of the sky promises heat, and by the time she has made coffee and brought it outside it is warm enough to slip off the jumper of Tom's she had thrown on. She sits at the little table, puts her feet on the seat of the other metal chair, tips her face up to the sun.

~

They spend most days by the pool; Rachel has brought four books, and finishes all of them with a day to spare. The advertised WiFi is virtually non-existent, but after a day or two Tom seems to adjust, if somewhat reluctantly, to the idea of being out of contact with his office. They swim a lot, and exchange brief pleasantries with the other guests – an English couple, slightly younger than themselves, and a family from Naples with three teenagers who alternate between staring at their phones and noisy games of water polo. Rachel does not mind the shouts, the occasional splashes of water on the sunbaked pages of her book. If she had the choice, she would never leave.

The night before they are due to fly home, they cook thick steaks on the brick-built grill on the patio, and eat them with salted bread and the heavy, overripe tomatoes they have bought at the market in the town. Afterwards, Rachel lies back in her chair and stretches out her legs. She feels like something over-ripe herself – too much sun, and red wine, and long afternoons in bed with Tom, the filmy white curtains drawn against the heat of the day. That, too, has felt different since the wedding. Oh, she is aware how ridiculous this sounds – they have lived together for nearly two years by this point, there can be no more mysteries surely – and yet she knows at the same time that it is true. She is more relaxed, more present, and he is different too – slower, more tender, more serious somehow.

Beside her, on the table, Tom's phone lights up and then starts to ring. Bernie's face flashes on the screen. Rachel sits up; Tom is in the bathroom. She debates letting it ring out, but she can never bring herself to do it.

'Bernie. Hi.'

'Rachel. I didn't wake you, love, did I? I'm only remembering now about the time difference.'

'Not at all, we've just had dinner. Tom's in the loo.'

'I won't keep you, so. I just wanted to wish you luck with the journey tomorrow. I'll say a prayer.' In Bernie's world, short hops with Ryanair are something best undertaken after divine intercession.

'We'll be grand, Bernie, don't worry. I'll get Tom to ring you when we get home.'

'And has it been a lovely trip?'

'The best.'

'I'm so glad for you, pet. And for Tom. He was so anxious coming up to the wedding, God love him. I've never seen him so bad.'

This strikes a discordant note in Rachel's mind; she had not seen Tom as stressed. But this is typical Bernie, with nothing else to worry about.

'Well. He seems fine, now, Bernie, he's having a good time.'

'I'll let you go, so, Rachel. Give Tom my love. We're dying to see you.'

'Thanks, Bernie. Good night.'

As she hangs up she hears Tom's footsteps behind her, and she closes her eyes as his arms wrap around her shoulders and hold her to him.

'Did I just dodge a call from my mother?'

'You did. You're welcome, by the way.'

'I knew there was a good reason I married you.'

She tips her head back, and he bends low to kiss her.

AFTER

Three Months

The Part of Her That Is Familiar

The hairdresser is visibly reluctant.

'All of it?'

Rachel nods. 'Up to here.' She touches her chin again. 'And the colour as well.'

He nods, slowly. 'All right, so. It'll be a big change for you.' His voice rises in a question, giving her one last chance to change her mind. But she is sure.

He cuts the hair first, long hanks of it falling around his feet. Rachel turns the pages of a magazine, not reading but watching the transformation from beneath lowered eyelids. It has never been so short, not since it first grew past her chin as a toddler; even in the first-day-of-school photograph that still hangs on the wall of her parents' sitting room, it is already a wild tangle reaching halfway down her back.

'We'll do the colour now, and then I'll shape it for you.' He is enthusiastic now, relishing the opportunity to effect something dramatic.

She is there for hours, three cups of tea growing cold as she sips slowly from them. There are long periods when she is left alone, her head an alien helmet of paste and foil; every so often the stylist will approach, unwrap a single clump, gaze at it consideringly. Eventually it is all washed away, and he snips again with his scissors, shearing off infinitesimally smaller and smaller pieces of hair until at last he pronounces it satisfactory and begins to blow it dry. In the mirror she watches herself emerge, a new woman. A stranger.

Finally it is done, and with great ceremony he hovers a hand mirror behind her head, angling it this way and that. She finds that she cannot speak, but nods and smiles enthusiastically, declaring herself delighted. As she stands to follow him to the counter, she cannot believe that all the hair under her feet has come from her own head; it feels wrong, somehow, to leave it lying there abandoned. The price is astronomical, but she hands over her card without a murmur, and accepts the compliments the receptionist offers along with her jacket.

As she walks along the street she cannot stop staring at herself in the shop windows she passes; it takes a second, each time, to pick out her own silhouette from those moving around her. But these ghostly glimpses are not enough, and she goes instead to the public toilets on the top floor of the shopping centre and studies her new reflection as she washes her hands pointlessly in the sink. She feels that she could walk down her own road now, and nobody would know her, and there is a strange comfort in this.

She pushes the new hair behind her ears, and as she watches herself doing this in the mirror a memory hits her, unbidden; her daughter, only a few months old, reaching up chubby hands to twine them in her long hair and laugh. *They wouldn't recognise me now*, Rachel thinks suddenly, and this strikes her as something very terrible, and she has to hold on to the sink to keep herself upright. The woman with the little boy washing his hands at the other end of the row looks at her strangely, and she counts silently until they leave, the child rubbing his

43

wet hands on his tracksuit bottoms to dry them. She stares hard at herself in the mirror, searching for the part of her that is familiar.

~

Driving home, she finds herself without warning on the road where her daughter's Montessori school sits tucked between a florist and a slightly down-at-heel solicitors' firm. She had not meant to come this way. She has been avoiding it, consciously at first and then by habit, for months now, although it is on the main road home and rerouting often costs her several minutes. But today, distracted perhaps by the glimpses of her unfamiliar self in the rear-view mirror, she has gone straight on instead of indicating left, and it is only when she sees the little knot of parents standing outside the brightly coloured door that she realises what she has done.

She slows the car; she cannot help herself.

They had spent months selecting this place from the several similar ones in the area, the task taking on an importance that seems ludicrous now, looking back, for it is all nursery rhymes and coloured paper at this age; and surely they must all be kind, the women who run these places? You would not devote your life to fingerpainting and sand tables and putting on endless pairs of shoes for minimum wage if you were not kind. And yet it had seemed like a monumental decision, at the time. And it was the right one, in retrospect, for their daughter had flourished here, coming home each day with tales of new friends and lunchbox contents and who had bitten whom. Worse to be the parents of the biter than the bitee, Rachel and Tom had decided after much debate, although thankfully they had never found themselves in either position.

44

She realises, in a detached, observant sort of way, that she has parked the car and is gazing now into the wing mirror at the group of parents, five or six of them – the same early birds who would always be here at five minutes to the hour, stamping feet against the cold or removing sun hats from fractious babies. They chat idly as they wait for the children to come out. Rachel's fingers hover just above the handle of the door. What if she were to join these parents, to stand outside the shop-front with its rainbow mural discreetly shielding the children from prying eyes, and chat in that polite, awkward manner about the weather and the roadworks at the roundabout? Who would challenge her?

Almost without awareness (although perhaps this is a cop-out, perhaps she knows exactly what she is doing) she unbuckles her seat belt – slowly, as if trying not to make a noise. She pulls once on the handle of the door, feeling its soft click against her palm, and then she is out, standing on the road beside the driver's door and shielding her eyes against the sun. She recognises the parents by the child to which each belongs – there is Sadie's mother, and Sophie's, and Emily's dad, chatting in a cordial, smiling knot; their pretty daughters are fast friends, already exhibiting the insular camaraderie of much older children. A little away stands Daniel's father, and then over near the curb are the mothers of Lily and Fionn, two women who look alike enough to be sisters, although she has never asked. They will all know her.

She is moving now towards them, this little cluster of mothers and fathers whose lives have been allowed to continue on unexploded, whose very ordinariness is an insult to Rachel and her family. It is an outrage, really, that they still gather here every day, as if nothing has changed. But she is not, of course, going to make a scene. No, she will just stand quietly with them, and make easy small talk, and wait for the yellow

45

door to open and the children to come tumbling out, one bright, shining mass of energy.

They have not seen her yet. Any moment now.

Now.

Sophie's mother laughs, her high, rather bleating laugh, and as she does so her head turns slightly, blond hair swinging, and for just a moment her eyes meet Rachel's. Rachel's stomach seems to fall away, the sudden horror of what she is doing, but then the woman turns around again, her lively conversation continuing undisturbed, and Rachel realises that she has not been seen for who she is, that her new hair and her big sunglasses have precluded any recognition at this distance. She lets out a noise, a gasp of relief that is almost a grunt, and stumbles back to her car.

She drives only around the next corner, where she parks again, and lets her head fall to her knees. She cannot breathe. She cannot breathe. She cannot breathe.

BEFORE

Five Years

Like Something Sacred

His face is not the face of a man who has been given good news.

'Pregnant?'

'Yeah.' Rachel laughs, bemused. 'It's hardly a shock, is it?'

'No. No, I . . . sorry. I just wasn't expecting it so soon.' He runs his hand through his hair. 'Are you sure, like?'

'Yes, I'm sure. Jesus, Tom.' She throws the test at him, this little wand of plastic and pink dye that only a moment ago had felt like something sacred. She feels like storming out of the house, but it is nine o'clock on a Sunday morning and they are both still wearing pyjamas.

Tom picks it up, the cheap plastic test, and looks at it as if he has never seen such a thing before. Which, to be fair to him, he probably hasn't. When he raises his head again his face is stunned – and then, seeing hers, immediately contrite.

'I'm sorry. Rachel. Come here.' But she does not go to him; she makes him come to her, and pull her to him, and stroke her hair.

'I'm really sorry. I was just surprised. And . . . nervous, I suppose.' He presses a kiss into the top of her head. 'It's a big fucking deal.'

'It's supposed to be good news, though.' Her voice, to her own ears, still sounds slightly petulant. 'We planned this, like. We were trying for it.'

47

'It *is* good news. Obviously. I'm delighted.'

She looks at him then, and it is true, he is smiling and even a little tearful, and so they hug, and study the test together, and agree not to tell either of their families for as long as humanly possible. When he goes to make her coffee he asks her anxiously if she should be drinking decaf now, and they look it up online, and decide to avoid the caffeine just in case. And later they go out and walk around town, and in the basement of a bookshop Tom finds a copy of a *Spot the Dog* book which they both remember from their separate childhoods, and they place it almost reverently on the counter in front of the teenage cashier. That evening they go to the Italian place beside the pub, which is not great but is good enough; they toast each other over dinner, she clinking her lemonade against his glass of beer, and they talk about names.

~

She waits to feel different; to feel something, some fluttering or stretching, some sign of new life emerging. Of green shoots. For weeks, though, there is nothing at all, not even a vague sickness, or the incredible fatigue that other women have told her about. There is at least the visit to the GP, much anticipated and then faintly underwhelming, where she fills in a form and submits a urine sample and promises that she is not a clandestine smoker; she is glad, in the end, that she has not asked Tom to come along. The days seem interminable, and she starts to believe that it is all some great hoax, or the most embarrassing of mistakes, and so when finally they have the first appointment with the obstetrician and she pushes the probe deep into Rachel's belly and the screen fills suddenly with something that looks, despite her better knowledge, unmistakably like a fully formed baby,

48

Rachel lets out a shocked, involuntary gasp. Tom is there too, this time, hovering close by, and she feels him turn to look at her quizzically. She does not cry; she is, in fact, slightly embarrassed by even the gasp, the unintended show of emotion, and for the rest of the visit she is calm and businesslike in a studied way, asking only questions that she has vetted internally for sense and practicality. But when she is alone in the bedroom that night she takes out the little sheaf of pictures and examines them under the lamp, running her fingers over the shiny surface, the spectrum of grainy whites and greys. It still does not feel quite real, but at least now there is some proof.

$\sim$

Her mother's joy knows no bounds. It is, being honest, a little much, especially considering the fact that this will not even be her first grandchild. When they are all together, the family, with Rebecca and Doug, Rachel cringes at her mother's unrestrained excitement – so clueless, so inadvertently hurtful. But as much as Margaret adores her twin grandsons, Rebecca's pregnancy the previous year, so clearly unplanned and then kept hidden for months, with a man from thousands of miles away whom her parents had barely been introduced to – no, this had not been the ecstatic milestone that their mother had imagined for herself. And so, instead, everything has come down to Rachel. In the first few weeks after they had broken the news, to tearful raptures and much clutching of hands, she had texted Rachel constantly with enquiries about her health, reminders to avoid eating liver – which Rachel has never been able to stomach, in any case – and recommendations for ginger biscuits. This has eased now, but even still when they are together Rachel finds her mother touching her – stroking her hair, rubbing her back, placing solemn hands on the soft swell of her barely visible bump – in a way she has not done since she was a little girl.

Two months before the due date she brings Rachel into town for a shopping spree, and together they buy sleepsuits in yellow and green, and snow-white vests of impossible smallness. In the café upstairs in Arnotts they push their bags under the table and study the menu, and then both order the soup. Rachel rubs her face.

'You're tired.' The tone is accusing. 'Did you sleep last night?'

'A bit. It's hard to get comfortable.' She squirms now in her chair.

'Oh, I remember it well.' This is her mother's favourite aspect of the whole thing, it seems – the licence it gives her to reminisce. 'And having to get up to go to the toilet twenty times.'

'Yeah.' Rachel tries to smile; she knows she is not being brilliant company. And it is good, really, to get the last of the shopping done. The big things, the cot and the car seat and the enormous buggy that apparently they must refer to as a travel system, have been bought months ago, and are crammed into the spare room to await their tiny occupant.

'How are you feeling about the birth? Are you nervous?' Her mother tilts her head, places one slightly gnarled, carefully manicured hand understandingly on Rachel's wrist. Begging for confidences, as she has done ever since Rachel's childhood exuberance started to fade and she developed the watchful reticence of every teenager.

'Well. A bit, I suppose.' Rachel shifts her weight in the chair. 'It's all so unknown, isn't it? Until you actually go through it, I mean. You don't know how you'll cope.' Sometimes it is easier to give her mother what she wants. In truth Rachel has not really let herself think about the actual birth, the mechanics of which she understands but has no real wish to dwell on. She has started

50

having dreams of nursing, though, her arms replete with tightly swaddled joy.

Her mother sits back, apparently sated by this brief show of vulnerability. 'You'll sail through it. You forget it all afterwards, that's the blessing. You won't believe me, now, but it's true.'

'So I hear.'

'Is Tom all right?' Margaret's voice is different now, and Rachel realises this is no longer idle curiosity.

'Yeah, of course. Why?' She tries not to bristle; everything is annoying her today.

'Oh, nothing really. I just thought he was a bit off, the other day. When you were down for dinner.'

Rachel thinks back. Sunday lunch at her parents' house – reliably heavy food, an excess of desserts, lots of coy jokes about Rachel being off the wine. Tom had been – well, himself, really, as far as she can remember. He had spent most of the afternoon watching the rugby with her dad; a sport he had no great interest in, but enough knowledge of to be able to keep up with Frank's running commentary. Had he, perhaps, been a bit quieter than usual? Maybe so; but then, what of it?

'He's very busy at the moment, with work.' She tries not to sound defensive. 'It's not easy, getting things off the ground.' It is only in the last few months that the architecture firm has reached a point where it can pay both Tom and Gavin, and Tom has finally given up his day job, with its monthly pay cheque and its pension contributions. Rachel has tried to see this as a happy milestone reached, and not a blind leap of faith.

'No, of course.' Her mother, having planted her seeds, is all comfort now. 'And of course he's probably nervous about all this as well.' She waves vaguely towards Rachel's stomach.

The waiter brings their soup; the bread is laced with sun-dried tomatoes, the butter whipped like cream.

51

'Your dad was no use at all when I was expecting you.' Margaret spoons her soup in the proper way, blowing on the surface gently. 'I think they just feel a bit helpless.' She smiles tolerantly; *what can you do?*

Rachel is already weary of this trope, and the baby is not even here yet.

'Well, Tom's not like that, Mam. He's very excited. And he'll be a great dad.'

'Oh, sure I know that.'

Her mother doesn't speak again until she has finished her bread, and when she does her voice is different – plaintive, even.

'He's good to you, isn't he, Rachel?' Her face looks all of a sudden naked behind its powdery caking.

'Jesus, Mam. Of course he is.'

Rachel pushes her bowl away, suddenly impatient to be gone.

~

And when – not that night, but another night soon; it is shortly before Christmas and she has taken to going to bed before nine o'clock, the late-pregnancy fatigue very much real – she wakes thirsty at three in the morning and walks silently downstairs to find Tom still up, bent over his laptop and muttering to himself words she cannot make out, she stops on the second-to-last step and sits down, careful not to make a noise. Tom is on the couch, the computer open on the coffee table in front of him. The glow of the screen is a spotlight on his face in the otherwise dark room. As she watches he looks up from the screen, towards the blankness of the wall over the fireplace, and frowns as if in silent argument with some unseen opponent. She thinks she sees his lips move, although she cannot be sure. Then he bends his head low again to tug viciously at

52

his hair with both hands, a movement that is as familiar to her as the smile on his face, the muted wave he gives her when he spots her across a crowded room.

Rachel sits there for a long moment, and then she slowly stands and retraces her way up the stairs. She is so tired. Her life is about to change, in numerous and unquantifiable ways; all her energy, her focus, must be directed to this seismic upheaval. Some things are choices, and in the same way that Tom has made the decision to behave as if her pregnancy is something he welcomes wholly, unsullied by fear or concerns for the future, Rachel has chosen to believe him.

AFTER

Four Months

If This Is Her Life Now

It is too soon. That's what they all say – her mother, and her friends, and the nice GP; and even when she spoke to her manager over the phone and told her she was ready to come back, she could hear the eyebrows rise at the other end of the line. Rachel doesn't care. She has to get out of the house; she will go mad, if she has not gone mad already. Some days it is hard to tell.

She starts on a Wednesday, the first of three long days. It feels strange, to set the alarm on her phone, to be dressing once more with some deliberation, to have a deadline for leaving the house. She is not hungry – she is never hungry in the mornings, and only mildly at any other time – but she forces down a reheated croissant with her coffee, and settles into the car. Tom's car, really, the bigger, family car having been the one in her name, although in practice they used to swap them regularly depending on who needed to ferry the children around on any given day. That car is gone now, anyway, and this smaller one more than adequate for her needs. She has not lost her enjoyment of driving. Tom has not stolen that from her, although travelling in the passenger seat is a different story, and on the rare occasions when she is unable to avoid it she sits closed-eyed and trembling the entire duration, her breath coming in shallow, ragged gasps. But today she sits behind the wheel with a sense of, if not satisfaction, at least some sort of purpose.

The drive to the hospital is just under half an hour – not long enough, before a shift, to transition comfortably into work mode, and yet always much too long at the other end of a busy day. She parks in her usual spot, and by the time she has clocked in and snapped her ID badge onto the crisp white pocket of her uniform, it feels like she has never been away. Her locker has a smell, a ripe mustiness, and in the back she finds a plastic lunchbox containing the desiccated core of some long-eaten apple.

It is not the same hospital they brought her to that night. That one was near the coast, the other side of the city, a place she had never been to before as either staff or patient. No, it is not the same hospital; and yet it is, because they are all the same, these places, cut from the same starched and laundered cloth, and the strange world inside them is the same strange world, no matter what the name over the gates. As she steps out of the lift and turns down the long corridor, a porter in red and grey is pushing a wheelchair that bears an old, old woman, her hair a cirrus mass of white. A nurse walks alongside, unhurried, the chart in her hands threatening at any moment to spill its papery contents onto the floor. The squeak of the wheels is the same squeak Rachel had felt piercing through her as another porter, black-clad this time, pushed her through the double doors marked Chapel of Rest.

She reaches the ward in time for handover, and slips into a seat at the back. There is a flurry of nods, of faces breaking open in recognition; she sees, so familiar now, the complex play of emotions that crosses them – realisation, self-consciousness, pity. But Denise, the clinical nurse manager, has already started speaking and so she is not called on to respond just then, beyond a brief lift of her hand. There are new faces, even in the few months she has been away; that is

55

the way of it, in nursing, it is all agency cover these days and newly qualified graduates deciding to chuck it all in for the charms of Bondi Beach. But Lynda is there, just finished a night shift, and Rob, whom she hasn't seen since the funeral but who texts her fairly regularly, usually memes that are gently funny and require no response. He catches her eye and she nods in greeting, her lips pressed together. She supposes that the new ones will still know who she is; there may even have been a meeting of some sort, prior to her return. An informal gathering in the break room, where Denise would have cleared her long throat and reminded everyone that Rachel was back to work tomorrow, and faces would have turned immediately grave and sympathetic, mouths pursing restrainedly, ears tipping gently towards understanding shoulders. She shudders to imagine it.

'Right.' Now Denise's tone changes slightly, and Rachel looks up; unprepared, although this was surely inevitable.

'Just to say that Rachel is back with us from today, and how – how pleased we all are to see her again.' And that is all, and yet it is scarcely bearable. Rachel holds her breath as people start to rise from their chairs, steeling herself for the inevitable press of bodies around her, the hugs and enquiries, the hushed questions to which there can be no real answers. And they come, but she is surprised to find that it is not as bad as she had feared. They are her friends, these people, they want only to know that she is OK; she must keep reminding herself of this.

And they are not, after all, people unacquainted with death.

The meeting breaks up at last; the night shift trail off to sleepy journeys home and breakfast dishes in the sink, and the day begins.

~

Mid-morning, she does obs on her fourteen patients. The other nurse working with her is a fourth-year student, a girl from Donegal named Jenny with a face like a postulant nun, and Rachel finds her soft voice and her calm, unhurried movements restful. Together they must look after the two six-bedded bays, one male, one female, and the adjoining single rooms, these much in demand and allocated according to some complicated algorithm meant to be strictly clinical, but often carrying a suspicious whiff of the political. They do their obs, wrapping blood pressure cuffs, checking pulses, pointing thermometers into willing ears. They are mostly older people in her bays, apart from the young girl with the jaundice and the scars on her arms, who smiles wanly at Rachel but says nothing. She does not think that any of them recognise her. The man in Two should be on the Stroke Unit by rights, but the Stroke Unit is full, and so until they can find a more suitable bed for him he will lie here with his newly useless right arm and the mouth that will no longer do his bidding, and hope that the physio and the speech therapist can find their way from the other end of the hospital.

The woman in Five has dropped her oxygen levels again, and her colour is terrible. Rachel bleeps the team, and a worried-looking intern comes and stares at the chart for a few minutes, and then the registrar arrives and for a while there is a bit of fuss. Within half an hour the woman is being trundled along the corridor to the High Dependency Unit. While all of this is going on the other patients in the room lie silent and watchful, determinedly buying into the delusion that the curtains pulled hastily around the woman's bed have rendered the cubicle soundproof.

By the time Rachel gets back from handing the patient over, it is time for lunch. She cannot face the canteen, not today, and instead she murmurs something about a phone call and escapes out into the grassy area behind the Day Ward, which is usually empty. She has brought a sandwich, sliced turkey and coleslaw, and she eats this sitting on the grass with her back to the wall, closing her eyes to the sun. She wants tea, but not enough to face the queue at the coffee dock in the lobby, which at this time will be full of people she knows. Still, she has a bottle of water in her bag, and the air is warm and balmy.

As she finishes her sandwich there comes a thunderous noise from overhead, and although she knows what it is still she opens her eyes and looks up, squinting against the sun. The red and white of the coastguard helicopter is close enough that it seems impossible it will clear the trees that line the perimeter, but somehow it does, and sinks lower again towards the landing pad on the first-floor roof. Its noise is apocalyptic. It is always on these hot summer days that it comes, a winged beacon of disaster; comes from one or other of the beaches that on a day like this will be teeming with sunburned teenagers and overconfident swimmers, parents who have turned their heads for just a moment too long. She knows that later she will hear the reason for its arrival on the evening news, and already she dreads it.

After the noise has died away it is very quiet. When the girl steps out onto the grass, Rachel knows that she thinks she is alone; she is unguarded, undone, her face collapsing into itself as soon as the door clatters shut behind her.

'Did you want some privacy?'

The girl swings around, her eyes huge, and Rachel sees her take in her uniform, the insignia of someone older and more senior, and potentially with some power to wield. She pushes the back of her wrist to her nose.

'I'm sorry.' Her eyes fill again, she is powerless in the face of whatever grief or shame this is. 'I didn't know there was anyone else here.'

'It's all right.' Rachel gives a half-smile. 'I won't tell on you.'

The levity passes her by; she is too aware of Rachel's uniform, of the status implied by the lightly pinstriped white smock. Her own tunic is the dark blue of the student nurses, her ID badge showing a child's round, guileless face.

'I got in trouble for something. I just needed to – I'm on my break,' she finishes in a rush, as if suddenly afraid she will be punished for dereliction of duty as well as everything else.

'Have you just started?'

She nods, sniffs twice. 'Last week. It's my first placement.'

'So what happened?'

'I threw out some urine, I didn't know they needed to measure it first. I think it was really important.' Her voice wobbles, threatening to betray her again.

'Who was it gave out to you?'

The girl names a senior nurse Rachel has known for years, her temper and her utter humourlessness things of legend.

'Yeah. She's a bitch, that one. She always has been.' Rachel sits back, closes her eyes again. She can feel the girl's uncertain gaze on her, her sudden doubt as to Rachel's position here. Her language is not what she has come to know, in this place of safety statements and inclusion days.

'Honestly. Wagons like her have been torturing students for decades, and they'll go on doing it. They should be strung up.'

The girl sniffs. 'She was right, I suppose. It could have been really serious.'

Rachel is disappointed in her, her lack of gumption. She wishes for hellfire and blood revenge, not this snivelling acceptance. Although she knows she herself would have reacted in the same way, back in the days when a bollocking from the ward sister was the worst thing imaginable.

Still. If this were her daughter, she would scratch the woman's eyes out.

She stands up, brushing crumbs onto the paling grass.

'Listen. Go back in there now in a minute, when you've got yourself together again. It'll all be forgotten about. She's not important, that one. She'll still be here in ten years' time when you've moved on. Don't let her spoil it for you.'

The girl nods, silent and unconvinced, and Rachel pats her arm once and slips past her and in through the door.

~

Her exhaustion that night is a surprise, and a welcome thing. She thinks with wonder of how, before Tom, before children, she would finish a twelve-hour shift and go straight to the gym for a stint on the treadmill, or into town if it was a Friday or Saturday night. Her practised hand steady with the mascara wand as the bus plummeted into potholes and over speed bumps. She feels tired now into the very core of her, as if her individual cells and organs are switching themselves off. She changes into pyjamas and lies on her own bed and closes her eyes for just a minute, and when she opens them again it is fully dark and the clock on her phone reads 03:42. She is hungry, she finds; ravenous in a way she does not remember being since the early days of motherhood, when her babies' constant feeding would render her insatiable. She goes downstairs now, and pours herself a bowl of cereal, and takes it to her spot on the couch where she watches the sun come up.

She wonders, in a neutral sort of a way, if this is her life now.

~

Driving home on the third night, she has a sudden impulse to call her sister. It is bright still, just past eight, and she drives

60

with the window down and the still evening air cooling her skin. They are supposed to change out of uniform before leaving the hospital, but instead she has thrown a cardigan over her tunic, too warm now, and underneath she can feel a thin film of sweat drying on her body.

The phone rings seven times before Rebecca picks up.

'Rach. You all right?' Her voice fills the car.

'Fine. Just driving home.'

'God, of course. Work. How is it? Is it awful?'

'Only in the same way it was awful before. It's fine, really.'

'Well, you know. *Nolite te bastardes*, or whatever.'

Rachel holds her mouth tautly open as she changes lane. 'Listen, I'm not far from you, will I drop in? Are you busy?'

'No, not busy.' A pause, then. 'I'll come to you. You head on home.'

'But I'm in the car already. It's fine, honestly. I don't want to be dragging you out.'

'I could do with the break. Let Doug sort things out here for once.' *Things* being bedtime, Rachel knows, baths and teeth and stories for the two sandy-blond carthorses her sister and Doug – young, heedless, barely more than strangers to each other then – had somehow produced. Rachel remembers staring at them in their side-by-side incubators with disbelief, their sheer physicality a wonder to her then childless eyes.

At home she pulls off the limp uniform and changes into a pair of linen trousers, a well-washed T-shirt. She opens the back door, and the airless kitchen starts to cool. It is very quiet, and when Rebecca's car turns onto the street she can hear its purr long before it has parked.

They hug in a perfunctory way. Rebecca is thin in the kind of way that sometimes draws second glances, the remaining vestige of a largely resolved eating disorder, which for four years of her

61

teens had consumed the entire family so absolutely that Rachel is sometimes taken aback now when she remembers it, and realises that she has not thought of it for some time.

She has brought a bottle of something red, and Rachel gets glasses – she has to wash the second one, which wears a thin coat of dust – and carries them outside, where there is one of those tiny iron bistro tables and four chairs that do not match. Rebecca pours them both enormous glasses and sits down, reaching with one foot to drag another chair towards her. She props her feet on it with a sigh.

'So tell me about work.'

'It's the same.' Rachel stretches out her own legs, the cropped trousers revealing slices of ankle that are pale and smooth. 'It's exactly the same, like. Feels like I was never away. I don't know if that's a good or a bad thing.'

'Doesn't have to be either, I suppose. Were you right to go back, do you think? So soon, I mean.'

'Who are you channelling now, Mam?' She shakes her head, dismissive. 'Ah, no. What's the alternative, really? Stumbling around here like some madwoman. Neighbours crossing the road to avoid me.'

'Rach.' The admonishment is gentle.

'Sorry.' She swirls the wine in her glass, watching the pink film it leaves on the surface. 'No, I know what you're saying. And maybe it is too soon, but, like . . . so what? If it is, it's only me who'll suffer.' And then, hearing the reproach in her sister's voice before she even opens her mouth, she hurries on. 'I don't mean that the way it sounds, I'm not being a martyr. It's just – the stakes are lower now, I suppose.'

They are quiet for a few moments. There is no breeze, on this early summer evening, and the swing set at the end of the garden is still.

Rachel clears her throat, then takes a large sip of wine and clears it again.

'When are you going to let me come around to the house again?'

The pause before her sister answers tells her that her meaning is not unclear. When Rebecca does speak, her voice is careful.

'What do you mean?'

'Becca. Come on.' Rachel angles her body towards her sister, who is staring down the length of the garden. 'I haven't been there in months. Every time I suggest it, there's some excuse.'

'I'm sorry. I didn't realise.' She plays with the stem of her own glass, avoiding Rachel's eye. High above them, a plane crawls lazily across the evening sky. 'It's not deliberate.'

'It's OK. I'm not cross. I understand, I mean. But we can't do that forever. I'm not afraid to see them, Becca. I see kids all the time; they're everywhere, believe it or not. I'm not going to collapse in a heap. And I love the boys. I miss them.'

Rebecca is silent for a time, and when she speaks her voice is very low.

'I'm not afraid for you to see them. That's not it.'

'Well, what is it, then?'

And to her credit, as Rachel thinks later with a grudging admiration that is bitter in her mouth, Rebecca's voice does not waver. 'I'm afraid for them to see you.'

Rachel turns abruptly, meeting her sister's gaze. 'You think it's going to upset them, seeing me? Jesus Christ, Bec. What do you think I'm going to do? I haven't changed that much.'

And is amazed to see Rebecca's eyes fill with slow, heavy tears.

BEFORE

Four Years

All the Things She Should Be Doing

A girl! A little girl, just as she'd hoped – a secret hope, though, for the official answer must always be *oh, just as long as it's healthy*. But in her head Rachel had always imagined a serious-faced child with her eyes and Tom's dark curls, the gossamer-light dresses and superfluous hair clips. And now she is here, and it is just like she has dreamed, only better, because there is a heft to her, a weight she hadn't imagined; she is something solid and very real. The tiny, slightly puffy face emerges blinking slowly from the cushion of the blanket they have swaddled her in, and she grabs on to Rachel's finger as if she too has just realised how very small and fragile and dependent she really is.

The labour had frightened her – she had always secretly thought of herself, not without pride, as something of a stoic, and it shook her, how unmoored she had become, how over-whelmed. The sheer physicality of it all. And the hours and hours it had taken, eventually uncountable, day running into night and back again. But there had been, at some point, an epidural, which turned the whole process into something quite different, and it seems comical now, looking back from the safe distance of the postnatal ward, how quickly her dignity and her manners had resurfaced once the pain was taken away. As if the woman squatting on the floor and baying through gritted teeth had been someone quite different. Until it came to the pushing,

64

when all that was lost again, although by then it was a different, productive sort of chaos, a sense that her body was doing exactly what it was meant to, and that there was a definite goal to be reached. When she heard the baby's first, tentative cry, she was hit with a euphoria that did not abate for days.

She thinks of Tom's face as the baby was placed into his arms. He had looked terrified, and very young, in days-old clothes and stubbled face; something like the boy he must have been before she ever knew him. But then he looked up at her, his eyes misty – this, too, was a first – and she was struck with a love for him that seemed to have taken on a new dimension – one of protectiveness, and a sort of pre-emptive nostalgia, and fear. Everything seemed suddenly infinitely more precious, and more fragile.

They all came, that first evening, through the cold and the rush-hour darkness – her parents and Rebecca, Bernie and Joe. They brought fruit that was welcome and flowers that were beautiful but inconvenient, a tiny pair of patent-leather shoes so breathtakingly impractical that Rachel could think of nothing to say. The curtain around the bed bulged as it tried to contain this transgressive number of visitors, but the staff seemed to turn a blind eye, the rules of the ward apparently in abeyance for this two-hour period. Tom's pride as he laid the baby in his mother's arms was like something tangible, it flowed out of him as if his body was not enough to contain it.

Now she watches as he fusses over the car seat, this fledgling child strapped so tightly that she must feel like she's back in the womb again. He feels her watching and looks up, sheepish; he wants so badly to do everything right. She leans down and kisses him, pressing her forehead for a moment to his. They are both just learning.

~

At home she sits surrounded by cushions with the baby in her arms. There is a huge bunch of flowers on the sideboard, sent by Gavin on behalf of the firm – although the firm, at this point, is only Tom and Gavin and a woman who comes in once a week to do the books. Still, the flowers are beautiful. Tom brings her tea and huge plates of the food her parents have sent over, and she feels, if only briefly, like a queen.

Then reality hits her, the great thumping fist of it, and she finds herself swinging wildly between moments of euphoria and sudden bouts of panic about all that she has left behind. Tom reads aloud from the leaflet given to them by the midwife and tells her that it is the third-day blues, and she blows her nose and knows that he is right and yet she does not believe that she will ever feel normal again.

Helen visits, and holds the baby with a rapt stillness that Rachel would not have thought her capable of. Rachel sits back on the couch, and feels her eyes immediately begin to shut. She had not realised it was possible to survive on so little sleep; she is not yet completely sure that it is. Through the open kitchen door she sees the pile of clothes on the counter, the bin so full that the lid will not close. Her own T-shirt is a landscape of tiny indeterminate stains, and she is sure that she smells. She lets her eyes close.

~

One afternoon, a week or two after Tom has gone back to work, she drives to the post office to collect a parcel that the postman had tried to deliver during their morning walk. By the time she has parked outside the long, low building, the baby has fallen asleep. She looks at the distance to the door of the sorting office – it is a few feet only – and at the short queue of people visible through the window. She looks at her sleeping daughter. She knows that she will not be able to carry both the parcel and the baby seat, if she brings it into the office with her.

She cannot come to a decision, and eventually she turns the key in the ignition again and drives home.

~

She lies with the baby for each of her naps, which are the scaffolding around which the whole day is built. It is bliss, that, the feeling when her tiny mouth releases its hold on Rachel's breast and she sinks into the full depths of sleep, her curled fist opening like a flower. Rachel knows that she too should sleep when the baby sleeps – it is not wrong, that oft-mocked advice – and yet she finds she cannot relinquish the opportunity for the forty minutes or so that is completely her own in mind, even while her body lies there next to her daughter, a bulwark against the vague and murky terrors of sleep. Sometimes she reads, trying to force herself away from mindless browsing to something more concrete; sometimes she just lies there, letting the diffident stream of her thoughts ebb and flow. Until the baby stirs, and cries, and with a mixture of relief and disappointment she presses her lips to the sweaty forehead and murmurs words to soothe and comfort her. *It's OK. Shush now. I'm here.*

~

Michelle from over the road, a woman with whom Rachel has never passed more than a few words before this, calls one morning. The baby is about four months old. Up to now, it seems that she has spent most of her life asleep or attached with a grim determination to Rachel's breast, content as long as she is in someone's arms. But just in the last few weeks she has woken up, like a small animal after the winter, demanding activity and stimulation, and the day stretches out now before Rachel with a daunting lack of structure or purpose.

By half past nine, when Michelle rings the doorbell, they are both dressed, and the baby has had her first nap of the day. She is in the sling now, solemnly observant, and Rachel is making some attempt to tidy the kitchen, which seems to have developed a thin but tenacious scum on every surface.

'Michelle!' She hopes the rising inflection in her voice indicates surprise, which is what she feels, and not displeasure, which is what she is afraid it sounds like. She is acutely aware of how long it has been since she has showered.

'I'm sorry, calling unannounced like this. I won't keep you.' Michelle's own child sits astride her hip, one chubby thumb plugging his mouth. When Rachel smiles at him – it is reflexive, how can you not smile at a small child? – he turns and buries his face in his mother's neck.

'I've been meaning for ages to drop this over. I got a big size, though, so hopefully it still fits.'

She holds out a gift bag, a cloud of white tissue paper spilling from its top. Rachel takes it, and wipes her hands on her jeans, and lifts out a little dress, a sleeveless linen with huge sunflowers all over. She holds it up to examine it.

'This is just gorgeous.' She looks at the other woman, squinting into the late spring sunshine. 'Honestly, Michelle, that's one of the nicest things she's been given. I love it.'

Michelle looks pleased. 'I thought it might be nice, for the summer.' She lifts a hand, and as Rachel nods in answer to her unspoken question she runs the back of one finger down the baby's velvet cheek. The baby stares gravely back at her.

'What a little dote.'

68

Rachel steps back to open the door wider. 'Come in, sure.'

'Ah no, I won't. I always hated when people just dropped in when I'd a small baby. But listen, I'm on my way down to the playgroup behind the church. Would you want to come down, maybe? It's a nice group, and they've tea and coffee and stuff.'

Rachel hesitates, looking at the baby who is surely too young to get anything out of a playgroup. She thinks of the untidy kitchen, of the bathroom that has not been cleaned in weeks.

'Oh God, I don't really think . . .' She trails off.

Michelle puts her head to one side. She is pretty, with a rounded, rural look to her. She has very dark hair, almost black, and ruddy cheeks that make her look permanently embarrassed. She smiles as someone who is self-conscious about her teeth.

'Are you sure? It might be fun.'

Her unwashed hair. Her ongoing inability to master feeding in public without a profusion of muslins and at least two cushions.

'No, honestly. I'm fine. Thank you, though. And for this.' She holds up the dress again. 'Really. You're very good.'

When the door has closed behind Michelle and her son, who gives Rachel a shy wave as they leave, it is suddenly very quiet. Rachel thinks again of all the things she should be doing. And then of the emptiness of the house all day, herself and the baby floating restlessly around it. She is seized with a sudden panic.

She finds her keys, her purse, the baby's changing bag, over-stuffed and unwieldy. Then she runs down the drive, calling after Michelle, hoping she is not too late.

~

Her parents have given them a voucher for a family photo-shoot and so, one warm, overcast day in early June, they dress

69

in various shades of blues and creams and drive down to the beach at Dollymount. It is a weekday, and early enough that there are few people around save the handful of dog walkers who are always there, hurling sticks into the surf to be retrieved with loud and joyous splashes. The photographer is there before them, sitting on a rock in the dunes; Camille, her name is, and Rachel knows from her website that she comes from Belgium and has been living in Ireland for eight years. She wonders how her mother came across her.

'Hi.' Rachel gives an awkward wave, trudging across the soft sand with the baby in her arms. Tom is just behind, with the changing bag.

'Hello.' The woman stands and smiles, her long dark hair moving in the warm breeze. 'A fabulous day, isn't it?' There is only the faintest trace of an accent.

They shake hands, and Camille strokes the baby's cheek, and Rachel likes her immediately. It is a scandal, how easily her loyalty can be bought with the merest homage to her child.

Tom gestures to the sky. 'It's not too cloudy, for photos?'

But Camille dismisses this with a tiny shake of her head, a gesture that strikes Rachel as very European and chic.

'No, not at all. This is better, this cloud. Better than a very bright day.'

She has brought, along with various camera bags, a box of accessories, and now she squats down and starts to lay these out on the sand – a thick and fluffy blanket in snowy white, a selection of stuffed toys, a tiny straw hat. She gets Rachel and Tom to stand, first, the baby between them, and urges them to look at each other, at the baby, at the sea – anywhere but at the long lens pointed towards them. Rachel tries to shake off the self-consciousness that sweeps over her any time a camera is aimed in her direction. She bends her head towards the baby, hiding behind the veil of her own hair.

Then Camille suggests they put the baby down on the blanket – at nearly five months she cannot yet sit without assistance, but Tom stretches out on the sand beside her and props her against his legs and she reaches for the nearest teddy and pulls it towards her mouth. When Camille places the straw hat on her head there is a collective exhale from all three adults, an 'Aaaah' of spontaneous delight at the impossible loveliness of her.

Camille turns to Rachel, gestures towards the blanket. 'You, too.'

'Let me just—' She moves to where she has left her bag on the sand, and roots through it for the hairbrush she had thrown in at the last minute, and pulls it through her wind-blown hair. When she turns back to the blanket Camille has started snapping away again. Rachel watches the way Tom dips his head towards the baby, whispering to her in their secret language; the way their daughter's face becomes instantly rapt with attention. She thinks she has never seen Tom so relaxed, so at ease with himself. It seems very important, suddenly, for this to be captured.

She waits, silent and smiling, hoping they will forget about her.

AFTER

Six Months

Things She Must Surely Have Missed

He is fat now. That is the first thing she sees, when she walks into the room and he is sitting there, this man who no longer looks like her husband. Fat, and the clothes he is wearing are nothing like the ones he would have worn before. She wonders where these clothes came from, if there is some room down one of these long Victorian corridors filled with thin T-shirts and white canvas runners left behind by previous inmates. Or maybe his mother brought them in, in their carrier bag with the tags still on; bewildered, more now than ever, Bernie, but clinging on to this one job she can do. She has, after all, been dressing him since he was born.

So, it is a stranger in cheap cotton who sits there, his hair longer now and greasy where it meets his scalp. He looks up as she enters the room, but the movement is slow, as if he must turn his head against some resistance, and when he finally meets her eyes his own are blank and unfocused. And then they clear, and a slow smile spreads across his face, and he says her name.

'Rach.'

There is such gladness in his voice, such relief, that she thinks she will not be able to bear it, and wants to run from the room. But the nurse is ushering her forward, to the chair placed opposite Tom's one, and it is easier to acquiesce. She sits in the chair, which exhales beneath her weight.

They look at each other for a long moment. Tom is the first to speak.

'I was hoping you would come. I keep asking them.' He nods towards the nurse, who has seated himself in the corner and is pretending not to listen.

'Well.' She shifts her eyes; it is too hard to look at him, this person who both is and is not the man she married. The man she loved, once upon a time.

'It's really nice to see you.' His voice is different too – slower, and there is a thickness to it, as if he has to speak around something in his mouth.

She wonders how long she must stay.

~

'Tom is happy for me to speak with you today.' The doctor had let a pile of the brown cardboard charts slip from her hands onto the desk, already overburdened with paperwork, and it teetered there unsteadily, threatening at any moment to fall. She was maybe fifty, or a little older, and looked tired, in the way every doctor Rachel had ever known looked tired. The make-up lay thickly in the creases of her face.

They had asked her to arrive half an hour before the scheduled visit so that she could meet with this woman, this consultant psychiatrist, and be brought up to date on Tom's condition. Rachel was not sure she wanted to know any more than she already did, but it didn't feel as if she had the option to refuse, and so there she sat, in this untidy office with stacks of paper on every surface and smiling graduation pictures in silver frames on the desk – a boy, a girl. Christine Trelawney, the doctor had introduced herself as, and although the name did not sound Irish to Rachel's ears, her voice was pure Cork.

Rachel took the chair she was directed to, in front of the window; outside there were small groups of people walking in the grounds. She couldn't tell from here which ones were patients and which ones visitors, or staff; they did not give off a cautionary aura. She thought suddenly of lepers forced to carry bells; *unclean, unclean.*

The doctor sat heavily into her own chair and rolled it towards the desk. 'Some of this may be repeating what you already know, but I just want to make sure we're on the same page.'

'That's fine.'

'Tom has been diagnosed with a major depressive episode with psychosis. I know he had had a history of depression for a number of years – there was a recent hospital admission, I understand – and you were aware he had been prescribed medication for that. It seems that, in the few months leading up to the car accident, he had unfortunately stopped taking it.'

'I didn't notice.' Rachel felt a need to justify herself, to explain. 'He never talked about it really, and I – I was working a lot, since his business fell through, and with the kids and everything . . . I'd kept an eye on them at the start, his tablets, when he first came out of hospital, but then – I just lost track.'

'Not your job,' Dr Trelawney said brusquely. 'I'm not saying this to apportion blame at all, his actions were not your responsibility. I just want to give you a clear picture of what happened.'

Rachel nodded. She felt she spent her life nodding at people now. She had become something almost entirely passive.

'Tom's depression was extremely resistant to treatment. He was started on medication as soon as he was admitted here – before that, in fact – but we had to trial a number of different treatments before we saw a change in his condition. He's now on a combination of drugs that seems to be working well for him. It's been a slow process.'

74

'So is he – better, now? I know it's not a case of being cured, but . . .'

'He's certainly improving. He has a better sense of reality now; the very disturbing thoughts he'd been having have gone away, largely. He's sleeping well, which helps. But it's all still quite fragile.'

'Does he . . . How much does he understand? Does he know what he did?'

The doctor spoke slowly. 'It fluctuates. We have spoken about it, and he's been having sessions with the psychology team. It's not a – a linear process, if that makes sense. Some days we have to start at the beginning, as if he's unaware of it all. Which may be a protective mechanism, of course.'

The doctor straightened the small stack of notes in front of her, moving her hands from top to sides and over again until the edges aligned. She kept her eyes on them as she went on speaking.

'He is very keen to see you today; he has been asking for you, a lot. And obviously it must be an incredibly difficult thing for you to do, to see him for the first time; we all understand that. But our primary responsibility is to Tom himself. If there were to be any – any altercation, or any – emotional outburst, I suppose – I feel that would be likely to affect his progress in a negative way. Does that make sense?'

She looked up, finally, and Rachel nodded, unable again to speak.

'If you feel you won't be able to control your emotions – which I would understand completely – then it may be better not to visit him today.'

Rachel found her voice – or someone else's voice, deep and throaty; it did not sound like her own. 'It's OK. I'm not going to – I won't do anything. I just want to see him.'

75

The doctor took off her glasses, and rubbed her eyes with the pads of her fingers. There were smudges of black beneath them.

'It doesn't seem fair of me to ask that, I know. It isn't fair, really. But it's for the best.'

~

Now Rachel sits opposite her husband and wonders if she was crazy to come. She does not know what she was hoping for exactly, but it was not this, this awkward *tête à tête* with a man she barely recognises. Would she have known him, if she had passed him in the street?

'How are you, Tom?'

'I'm all right. It's funny, in here. Strange old place.' He nods towards the nurse, who is reading a magazine in the corner. 'They're nice, though. Good to me.'

'Do you—' She has to clear her throat, and start again. 'Do you get many visitors?'

'My parents. Well – Mam, mainly. Dad came once, or twice maybe. You know what he's like.'

Rachel does know what he's like, and she nods, and then she finds that she cannot think of anything else to say. It is impossible to talk with him; how can they talk, when the thing they cannot speak about is everywhere around them, a giant prowling beast they cannot escape? It has sucked up all the air in the room, and now it is sniffing at their ankles; at any moment it may pounce, and bite.

Tom smiles at her; the smile is shy, uncertain.

'You changed your hair.'

She puts a hand to it instinctively; she had forgotten, already it has become an ordinary part of her.

76

'It's nice.' He nods towards her, that same unfamiliar smile on his face. 'Suits you.'

'Thanks.'

You tried to kill me. The words come into her head completely unbidden; it is not a thought she has ever articulated to herself before, and the realisation of this is as much of a shock to her as the idea itself. The children are so much at the forefront of her thoughts, of everything she does, that the sudden knowledge that she, too, was meant to die hits her like a blow to the face.

Why has she come? Because she was curious; she had married a man, and one day he had become a monster, and she had not noticed. She is looking for signs, for things she must surely have missed. And because she hopes it might help her to sleep at night, might give her that elusive 'closure', a word that is both an insult and a joke.

And because she misses him. That is the truth of it, the bit she cannot admit even to herself. She misses her husband around the house, the smell of him in the bed next to her, his heavy footsteps on the stairs. She misses hearing him lock up the house at night as she lies already drowsy on her pillows, and the way he would bring her a cup of tea unbidden as she sat in front of the TV with the kids on a Sunday afternoon. All of it, all of it is gone now. She will not find it here.

She shifts herself forward in the chair. 'I'll go, Tom.'

'Are you sure?' He is disappointed, but he looks exhausted too. 'You could stay a bit.'

'No, I need to go.'

'Will you come back?' His eyes are like those of a child. The want in them.

'I don't know. Maybe.' She knows this is a lie.

She stands, but he stays seated, so that she is looking down at him when he suddenly lifts his head and speaks again.

'How are the kids?'

The very room seems to hold its breath; a second, only.

'The kids are gone, Tom.'

'Yes. Yes. I knew that. Sorry.'

She nods, and her eyes are full of tears now, but for the first time she is looking into his eyes too, and neither looks away. And it might be a moment of understanding or it might only be a memory of something once shared, she does not know. And then she is out on the corridor again, following a different nurse this time, and she looks back only once and sees through the reinforced glass pane in the door her husband still in his chair, and the red-haired nurse leaning over to say something to him, and laying a large hand on his shoulder.

She cannot say any more that she loves him; nobody could ask that of her. But she finds that she does not hate him either. There is so little of him left to hate.

BEFORE

Three Years

Something She Already Knows

'I don't understand.' Rachel is impatient, jiggling the baby on her hip while she tries to coax her daughter to eat some of the pasta scattered cold and gluey on the tray of her high chair. Two babies in seventeen months; it was insanity, what they had done, that decision. Although *decision* is not really the word.

'We thought there'd be more work around.' Tom's voice is flat. 'It's all just dried up, since the crash. Nobody can afford to build anything. Even small extensions, all that sort of thing – it's just gone.'

'But what about the money from Gavin's dad?' She had never been truly happy with this arrangement, the idea of borrowing from family fraught with potential hazard and the amount itself frightening, but Tom and Gavin had been full of reassurance, and their very confidence was somehow infectious. And they had worked hard, she could not fault them for that. So many long evenings spent in the office they had rented in Fairview, its slick, minimalist signage and expensively designed logo, while Rachel paced resentfully at home with one fretful baby or another. It was all supposed to be worth it in the end.

Tom stands and opens the fridge, peering inside for a long moment. She stares at his shoulders, wondering if he really thinks she does not see this stalling tactic for what it is.

'Tom.' She tries to keep the rising anger from her voice. She can cope with the news, but this avoidance is too much.

'It's all gone,' he says finally, turning around. 'That last big marketing push, we had to try and give it everything. It just – there hasn't been the return on it. And now there's nothing left.'

Nothing left. 'But—' She knows what she is wondering, but she is struggling to find words that will not make it sound like an accusation. 'How could it happen so quickly? Things were fine up to recently, weren't they? You said they were fine.' The accusation is there, of course, despite her best efforts. *How did you not know?*

Tom doesn't answer, and when he eventually lifts his head to meet her gaze she sees that this is because there is no answer. She is suddenly frightened.

'We're not – we're not bankrupt or anything, are we?' The word is so alien. It is not her world, this; she has no experience of self-employment, of the dangers that lurk outside the cosy embrace of the public service.

Tom's reply is swift. 'No, no. It's nothing like that. Our own money is separate, the house and stuff. I just – we have to wind things up, me and Gav. And I can't draw a salary any more.'

'Shit, Tom.' She hands him the baby, unthinking, and wipes her hands on the legs of her jeans. 'What are we going to do?'

Tom's whole body is a shrug. He presses his face into the top of the baby's head.

'I don't know, Rach. I'm so sorry.'

'No, that's not . . .' She shakes her head, dismissing. 'It's not your fault, I know that.' This is the right thing to say; she does not allow herself to examine whether she really believes it.

She lifts her hands, defeated. 'I'm going to have to go back full time.'

She has only just gone back to work after her maternity leave, never long enough, the part-time role lobbied for and hard won. Even with that the busy days are almost unmanageable, and her days off a constant cycle of trying to catch up. Going back to a full roster seems inconceivable.

Tom's face contorts with apology. 'I'll get another job. I will, Rachel. I'll start looking tomorrow.'

'I know.'

She smiles, a glum sort of smile, and they look at each other. Sometimes, she knows, this sort of crisis brings people closer together.

~

She believes that he is sorry; she knows that he is, that he feels genuine regret and guilt and, presumably, failure and emasculation and all that other shite, all those complicated emotions that, for men, seem to be hopelessly enmeshed with their ability to provide for their families. And yet this knowledge does little to assuage the resentment that she feels building up inside her over the next few weeks, as she negotiates the messy return to full-time work and the myriad other arrangements this entails. For a time they are busier than ever, because even though there is no longer any income from it, it turns out that there are a thousand and one things entailed in wrapping up the business, all of them thankless and dispiriting. The premises have to be cleared out, and stacks of paperwork and now useless office supplies brought home to reside indefinitely in the spare room. She becomes petty; not a cup is left unwashed in the sink without her mentioning it; not a forgotten toothbrushing, revealed by an obliviously treacherous daughter as Rachel tucks her into bed five minutes after returning home from work, does she allow to go unremarked. They have to drop the childminder, with whom their children have just started to settle – they cannot afford to continue paying her, and in any case there is no need now with Tom home all the time. To her everlasting horror Rachel cries when she calls around to tell her, and the woman, a large soft woman with a bosom which is broad and comfortingly maternal, ends up sitting Rachel down and making her tea and promising her that everything will work out in the end. But although she urges Rachel to get back in touch with her once Tom is working again, Rachel knows it is impossible that she will not have been snapped up by a hundred other desperate families by then, and she will have to start the whole exhausting search all over again. It is just one more thing for which she can blame Tom.

It cannot go on forever, this cold war; she knows this, that it will eat away at their marriage if she allows it, sending poison to its very core. She knows, too, that Tom's guilt and his solicitude towards her will not last indefinitely, if they continue to meet the brick wall of her animosity. As she sits pumping breast-milk in a storage cupboard off the ward, eating her sandwich because there will not be time to do it when she has finished, she forces herself to breathe in and out slowly, trying to blow away the anger and the betrayal she feels. There was a time she felt she would have forgiven Tom anything; now, though, she finds it impossible to summon that reserve of goodwill. Now, she knows she will have to pretend, until with a bit of luck the feeling eventually becomes real.

~

With no real sense of what she is hoping for, she phones her mother-in-law. It is a Saturday morning, and Tom is giving the kids a bath. She resists the urge to remind him that the baby cannot sit up yet.

82

'Rachel, love. How are you?' Bernie's voice is pleased, and Rachel reminds herself that she really should try to ring her more often. Although she cannot imagine Tom ever phoning her own mother just for a chat.

'Grand, Bernie. I'm grand. How are you?'

'Ah, sure. You know yourself. This knee of mine – I was in with the specialist last week.'

'Yes, you were telling me.' Rachel says it brightly, both to demonstrate interest and to make it clear that Bernie does not have to go through the whole story from the start. This tactic usually proves futile, but she gives it a go.

Today, though, Bernie for once keeps it brief, and when there is a pause then in the flow of speech Rachel can hear the worry that is never far from Bernie's voice.

'Were you ringing for anything in particular, pet? Are the kids all right?'

'They're fine. Tom's giving them a bath.'

'Oh, they love that.'

'It's me, I suppose.' This already feels a disloyalty, but she plunges ahead. 'I've been – since things went under, with the company, it's been hard. Managing work, and everything.'

'Oh, of course. I feel so sorry for you all, love. If we were closer—'

'Ah no, no. It's not that.' She entertains a brief fantasy of having Bernie and Joe next door; the convenience, the horror.

'The kids are fine, they love having Tom home all the time. I just – I don't feel it's good for him, I suppose. He's a bit low.'

Bernie, for once, does not interject, and Rachel is forced to go on.

'He never wants to do anything. And his body clock is all over the place. Not sleeping at night, you know, and then if I've a day off he'll go to bed, sometimes, in the middle of the afternoon, and sleep for hours.

Bernie sighs. 'He gets like that, Tom, when he's a bit down about something.'

'I've never seen him like this before, though.'

'This is what he was like, now, back when he was a teenager. That time he went into hospital.'

The world freezes. There is a brief moment, an eternity, when Rachel could choose to pretend that this is something she already knows. But she hesitates too long, and when Bernie speaks again her voice is full of horror.

'Oh, Rachel. I'm sorry, Rachel. I thought he would have told you.'

'No. No, he didn't tell me.' She opens the back door and steps outside, looking up to make sure the bathroom window is closed.

'It wasn't a big thing, love. He got a bit low, and the doctor put him on some tablets, some sort of antidepressant; I don't remember the name of it now. But it didn't really work, and he ended up having to go in for a few weeks.'

'I never knew that, Bernie. Tom never told me.' She tries not to sound petulant.

'I'd say he's forgotten all about it. It was years ago.' This seems unlikely, but it is hardly the point.

Rachel wipes a spill of rain from the seat of the swing, and wedges herself into the narrow seat. She wonders if Bernie is in her own garden; that is where she most likes to make calls, her voice echoing up the hillside.

'And was he – was it bad, Bernie? Was he very unwell?'

'No, no. I'm making more of it than it was. He was just very down in himself – didn't want to get up or go out of the house or anything. We didn't know what was wrong with him.

84

He was only in there for a week or two, now, and then he was on more tablets for a bit, and after that he was fine. He went back to school the next year.'

'He missed a year of school?'

'Ah, well, not really. Half his friends had done the Transition Year, so he just joined back up with them then for Fifth Year. It didn't make any difference in the long run.'

Suddenly Rachel has to get off the phone. Her feelings of anger and hurt are, she knows, misdirected. She could hardly have expected Bernie to divulge all this to her, behind Tom's back. And yet the betrayal feels monstrous, unforgivable.

'I have to go, Bernie.'

'Ah Rachel. I'm sorry. Have I upset you now?'

'No, no.' She swallows hard, against the sudden unyielding ball in her throat. 'Thank you for telling me, I appreciate it. It – it helps, to know.'

'I'm sure he's not going to get like that again, Rachel. It's just the job. Sure that would hit any man hard, the disappointment. Once he finds something else, now, he'll be right again.'

'Yes. I'd say so.'

She knows how she sounds, but it is beyond her just now to try to relieve Bernie's anxious tremblings. She says goodbye, and does not wait for a response before she hangs up. For a time she keeps swinging gently back and forth, keeping her eyes on the bathroom window, where Tom's tall silhouette is dark against the frosted glass.

AFTER

Ten Months

All Your Private Business

They meet at the house. Rachel was reluctant, at first; it feels like an intrusion, which of course it is, and she does not want this woman examining the lines of dust on the windowsills, or pushing open the doors to the children's bedrooms on the pretext of using the loo. And yet the alternatives seem somehow worse; she has no desire to have this conversation in public, in some quiet coffee shop or hotel lobby, and nor does she want to go to the offices of the newspaper, where she imagines reporters at their desks falling respectfully silent as she passes. The house is better; it is her own domain at least, where there is a chance she might feel some illusion of control.

She had wondered if there would be a photographer too, but no, the woman had said they would get the pictures later, and it is a relief, not to have to think of dressing up or getting her hair done. But she dresses up anyway, a bit, in fitted grey trousers with a high waist, and a cashmere jumper in a sort of heathery blue. She blow-dries her hair carefully, and puts on a bit of make-up, her hands trembling only slightly; she starts to apply eyeliner, but then has a sudden vision of a piece that opens with the line 'For a woman in mourning, Rachel Callaghan cuts a remarkably glamorous figure,' and wipes it off again.

Once the house is as tidy as it can possibly be – a job that is so much easier, now, and one that for the first time in her life she finds soothing – she stands in the hall, trying to see the place through a stranger's eyes. To her, of course, it looks empty; the living room is denuded, now, of the acres of brightly coloured plastic, the scraps of sugar paper and uncapped markers. It has taken her ten long months to get to this place, where she could take the terrible but necessary step of starting to pack away the leavings of her children's lives, and for the last few weeks it has consumed her. She refused all offers of help; she could not bear, somehow, the idea of somebody else's hands doing this work.

They are still here, their things, but stowed safely away now in their bedrooms, which remain individual shrines to their former inhabitants; a reckoning set aside for another day.

~

Her mother thinks it a terrible idea. Her father too, for that matter, but on this sort of thing his opinion carries little weight; he is the type of man who thinks birthday greetings posted online a gross invasion of privacy. But her mother – who is, in fact, a great fan of the journalist, regularly passing on to Rachel nuggets of wisdom from her weekly columns – had paled visibly on hearing of Rachel's plan to go ahead with the interview.

'Do you think it's a good idea?' Her hand at her cheek; some-what over-dramatically, Rachel thought.

'I don't see why not. It's a proper newspaper, it's not one of the rags.'

'No, I know that. But just – it'll be very invasive, Rachel. They'll want to know everything. All your private business.'

'I don't really care.' This could not be true, surely, but she threw it out regardless. Defiant. 'They know it anyway. It's all been written about before.'

Rebecca moved behind them, carrying bread to the table. It was three days before Christmas, and they were all at Rebecca and Doug's place for lunch after the boys' nativity play. Rachel had not gone to the play – hadn't a notion of going into a primary school full of excited children and doting parents, although this had not stopped the quick flash of resentment when Rebecca suggested she might prefer to meet them at the house afterwards. But she had come anyway, and now she prepared lunch with her mother and sister while Doug and his father-in-law took the children for a quick run around the park. It was with only slight smugness that Rachel noted to herself that for all Rebecca and Doug's lack of conventionality, the old gender roles refused to be held at bay for very long. She looked around her sister's small and narrow kitchen, the clash of red cupboards against the blue of the walls. There were piles on every surface, papers and artwork and unidentifiable bits of plastic; clean but crumpled clothes. She knew it made her mother itch to sit amongst it all.

'I suppose it can't do any harm, Mam.' Rebecca was not used to taking on the role of peacemaker; it sat uneasily on her. Still, she made an effort. 'She's right; there's been so much written already. At least this might be halfway accurate.'

This was part of it, Rachel thought; the part that was explainable, anyway. It had been one of the strangest aspects of this whole unreal time – the thousands and thousands of words written about her family, written by strangers who had never met any of them, and never would. She had read them all, every news report and column, every mention online, like so many lashes on her back. Some of it was, predictably, awful, even the basic facts of her children's lives mangled. The more thoughtful ones got most of it right; and yet. Somehow it was never quite them, the family depicted in these lines of inky print; somehow it was like reading about a family in a story.

She tried again.

'I'll have full control over what's written. They've told me that; they'll let me see it all before it goes to print.' This was not precisely what the journalist had told her, when they spoke on the phone. She had been instead generally reassuring, in a way that was not quite specific enough. But by then, Rachel thought, she had been looking for a reason to say yes.

Her mother sniffed; a dry, deliberate noise.

'I would have thought you'd have more dignity.'

Maybe, if it was not Christmas; maybe, if she had not had to walk past the fireplace in Rebecca's sitting room with its two enormous stockings hanging side by side. Maybe, if that morning she had not stood for twenty minutes staring into her medicine cabinet and wondering if any combination of the pills inside would allow her to drift into a dreamless, endless sleep.

'Well, I would have thought you'd have more compassion, I suppose, Mam. Especially when it's absolutely fuck all to do with you.'

The very air in the kitchen seemed to freeze. They were not a family who swore at each other. But this too, Rachel thought in the sudden silence, this steel in her voice – this too she had inherited from her mother, along with the wavy hair and the hay fever, the horror of precocious children.

Rebecca jumped up from the table, clasped her hands together.

'Maybe we should all have a little drink.'

'Oh, for God's sake, Rebecca, it's not even twelve o'clock. Have a bit of cop on.'

Margaret sniffed again, having managed to be offended by both her daughters for entirely different reasons.

They worked on in silence, three women side by side.

~

She arrives exactly on time. Rachel hears her footsteps on the gravel path, but she waits until the ring of the doorbell, too loud always in this empty house, and there is a yawning hollowness in the pit of her as she moves slowly to open the door. The journalist is older than Rachel had expected – the picture at the top of her column, she realises now, has been unchanged for years – and very tall, with a mass of wavy hair. She flashes a bright, professional smile.

'Rachel?' Her voice seems to strike them both as too loud, too cheerful, and her next words are almost comically muted. 'It's very good to meet you. Darina Byrne.' The hand she stretches out has dark crimson nail polish, and the nails are short and squared off.

'Come on in.' Rachel steps back and the woman moves past her, exclaiming as everyone does about the light in the hallway. Rachel leads the way to the kitchen, which she has decided is the easiest place to be, with the bulwark of the big table between them. She has laid out mugs, and a plate of Danish pastries, and water in a glass jug. She had meant to slice a lemon but has forgotten, and now it is too late.

'Sit down. Please.' She moves to the sink, unable yet to meet the woman's eyes, and fills the kettle. 'Can I get you tea, or coffee?'

'Water is fine, thank you.'

'Help yourself.'

She decides against boiling the kettle just for herself, unwilling somehow to be on an uneven footing, and dries her hands instead on a tea towel before sitting down. The woman has taken off her coat, long and many-tasselled, and hung it on the back of her chair; now she is busy setting down a notebook, two pens, a small black device on the table in front of her. She arranges these neatly, squaring off each one before moving on to the next. Rachel wonders if she is nervous too.

Then she looks up; there is the bright smile again.

'Rachel. I want to thank you, first of all, for agreeing to speak to me today. I appreciate it can't be easy.'

Rachel shrugs, the movement small and constrained. 'That's all right.'

'With your permission, I'm going to record our conversation. It makes it easier to accurately transcribe later on.'

Rachel nods; she is prepared for this, they had discussed it during the initial phone call. Which had happened eventually, long after the first of the two emails, which she had read quickly and immediately deleted. But she had lain awake that night, regretting the haste of her decision, although not enough to retrieve the message from the Trash and read again the polite but firm enquiry. The second email had come ten days later, and this one she had read over and over, parsing every word for hidden meaning. Still it had taken her nearly a week more to make the decision to reply, and then she had sent it off quickly without pausing to proofread, and had lain awake again long into the night. Darina had called the next day, her voice clear and instantly recognisable from the Sunday-morning radio shows, where she was a regular contributor.

Now as Darina presses buttons on the little recorder, testing that it is working, Rachel cannot remember why she has agreed to do this.

'So.' Darina clasps her hands together and sets them down on the table. 'Tell me how you and Tom met.'

Rachel is startled; she had not expected this, somehow. The story she has been rehearsing in her head for the last week is of the accident itself, the aftermath, her feelings about Tom now. She has not prepared herself to go back in time.

'We met – well, in a nightclub, to be honest. Not very original.'

'You were students?'

'No – at least, I'd been out for about a year. I'm a nurse,' she explains, and Darina nods as if she does not already know this.

'And Tom was – he's an architect, you know, and he'd just finished his exams, so he was working for one of the big firms. But it was always his dream to have his own set-up.'

'He was ambitious?'

Rachel is never sure what people mean by this. Everyone wants things, surely. Just not always the expected things.

'Yes. He was really passionate about it. I liked it – that that was his job, I mean. There was something very attractive about it.' She feels herself redden. 'It's silly, I suppose. Men in TV dramas are always architects, you know? I think it's just so that they can set things in very elaborate houses.'

Rachel hears herself, this toneless rambling, and wonders if it is coherent at all. She cannot imagine any of it written down.

'So yeah, we just – we hit it off, I suppose. We went out for a few years – four years – and then we bought the house, and we got married.'

'You were young. To get married, I mean.'

'Yeah. Yes, I suppose. I was twenty-six.'

'You were keen to start a family straight away?'

Rachel nods. 'Yeah. We both wanted that. Tom's an only child, I think he always felt he missed out a bit.' She looks up suddenly. 'But maybe don't say that bit? His mother – I wouldn't want her to be hurt.'

Darina nods, but does not in fact promise anything.

I got pregnant in the spring after the wedding, and our daughter was born then in January.

'And at that stage – were there any signs of Tom's illness? Anything you noticed?'

She shakes her head. 'No. Not really. He was a bit stressed, when I got pregnant. I think it happened more quickly than he expected. But he was fine, then; he was excited. He cried when she was born. I'd never seen him cry before that.'

Darina nods slowly, and purses her lips. 'So when did things change?'

'How do you mean?'

'When did you begin to see signs of Tom's true nature?'

Rachel shakes her head, frowning; the phrase sounds ridiculous, like the voiceover to a low-budget documentary. 'It's not like that. It wasn't – it's not like he was hiding something. But he – it was after our son was born, I suppose, that he seemed to change. Around the time that the business – they went bust, it wasn't his fault, it was the crash and everything.' Is she making excuses for him? She doesn't mean to. She is just trying to tell it the way it was. 'But they had to close down, and that hit him very hard. He became really depressed.'

'And how did that' – Darina uses her hands; a big, expansive gesture – 'manifest?'

Rachel struggles to remember. There was no one particular thing. 'He was just sad all the time. Moody. He had no interest in doing things – taking the kids out, or visiting his parents, or that. That kind of thing.'

'And did he seek help? Did he see a doctor?'

'Eventually. I was pushing him to go, but he really didn't want to, at first. But he went, and they put him on tablets, and for a while he seemed better. And then – well, there was a – an incident, I suppose you'd call it, he was in a shop and he was acting really strangely, they had to call me to come and get him. So then he went into hospital for a bit. And he got different tablets, stronger ones.' These calm, measured sentences; she marvels at their inability to do justice to the true horrors of that time.

'Did that help?'

'A bit. He stopped crying all the time – before that, I used to find him crying in our bedroom in the middle of the day. And up all hours at night, he could never sleep. That got a bit better, with the medication. He wasn't the same, though – he didn't go back to the person he'd been.'

Darina nods silently, her face a mask of sympathy. It is difficult to tell what is real.

'Go back a bit. Tell me what family life was like. Ordinary life, when Tom was well.'

And so Rachel does; this is the easy bit, she finds, talking about her children, which is something that the people close to her do not encourage her to do. It feels strange, to say their names aloud; she realises she has not done it in weeks.

'And was Tom a good parent, would you say?'

'He was a great parent. The kids were mad about him.' She has been expecting to cry, it seemed inevitable that it would happen, but even so the suddenness of the tears takes her by surprise. They hover for a moment at her eyelids, and then she blinks, and there is a slow spill down the grooves of her nose, the angle of her mouth. She presses her fingers to her face.

Darina leans forward. 'Let's take a break for a minute.'

'OK.' Rachel takes a deep breath, and pushes herself up from the table. 'Would you like something to drink now? I'm going to put the kettle on.'

'Coffee would be lovely, then. Thank you.'

There is something restorative in filling the kettle at the tap, finding the cafetière, measuring carefully the spoonfuls of dark, unforgiving grounds. By the time Rachel has set the two cups on the table and placed the sugar bowl between them, she is calm again.

'Would you like to see some pictures of the children?'

The other woman looks startled, and then – something else – moved, even? When she answers her voice sounds more real than it has up to now.

'Yes. I'd like that a lot.'

Rachel nods, unable again to speak, and they carry the mugs into the living room. The photo albums are in a row on the bottom shelf of the big bookcase, their spines blank and innocent. Rachel kneels on the floor; she means only to pull out the books before standing up again, but Darina comes to kneel beside her, the citrus tang of her perfume sharp in Rachel's nose. The woven rug, which she'd found at a market stall during her second pregnancy, is thin under their knees, and the floor beneath is cool.

'I never really print out pictures; people don't, now, do they? But I used to make a photo book, at the end of every year.' She pulls the albums from the shelves, slim matt volumes with a binding that is not leather, but purports to be. There are four of them – yellow, mauve, indigo, and a kind of sagey green. Her daughter had helped with that last one, picking out the photo for the cover, which is a shot taken by a helpful stranger on the beach in Kerry, the four of them squinting into the sun.

Darina lays a crimson finger on the cover of the first book, the pale-haired baby in Christmas pyjamas. Her round, nappied bottom is jutting into Rachel's laughing face, her tiny arms grabbing for Tom's neck.

'Was this her first Christmas?'

'Yes.' Rachel smiles. 'We went a bit mad with the presents, I don't know what we were thinking. She barely looked at them. She loved the wrapping paper, though.'

She turns the pages of the book. There is, she is discovering, something so seductive about talking about herself and her family, uninterrupted, here in this warm and quiet room. Outside, the winter sky is losing its light, although it is not yet four o'clock. She wonders idly if the little black device is still recording, forgotten on the kitchen table; catching perhaps just the echo of their voices.

Darina's voice is very gentle, so gentle in fact that at first Rachel does not understand the question.

'When did he first become violent?'

'Who?' she says stupidly, and then realises. 'You mean Tom?'

Darina nods.

'No, Tom was never violent.'

'Well.' The condescension in her voice is slight but it is there, inarguable. 'Until he was, I suppose.'

'No, that's . . .' She stops, unsure how to go on. She does not think of what Tom has done as violence, exactly; it seems too removed for that. He did not strike anyone, or strangle, or smother; he did not beat, or shout, or hold heads underwater. He just turned the car, and the rest took care of itself.

She tries to gather herself. 'What I mean is, before that day he had never hurt any of us. Or anyone at all; I never saw him get into a fight or anything like that. He wasn't that type of person.'

'Was he emotionally abusive to you?'

'No. No.' The answer comes quickly, but only after giving it does she think, and wonder. It is not a question she has asked herself before now.

Darina keeps pressing. 'But there must have been some signs?'

There must, mustn't there? It is impossible that you could live with a person, share his bed and his breakfast table, know every inch of his body intimately, and yet. It is not credible; she would not have believed it of somebody else.

But this is all too much, now.

'Just – excuse me a minute. Please.' Rachel hoists herself from the floor, her right foot numb and sponge-like when she tries to put weight on it, and half stumbles from the room. Upstairs it is very warm, the heat of the day having settled at the top of the house; Rachel imagines it hovering there, an unseen cloud. She closes the door to the bathroom behind her and turns the key in the lock, which has grown stiff with lack of use. In the mirror her eyes are puffy, and her tears have left faint streaks of mascara down her cheeks.

She will ask her to leave. It is her right; this is her house, after all, and she does not owe this woman anything. She does not owe the world her story, either, and the whole thing strikes her suddenly as something grotesque, the idea that people will read her words over their slow Saturday breakfasts, pausing now and then to flick crumbs of toast away from a picture of her children.

Downstairs she hears Darina moving; a soft, nasal grunt as she rises from the floor, and then firm steps across the living room and into the hall, where she seems to pause. Rachel wonders how long she has been upstairs. She looks again in the mirror, and wets some toilet paper to remove the smudges from beneath her eyes. She hears Darina enter the kitchen, and the scrape of her chair as she pulls it away from the table. It is not over, then.

She gives a final swipe at the mascara and drops the crumpled tissue into the toilet bowl. She knows that she would be perfectly within her rights to call the whole thing off, even now, but she knows too that having the right is not helpful if the awkwardness of exercising it would be more than she could bear. And she knows that it would be more than she could bear. Rachel runs a hand through her hair, and unlocks the bathroom door, and walks slowly back downstairs.

BEFORE

Two Years

Fragile as Glass

'What did he say?'

Tom says nothing for a bit; he is taking off his jacket, hanging it up, dropping the keys into the little dish on the hall stand. He straightens up and runs his hands through his hair. Rachel is impatient, eager to hear everything; she knows she has built this appointment up in her head to be the answer to everything, and she knows too that this is dangerous.

Finally Tom turns to her and shrugs.

'He thinks I have a depression.' He says the word as if he doesn't quite trust it.

'OK.' She forces herself to breathe. This is not news, but it is good, still, to have her own diagnosis validated.

'He wants me to start taking some tablets. Here.' He fishes in his pocket and pulls out a piece of paper, already crumpled and slightly translucent in places, and hands it to her. Rachel looks at it. The name is familiar, it is one she has dished out many times at work in the tiny plastic cups, round and white and innocuous. She wonders if it is the same medication that he took before, that mysterious time as a teenager; she cannot ask, because she has never told him that she knows, that his own mother had revealed the thing he so clearly wanted to keep hidden from her. She does not really know which of them she is trying to protect.

'OK, so.' She turns her face up to his. 'Well, this is good, isn't it?'

'I suppose. I don't know. I don't want to turn into a zombie.'

'Tom.' She tries to take the harshness out of her voice; it seems to be always there, these days, simmering just below the surface. It is just – Jesus. It is the idea that it would be the *pills* that would turn him into something dead-eyed and emotionless. God, he has no clue.

She tries again. 'They won't make you a zombie, love. They might just get you back to yourself a bit.'

He shrugs again; she is sick of the shrugs, of the non-committal everything of him.

'Maybe.'

The children trundle out into the hall, lured from the late-afternoon TV by the sound of their father's voice. Their son pads a few steps on his newly mobile legs and then sits down, made unsteady by the weight of his own nappy, which is heavy with damp. Rachel picks him up.

'What about a counsellor? Did he say anything about that?'

Tom frowns. 'Yeah, he was really pushing that. Some woman out in Clontarf that he says is good. I told him no, though. It's not my kind of thing.'

'Tom. You have to be open to things. To trying it, at least.'

'I'm not going to sit in front of some stranger and talk about private things.' His scoffing laugh is unkind, although she tells herself it is not directed towards her. 'I couldn't do it, Rach.'

Their daughter lifts her head from where she is playing with the laces of Tom's shoes, attuned to the different tone in his voice, and Rachel forces a smile into her own words.

'Well, why don't I go and get these now, at least? Get started straight away.' She does not allow room for argument. 'You take him – he needs a change. I'll be back in twenty minutes.'

She pushes the baby into Tom's arms and opens the front door. She has the keys in her hand already, and the precious bit of paper, the one that is going to make everything all right again. She does not look at Tom as she fishes for her purse in the pile of junk on the hall stand.

~

In the car she forces herself to breathe, to keep to the middle of the lane, to slow down at the turns. She had thought that the new job would be the solution to everything; that was the problem, her faith in Tom's return to work fixing things, and when this had proved not to be the case she had felt a disappointment that was like something tangible in her mouth, coarse and bitter. It had taken so long in the first place, for Tom to find the new job. He had seemed to try, all right, after those first unhappy weeks; she would come home from a long shift, her feet aching and swollen despite the winter chill, and find him at the computer, a collection of tabs with the right websites open in front of him. The children would be asleep and the house relatively tidy, and she would think *at least, at least.* But somehow the internet searches never seemed to materialise into anything, and even when she started looking through the ads with him herself, there was always some reason not to apply, some not-quite-clear unsuitability. When this job with the council had finally come up it was more a case of attrition than anything particularly appealing about it – although to Rachel the regular hours and the mention of a pension were reason enough. But in any case he had gone to the interview with a relatively good grace, and she had not been surprised when the call had come a few days later. People liked Tom, that was the thing – his boyishness, his slightly unsettling energy. When he switched it on, he could charm the world.

And now he was going to the job, and the pay was coming in, and although it was still not enough that Rachel could drop her hours again, they could all breathe a little easier at last. And yet Tom himself was – not. Not Tom, not himself.

She slows the car at the run of shops with the bright green cross of the pharmacy overhead, and waits for another car to pull out before slipping into the space. It feels like months that she has been nagging him to go to the doctor; twice she had almost picked up the phone herself to make the appointment. But always she had stopped short, aghast at herself for even considering the kind of infantilising behaviour from which she has always protected her patients at work. *Mammy won't be able to handle bad news.* No, it was something he had to do himself. And he had done it, eventually, although really it was hard to argue that her constant nagging was any less disempowering than simply making the call for him. A small niggly part of her had wondered if he would even go, if instead he would drive around for an hour and then come back, full of spurious reassurances from the doctor that the constant black moods and his inability to get out of bed in the morning were nothing to worry about. But no, he had gone all right; the piece of paper now lying on the passenger seat is proof enough, and once again she berates herself for doubting him. She is no sort of a wife.

~

By the time she gets back from the pharmacy – she has taken the long way around, because *why not?*, it is good to be out on her own for a bit – it has started to rain. It has been a rubbish sort of a summer, weather-wise, and although it is still only

July she finds herself hankering already for shorter days, for the excuse to close the curtains at half past four and throw some logs into the stove. Somewhere not far there is an ice-cream van on the prowl; she hears the tinny music jangle across the empty air with that slightly eerie quality, a deserted fairground at dusk. Summer sounds, echoing through the years from her own suburban childhood; games of Red Rover on the street, and British Bulldog, and Relievio; Atlantic 252 from the radio in next door's back garden, and *Come on, Tim!* from the TV in the corner of the sitting room where her father would sit glued to the couch those first two weeks of July. Her own house now is quiet, and when she puts her key in the lock and pushes the door in she is stopped short, the door jarring as if coming up against something immovable. It takes her a second to realise that the chain is on.

'Tom.' She waits a second, tries again, louder this time. 'Tom?'

This has never happened before. She wonders stupidly if they have gone out, and then realises that in that case the chain could not have been drawn across.

'Tom?' She can hear the fear in her voice, although what she might be frightened of she could not really say.

'Tom?!'

And then at last there is a noise and he is coming down the stairs, just his feet appearing first in the narrow gap that is all that is visible to her of her home, and then his long legs in the dark jeans, and suddenly she is filled with the sickening certainty that when his face appears it will not be Tom at all but some stranger, alone in the house with her children who are tiny and trusting and fragile as glass. She is seized with the sudden urge to vomit. And then he takes one more step and he is there in the gap, her husband, familiar as her own skin, and the relief of this fills her with a sudden rage so intense she fears she will claw at his face. He pushes the door briefly to and releases the chain with a metallic scraping, and then finally the door is open wide.

'What the hell, Tom?' It is almost a screech.

'Jesus, Rach. I'm sorry.' And it is true, his face is contrite. 'I must have put it on automatically when you went out.'

This makes no sense; the chain is only ever put on at night, and even at that they tend to forget it more often than not.

'Where are the kids?'

He looks at her strangely then, and she realises that her voice is still too frantic, and she tries to smile. It feels like a rictus on her face.

'They're upstairs, with the Big Lego.' They have all adopted this way of referring to the big clunky toddler bricks, bright and indestructible.

'OK.' And she realises she can hear them now from the bedroom, their high-pitched stream of chatter. She hears too her own breathing, heavy, as if she has been running.

'Rach.' He puts his hands on her shoulders, and somehow he has become the steady, sensible half of them, and she the one who must be cosseted. 'I'm sorry. It was an accident, honestly. I wasn't trying to lock you out.' He finishes with a little laugh, and it feels almost funny that it is this, this utter bullshit that has brought a smile to his face for what feels like the first time in weeks.

She pushes past him into the kitchen, and puts her bag down on the table. 'I got your tablets.' Her voice, she hears, is that of a sulky child. She pulls the forgotten package out of her pocket, and he takes it dubiously.

Rachel shakes her head before he can speak. 'You're to take them, Tom. You have to give them a chance.'

He looks at her, and he nods. It will have to do.

103

'OK then.' She tries to smile at him, to make the effort. 'I'm going to have a shower. Will you put on some chips or something?'

'Sure. You take your time.'

And his voice is for once so reasonable, so in control, that all her dark imaginings are rendered absurd. This is something she does, she knows – allows things to blow up out of all proportion in her unrested, overwrought mind. She steps out of her shoes, goes quickly up the stairs, slips into the bathroom before the children notice she is back and come clamouring for her with their endless delightful, suffocating needs. In the mirror she avoids her own gaze, tired suddenly of the endless loop of her thoughts.

AFTER

Twelve Months

In the Dark

It is one of those hotels meant only for people visiting Dublin on business; you would never walk through its doors otherwise. Everything about it is blandly anonymous and inoffensive – the grey and purple lobby, the barely audible piped music, the attractive, interchangeable staff. Although Rachel has never been inside one, she can picture the bedrooms – the wood veneer, the hot drink station; the beige and blue carpet, good for hiding stains.

A scrollwork sign over the arched entrance to the bar reveals that it is called The Arrivals Lounge, a name that seems to Rachel less and less clever the more she thinks about it. Inside, it is more of the same – smooth and agnostic, devoid of any atmosphere in a way that she finds curiously soothing. She takes a seat at the bar, hoisting herself awkwardly onto the stool in her unaccustomed skirt. She can't remember the last time she wore a skirt – this kind of skirt, anyway, black and tight and unashamedly wanting; maybe when she and Tom were first going out. Back when it seemed important to dress with a thought to other people's reactions.

She orders a glass of wine, white, and fingers the stem of the glass, trying to appear relaxed. There is nobody else sitting at the bar; there are only a handful of people in the place at all, it is early still. The only big group is in the corner, all men, ties loosened already and occasional brays of laughter which erupt gratingly into the hush of the bar. The girl collecting the glasses moves among them with practised fluidity, her tight smile unyielding, ignoring the cat calls and the sweaty hands that glance off her thighs as she brushes past. Rachel wonders who this performance is for; it cannot be for the girl, surely, for even the most deluded of these men could not possibly believe that she would look twice at any of them. It is for each other, then, and all the more baffling for that.

The barman points to her glass, and she nods, and watches as he unscrews the cap from the bottle and pours again. The wine is nothing special, but it is cold at least, and goes down easily. She should have had something to eat, something more than the single piece of toast she had forced down before leaving the house. She was already feeling nauseated by then, long before the wine, with the anticipation of what she might do. What she might allow herself to do.

~

It is nearly ten o'clock by the time he arrives. There have been other possibilities – an older man with silvering hair who chatted in broken English with the barman; a man with a Belfast accent whose thick dark curls reminded her of Tom's. The man who takes the stool next to her just before ten is dark-haired too, but shorter than her husband, and stocky where he had been lean, rangy. He orders a pint of Guinness, and the barman places a beer mat in front of him, and moves away to the taps. Rachel fiddles with her phone, both hands on the bar, and glances at him from under her eyelashes until eventually he happens to look up at the right time. He nods awkwardly, raises the brimming pint.

'Cheers.'

106

She lifts her glass, inclines her head towards him. He takes a sip of his drink, and smacks his lips with a grimace.

Rachel affects a shudder. 'I could never stomach that stuff.'

'No? I'm not too keen on it, to be honest. But, I just thought. When in Rome.'

His accent is English. London, she thinks, although not with confidence; she finds it hard to do more than separate the sawn-off Northern vowels of the soap operas from everywhere else. He is about her age, or possibly younger by a year or two; there is the beginning of a bald patch at the centre of his scalp. He is a good-looking man, for all that.

He turns his body now towards her, cumbersome on the stool, which seems too small for him. Rachel has a sudden vision of some circus act, an elephant on a unicycle, although this is hardly fair. He is not remotely elephant-like. She mirrors his movement, half turning her body towards his; an invitation.

'You're not from here.'

He laughs. 'No. No, I'm just in town until tomorrow night. Work.'

'What sort of work do you do?' She tries to keep her voice natural, to avoid the vampish tone that threatens to creep into the clichés of this script.

'Marketing.' He grimaces. 'It sounds worse than it is.'

She rewards this with a smile.

He looks around vaguely. 'How about you? Are you meeting someone?'

'I was.' She waves her phone at him mournfully. 'A friend, but she's had to cancel. I think I'll just head home.'

'Can I persuade you to stay?' He dips his head towards her glass, empty now.

She feigns hesitation, narrowing her eyes as if appraising him, then giving in with a rueful smile, a reluctant nod.

He looks delighted.

'What was it?'

'The pinot grigio. Thank you.' She settles herself now, on the stool, tucks her hair – she has had it cut again, shorter still, and she cannot get used to the weightlessness of it – behind her ears. She wishes she had remembered to put on perfume. She has hardly ever worn perfume in the last few years – she had stopped when her daughter was born, afraid that the smell would confuse or irritate her – but there is surely a bottle of it languishing in some drawer; a present from Tom, or from the kids on Mother's Day.

The barman has to open a new bottle of the wine. This one is ice-cold, and she traces a finger down the condensation which forms instantly on the outside of the glass.

'This is kind of you. Thank you.'

'Not at all. Nice to have somebody to chat to. I'm Sebastian, by the way. Seb.'

'Rachel.' For a brief moment she wonders if it would have been better to give another name; but no, that is a nonsense, she must not allow her mind to run away with her. They shake hands; his skin feels rough, as if he spends more time outdoors than the job and the suit would suggest.

'Is it your first time in Dublin?'

'I came here once as a student. But that was – you know.' He shrugs. 'Pubs and clubs and six of us in a youth hostel dorm. We did that Viking boat thing, I remember. That was good fun.'

'I've never tried it.'

He reddens slightly, embarrassed, and she is touched. 'Well. A bit silly, really. Kids would enjoy it.' He twists the thick silver band on his ring finger. She does not ask him if he has children; she does not want to know this.

There is a drop of water on the bar, and she pushes a finger through it, tracing patterns in the liquid. She feels him watching her, and she bites her lip. She had thought she would have forgotten how to do this – how to display herself, to perform attractiveness for a man who is a stranger – but she finds now that it comes back to her, this way of being around men.

When she looks at him again she can feel the change that has happened. He is looking at her directly now, and his back is straighter, and she can feel that he both wants her more and likes her less. She understands that already it has been decided they will go to bed together. And part of her wants to refuse, and thus to redeem herself in his eyes; but that is not the reason she came out tonight.

He raises his eyebrows at her, and she smiles with closed lips. His voice is different too, when he speaks.

'Another drink?'

She holds his gaze; holds it, holds it, just a second more.

And then.

'Why not?'

~

In the lift they do not touch, or talk, but stand in parallel facing the closed doors, and watch as the numbers slowly rise. Rachel has a sudden fear that the lift will stop on some intermediate floor and the doors will open, and standing there will be some person from her other life, her real life – Tom's old business partner, or her daughter's preschool teacher, perhaps. Her mother-in-law. But the lift does not stop, and the doors do not open, not until they have reached the fifth floor, and then he is leading the way out of the lift and down a long, dimly lit corridor with prints of Dublin bridges on the walls. He stops at one of the many identical doors. 512, she notices – deliberately takes note, in fact, in case she has to recount it at some later date; to whom, though? The police?

She is appalled at her own recklessness; this is dangerous, this is a dangerous thing to do, she tells herself, to disappear into a hotel room with this strange man and not a soul on earth knowing where she is. And she finds that the danger is what is making her do it, for the prospect of sex itself holds no more interest for her than running a marathon. No, it is the danger that pushes her forward, as he stands holding the door open and gestures towards the shadows of the room. She steps inside.

It is all dark for a moment as he fumbles at the card slot by the door, and then the lights come on and she sees the room, which is exactly as she'd imagined it, down to the colour of the bedspread and the trouser press in the corner. She sits on the end of the bed, her knees together, her back straight as if at a job interview. He is still standing by the door, unsure of himself now – had he ever actually thought that she would say yes to this? Maybe he is regretting it all now, Rachel thinks, and she finds that she does not care.

'Would you like another drink? There's a bottle of whiskey there; I found a place near Grafton Street, great little shop . . .' His voice trails off. She sees that it will be up to her, all of it.

'Sure, yeah. Thanks.' She forces the smile back to her lips.

His relief is immense. 'Great.' He rubs his hands together, then takes two glasses from the bedside table and unscrews the lid from the bottle. The liquid is golden and viscous-looking, and she can smell it from here.

'No ice, I'm afraid.' He hands her a glass. 'I could—'

'No, no. This is fine.' She holds the glass in both hands. Has she ever drunk whiskey neat before? Has she ever drunk whiskey at all before, really, save mixed with a healthy sluice of Coke at somebody's house party, back when you drank whatever was going? She raises the glass to her lips now, and takes a sip, and feels the long slow burn down the back of her throat.

He sits beside her on the bed, and she feels the mattress sag under their combined weight. They tap their glasses together, and she drinks again, willing on the heady feeling, the shedding of inhibitions she knows will come. His phone, tossed on the bed beside him, buzzes and lights up with a message, and as he reaches to switch it off she sees that the wallpaper is a photograph of a child, and she feels slightly sick.

Then his face is right in front of her, his mouth pressing against hers, and this part has happened so quickly that she jerks her head backwards instinctively, and he recoils.

'Sorry. Sorry, I—' He raises his hands slightly in blustering semaphore. *I am not a threat.*

'No, it's fine. Sorry. I just – I wasn't expecting.' She smiles, someone else's smile, and bends towards him again, and although it is strange at first and the taste of him is wrong, eventually they find a rhythm, and she finds if she keeps her eyes closed it is bearable. He is tentative when he undresses her, although not unpractised, and after that it is just sex, neither horror nor bliss, but he is tender enough, and he does not, thankfully, turn out to be the kind of man whose words become vulgar and cruel in the dark, or for whom a little light strangulation is all in a day's work.

She has not given a moment's thought to contraception. She realises this halfway through the act, and her eyes fly open, although he is deep in his own reverie by then and does not notice. She spends half a minute in frantic arithmetic, and decides that it is probably OK, and tries to relax again. When he comes it is with a shudder, but he does not call out, and Rachel knows that he too is used to sex being largely for stolen moments with a lightly sleeping child on the other side of the bedroom wall.

Afterwards they lie close but not touching, and they talk about a Netflix series they have both been watching recently, and it is without a doubt the most enjoyable part of the whole evening. But when he gets up to go to the bathroom she is out of bed immediately, and fully dressed by the time he emerges. The relief on his face is unmistakable.

'I'd better go.' She tries to smile, as if there is some regret in this parting.

He nods, spreading his hands. 'It was really great. Really nice.' And she knows that he will torture himself with this now, and a small part of her feels sorry for him, and wants to urge him to forget it happened, that what went on here tonight was not really what he thought it was.

But he had done it, after all. She cannot offer him absolution.

He offers to walk her out, to find her a taxi, but she refuses. At the door they hug briefly, and she grazes his cheek with lips that feel tender and swollen. She does not look back as she walks down the corridor, and before she has reached the lifts she hears the click of the bedroom door as it closes behind her.

~

In the taxi home she feels sure the driver can tell how she has spent her evening; she feels the secret of it seeping out of her, leaving a stain on the upholstery that will be impossible to clean. He does not, at least, try to make conversation; instead he sings along to Christian rock on the radio in a voice that is unexpectedly powerful and true. The streets are quiet at this time – it is past two o'clock, she sees – and they glisten with the earlier rain. As she fumbles her key into the lock of the front door, her feet suddenly afire in their ridiculous heels, she sees the driver turn the car in one easy, fluid motion and then pause by the kerb, idling there until she has coaxed the lock and stumbled safely into her hall. She lifts a hand in silent gratitude as he drives away.

In the quiet of the house she drinks glass after glass of water, cold from the tap, and then goes heavily upstairs and runs a bath. She steps out of her skirt in the bedroom and pulls the top over her head; it smells faintly of his aftershave, and of sweat which is her own. The tights she pulls out of her handbag and stuffs straight into the bathroom bin; she had not bothered to put them back on when she was getting dressed, afraid that he would return to the room at any moment to witness the undignified shimmy. She lowers herself carefully into the bath, the water as hot as she can bear. It is like heaven on her skin, which feels bruised and tender, although she has not been hurt.

Rachel lies there until the water has long grown cold, and then with an effort she pulls herself out and spends a long time towelling herself dry. She dresses in clean pyjamas, brushed cotton ones that were a helpless gift from her mother in those early weeks. As she climbs into bed she turns to look at the little clock on the bedside table; the time is 3:27.

She does not, of course, need to check the date.

She lies still, and waits for sleep to claim her.

BEFORE

Fourteen Months

The Worst Thing That Could Possibly Have Happened

She is three, and runs through the house like a sprite. Everything about her is pale, and thin – the flying legs, the fingers; the long, straight hair that Rachel combs after her bath.

She eats nothing. Rachel has moments of panic about it, the impossibility that a human life could be sustained on the few flakes of dry cereal and the nuggets of breaded chicken that, some days, are all she will accept. Chips – she will eat those too, would eat nothing else if she was let; and squares of toast that she inspects closely to make sure that her mother has not tried to sneak butter into her, letting it melt into invisibility before she presents the plate. Rachel resents it, sometimes with a bitterness that startles her, as she picks through the tinned sweetcorn to find the five or six acceptable pieces that her daughter may consent to eat. Tom is inclined to get worked up about it all, and against her own worried instincts Rachel urges him to relax; but it is true that the child is grow-ing, somehow, on fresh air and weak spring sunlight, on city fumes and playground screeches and the smell of the garden after rain.

Her fierceness – her fierceness is a revelation to Rachel, who does not remember being a fierce child herself. It is not that her daughter is mean-spirited – the very opposite, in fact – but she is fearless, and quick to anger, and determined to a lunatic degree in her refusal to back down, to admit fault, to wear the yellow boots instead of the purple ones, which are demonstrably too small now and leave her petal-like toes red and curling. And it is exhausting, of course, the constant battling with her infinitely stronger will; and yet. There is something so admirable about it all. Rachel envies her absolute belief in her own place in the world.

And she can be tender too; oh God, there are moments when she can be the sweetest thing on earth.

She will spend hours in the garden in all weathers, exploring under rocks and discarded plant pots, transferring insects from one green place to another with the care of a laboratory scientist. In her sand table she creates tiny universes, mountain peaks and crenellated towers topped with a particularly smooth stone or a stick that has taken hours to select from the scores of other, similar ones. And always, always she is talking to herself, whispered conversations with some unseen confidant. Sometimes Rachel tries to hover near, eavesdropping on her murmured commentary, but never can she be unobtrusive enough; always she is caught, and her daughter becomes immediately silent with a smile that is at once charming and accusatory.

One day late in the summer she trips and falls on the uneven paving stones in the back garden, and Rachel is already running to scoop her into her arms when she lifts up a face full of blood and spits a tiny tooth onto the ground before her. It is the first time Rachel has ever seen blood spill from her child. She, who has spent half her life wiping up the bodily fluids of strangers, is almost undone by the sight of her daughter's raw and gaping face. She holds her to her chest, trying to calm her sobs with the beat of her own racing heart. The tooth is milk-white and perfect, its root still long and pointed; it was nowhere near ready to be pushed from her tender mouth. Rachel holds her close, the blood seeping through the thin white cotton of her own T-shirt, and makes silent promises to her daughter that she will never take her eyes off her again.

It feels, for a moment, like the worst thing that could possibly have happened.

AFTER

Fifteen Months

One Who Is Dutiful

She sits now alone in the small and soulless room. The building in its entirety is far from what Rachel had imagined, although really her only experience of a courtroom is through television dramas, all monstrous wigs and 'May it please the court.' She wonders if they will be wearing wigs today; she has not thought to ask.

This building, anyway, is large and modern, more like an airport terminal than a seat of justice. The room she was led to is on the third floor, where the ceilings are lower and the atmosphere generally quieter, although every now and then there is a clatter of quick footsteps passing, and the rise and fall of intense conversation; Rachel imagines solicitors and barristers in frantic conclave. She does not have a solicitor of her own, which seemed like an odd omission, at first – that she would be left rudderless, floating free in this process. But she has come to understand that she is not, in any official sense, a party to the case, which is between Tom and the State. Instead she is a witness, and also of course a victim, a position that does not in itself seem to have any legal standing. That she is here to testify today is her own decision; she never fought it, although she is not sure what would have happened if she had, whether they would have compelled her to come anyway – she has the vague sense that they might have let her be. But really, what choice did she have? She was the only witness; it would have been ludicrous to refuse.

She wonders now if she is, in fact, really entitled to this room, and the privacy it affords her; she supposes not, but that she has been offered it as a courtesy, a means to escape the unrelenting gaze of the people amassed in and around the courtroom, for whom she is naturally the focus of all curiosity. She is grateful; this is all hard enough without having to sit for hours in the fishbowl of the corridor outside.

The door opens and Rebecca is back, the coffee cups small and flimsy-looking in her hands. It has been a long time since Rachel has drunk coffee from a machine, but here on the third floor of the court building there is apparently still one of these relics from the past. She takes it from Rebecca, and sips cautiously; it is hot, and surprisingly drinkable. Rebecca sits down with a sigh.

'Any updates?'

Rachel shakes her head. 'No. She hasn't been back in.'

It is the same family liaison officer, the nice blonde woman who has seen it all, who is here today, checking in on Rachel and her sister from time to time with updates about the running of the day. It is all delays, it seems to Rachel, for various opaque reasons which she does not question. Really, she is in no rush to get in there, to have to parse and defend her memories of that night; really, she would wait forever. According to everyone who has the authority to comment on it – and many who don't – the outcome of the trial is not in any doubt.

Rebecca sighs again – somewhat dramatically, Rachel thinks privately. 'God, it all takes so long, doesn't it? It's like being on a film set.' She tips her head back to look at the ceiling, one of those eggbox ones Rachel remembers from college.

'You've spent a lot of time on film sets, have you?'

Rebecca kicks her under the table. 'Well, I'd imagine. Waiting around all day to be called.'

'And the glamour of it all, of course.' She breaks a piece off the Styrofoam mouth of the coffee cup.

Rebecca's smile is fleeting. 'How are you feeling?'

Rachel closes her eyes, leans back in the chair. 'Jesus, I don't know. I just want it to be over. But I don't want to have to do it.'

'You don't have to do it.' Rebecca's tone is gentler than her words.

'I know that. But – like, who would I be serving, really? If I said no? Not Tom, God knows.'

Rebecca says nothing, and the room falls quiet again. There is a large, utilitarian-looking clock on the wall, the kind you'd see in a classroom. Rachel feels she will be hearing its steady tick long after she has left the room.

~

Her mother had not wanted her to come at all, of course. Her mother, in fact, would prefer if Tom's existence was never referred to again, if some other mythos could be built up around the inescapable fact that Rachel had once had two living children, and now does not. She cannot understand why Rachel would choose to, as she puts it, relive 'all that', which is the suitably vague euphemism she has chosen to cover events that are, to be fair to her, impossible to describe.

'But they're not making you go? Are they putting pressure on you?' It would have been March, or April or May; so many times they had had this conversation, and yet Margaret's eyes were again filled with a confused wonder that Rachel found so irritating she had to grip the edge of her seat with both hands.

'No. No, Mam. I told you. I just think it's the right thing to do.'

'But *why*, Rachel? Sure, they know what happened. You've told them everything. It's not like he's claiming he didn't do it.'

Rachel flinched. She could not help it; there was something so ugly in the way her mother spoke about Tom now, the contempt in her voice.

'It's not that. I just – I want to make sure they understand. What he was like, before, and that he loved them. That he was a good father before all this.'

Her mother was furious. 'Jesus Christ, Rachel. Jesus Christ.'

'I'm just telling them what happened, Mam. I'm not defending what he did.' That she should need to say this.

'Well.' Her mother could fit a surprising amount of scepticism into a single word, and its accompanying sniff.

There was a point, Rachel knew, at which unforgivable things would be said, and she felt that this point was suddenly very close. She stood abruptly; they were in her parents' kitchen, dappled yellow with tentative spring sunlight. Between them on the table was a plate of scones, the butter long melted in, and the chipped mug with the recipe for tomato soup, which had been her favourite since she was a little girl. Her mother's own teacup had a picture of a sunflower, painted by a child's careful hand.

'I'm not doing this, Mam. I can't. I'm sorry.'

'Rachel.' Her mother reached across the table for her hand, and Rachel allowed herself to be pulled down again.

'I'm only saying.' Margaret's voice is softer now. 'You don't owe him anything, you must know that. You're not responsible for what happens to him now.'

And Rachel thought how easy, how easy it was to say the right words, and how weightless and irrelevant they were.

~

Rebecca stands now, paces the length of the small room. She has taken a week off work for this, to be here, to be sitting in this room with her sister today, and Rachel is struck with a sudden gratitude. Rebecca works in the local social welfare office, although she is restless there, as she has been in every job she has had since Rachel can remember. She wonders if Rebecca misses the freedom she had once made such great use of – the ability to take off, birdlike, to Spain or Thailand or New York, as soon as she tired of a job or a boyfriend or a flatmate, as soon as Dublin began to feel ever so slightly small. A freedom Rachel shared, she supposes now, at least on paper, but never one she felt she could take advantage of. In every pair of daughters there is one who is dutiful, and one who is free. Rebecca had celebrated her twenty-first birthday on a collective farm in Cambodia; her suntanned face beamed over a grainy video call to the house in Glasnevin where Rachel and her parents sat with glasses of champagne below a foil banner spelling out her sister's name. After four minutes of broken conversation with a Rebecca who, Rachel suspected, was either drunk or stoned or both, the call had cut out, and they had sipped their drinks in the sudden silence of the autumn evening and told each other how well Rebecca was looking.

And now Rebecca has two children, and a house, and responsibilities, and it is Rachel who is free.

After a few minutes Rebecca sits down again, unable to settle.

'You haven't seen him since the hospital last year, have you?'

Rachel shakes her head.

'God.' Rebecca sits back, and blows a long sigh through lips that are, as always, dry and flaking. 'That's going to be weird, isn't it?'

'Well, he's not actually going to be there. It's a – a video-link, or whatever you call it.'

'But he'll be able to see you too?'

Rachel shrugs. 'I suppose.'

'God,' Rebecca says again.

Rebecca and Tom have never particularly liked each other. Rachel knows this now; knew it always, really, but when they were both a part of her everyday life it was easier to choose to ignore this slightly awkward truth. But she knew it then in the way that Tom would always affect a bemused tone when he spoke about Rebecca, as if her life and her choices were a vaguely ridiculous mystery to him; knew it in the slightly mocking look Rebecca's face would get when she was speaking to him, a look subtle enough that only a sister intimately acquainted with her specific brand of cruelty would spot it. She knows it now in the way Rebecca has never spoken critically of Tom, not once, since the crash, steadfastly saying nothing at all when the subject comes up.

Of course it is unimportant, really; people do not have to like their in-laws. But it makes Rachel self-conscious any time she mentions Tom now, even more than she would have been otherwise; there is sometimes a curious impulse to defend her earlier, more innocent self against things not yet said. *I always knew there was something. I told you so.*

~

Sometimes, almost as an academic exercise, she lists for herself all the times she could have stopped him:

She could never have gone out with him at all, of course. That would have been the easiest thing. That first time in the nightclub she could have said no to the drink, could have sought out somebody else with eyes that were just as blue, a smile that was just as persuasive. She could be living an entirely different life now.

When he asked her to marry him, on the cliff walk at Howth that early spring day, she could have said no. Could have pushed the ring away with a gentle hand and walked back alone to the car, the wind drying her tears.

When they were trying to get pregnant, some unsettling premonition could have moved her to quietly start taking the pill again, and make a plan to leave.

But the problem with all of these scenarios, of course, is that they involve the children never having been born at all, and there is no part of her that is able to answer the question that is never asked, but that she can see in everyone's eyes – *would it have been better?*

Simpler to stick to later things.

When the firm went bust, and his mood started to slip – then, then she surely could have asked him to leave, not to pollute their lives with whatever darkness was starting to smoulder inside him. Nobody would have blamed her.

And when he stopped taking the tablets, the summer before – why then did she not see this for the blazing red flag that it was, and gather the children to her, and run away with them to a place of safety?

She could have insisted on going with him to the doctor.

She could have told the consultant he needed to stay in hospital, that he wasn't ready to come home. (Had she really felt this? She does not know. But surely. But surely.)

There has to have been a moment, when she could have stopped it all.

She could have turned away, in the nightclub.

She could have tried to grab the wheel.

It seems only right, really, that she too should have to stand in a courtroom today.

～

There will, at least, be nothing new in what they can ask her. On the night of the crash, she had told the Gardaí everything immediately; there had been no sense of betrayal, of giving Tom up – she was only bewildered, trying to make sense in her head of what had happened. *He just turned the car.* It was only long afterwards that she had any realisation of what her statement must have meant, how it would have turned what appeared at first to be a tragic accident into something so much darker and less explicable.

She remembers the detective's careful questions, his gentle insistence that she speak accurately – had Tom said anything? Anything at all? Had there been something on the road, some animal perhaps, stark and frozen in the headlights? And then, of course, they had found the stuff on the computer – the maps, the letter – and the jigsaw pieces of Tom's careful planning had all fallen suddenly into place.

Rachel wishes, often, that she remembered none of it; that the crash had wiped her memory clean, even of just those few moments. That would have been something divine, an act of grace.

Instead—

Instead—

~

Rachel comes to into blackness, and at first she thinks that she must have been unconscious for a long time. And then gradually she realises that no, it is not darkness at the windows but the deep green fronds of fern and grass; the car has plunged so far into the undergrowth that the remaining daylight is completely obscured. The windows are at ground level now, because the car has come to rest on its roof, its four tyres up in the air; Rachel

124

imagines them waving helplessly, like the legs of some stranded turtle.

She hangs there against the seat belt, trying to orientate herself; to remember what has happened, and why she is here. It is very quiet. She could almost believe she is alone in the car, but she knows she is not alone; at the far reaches of her memory she scrabbles for the missing pieces.

A moan comes from somewhere beside her, or under her; directions are not reliable now, she is floating in space, unmoored. She turns her head, a slow, complicated movement which halts abruptly with her chin only just past the midway point; it is as if there is something rigid there, pressing against her cheek. She sees movement at the edge of her vision, a shape squirming and stretching, and the moaning sound too is coming from this shape, whom she recognises the next moment to be Tom. The word he is struggling to repeat over and over, emerging slow and mangled from his mouth as if from a record player that is running down, is 'No'.

She tries turning her head the other way. It is more free, on this side, and she finds she can twist right around to see behind her.

The back of the car is gone.

Where it used to be, where once there was a space with two windows and two car seats and a mishmash of biscuit crumbs and half-empty sippy cups – now there is nothing but darkness. Not even the space is there, because what used to be the roof of the car has now somehow been forced up to gently kiss the floor, and everything between them has simply vanished.

She is still trying to make sense of this when she hears the sirens fade in, and the darkness around her turns blue.

~

The single knock on the door is firm, authoritative, and then it opens before they have had time to react at all. There is a stranger there, a court official of some sort, Rachel thinks, and just behind him is the Garda liaison woman, her own cup of coffee in hand. She nods once, her mouth firm; her voice, though, is gentle.

'It's time, now.'

They rise, together; for a moment they are little girls again, frightened and obedient, and as Rachel is reaching blindly for her sister's hand she feels Rebecca's cold, clammy one grab hers, and they stand like that for a moment, not looking at each other. She is suddenly terribly afraid.

BEFORE

Twelve Months

The World of Men

He is nearly two; how can that be, that already he has been theirs for twenty-one months, and yet still there are times – after his bath, or very early in the morning – when he seems like something shining and new?

Before, Rachel would not have believed that so much of him would come predetermined; she had inherited her mother's belief in the dominance of nurture over nature, the importance of boundaries and routine. Now she looks at the solid lines of his burgeoning personality, so different from that of his sister but no less powerful, and wonders that she ever thought her own influence could be anything more than ancillary. His character is hard-wired, as immutable as the colour of his hair.

She carries him still, in the baby carrier she bought when her daughter was first born, ignoring the concerned stares of strangers purporting to worry about her back. She likes it, the ease of having her hands free, the way the extra weight makes her body work. He will fall asleep in it, indeed it is a foolproof method on days when the naps come hard; she only has to walk once around the block before she feels it happen, the way the weight of him changes as he slips into sleep. If it is a day when her daughter is occupied elsewhere – with grandparents, sometimes, or on weekends at home making Play-Doh creations with Tom – sometimes Rachel will walk on and on, relishing the unaccustomed headspace, the heat of his compact little body held tight against hers. She walks for miles like this, some days, while he sleeps; and sometimes she will look down and realise that he has woken up unbeknownst to her, and is looking about him placidly from the safety of his perch.

The smell of him is milk, and apples, and the sweet oil she rubs into his scalp to remove the last vestiges of cradle cap. This last smell lingers on his pillows too, and every time she changes the bedding – not often enough, for God, this is her least favourite of all the interminable jobs, she would literally employ someone just to do this one hated thing – she buries her nose for a moment in his pillowcase before bundling it into the machine and moving on. She thinks she will never get tired of that smell.

Tom refers to him as her shadow, and it is true; ever since he learned to walk (out of nowhere, for he never seemed to get the hang of crawling, and Rachel had a few months of secret fears that there was something badly wrong – she could feel it in her bones – and then one day he just stood up and took off running) he has trotted around at her heels, bound by some invisible tether. She feels sometimes that Tom is jealous; not in a boorish, proprietary way – she would not have stood for that, she tells herself – but she knows that he envies the absolute adoration. He imagined this for himself, when they had a son – an acolyte. Rachel reassures him that it will come later, that all small boys adore their mothers; it is the natural order of things. Later he will ache to be part of the sphere inhabited by his father, the world of men; for now, he belongs to her.

Although he no longer nurses – a grievous parting, that; she was not ready for the wrench of it, the way her body would keen for him – when he is tired he will often climb onto her knee and nestle his tiny hand in between her breasts. Sometimes he falls asleep like that, and she stills her breathing until her chest barely moves in and out, hoping he will stay there forever.

AFTER

Eighteen Months

Very Simple Things

Three days into the holiday, and Rachel still does not know if it was the right decision to come. Sometimes, like when she wakes in the early morning to the crash of waves on the pebbled shore, and lies watching the sunlight playing on the railings of the balcony outside, she feels an ease that is new and pleasurable. She stays there until hunger or the need for the toilet drives her from the bed, and then there is ease again in slipping into the lightest of clothes and running a brush quickly through her hair before going down for breakfast. The hallways are cool and dim, and echo with the slap of flip-flops on the tiled floor, and when she passes a porter or a chambermaid in their impossibly neat uniform, their murmured greeting is accompanied with a smiling dip of the head, which she returns. At breakfast she eats mostly fruit, and although the staff are polite and attentive, nobody attempts to make conversation beyond the briefest remarks about the weather, which shows almost no variance from hour to hour.

But much of the time she is restless, and conscious of how she must stand out, a woman alone. At the pool she selects the lounger furthest from the water, and pulls it even then a little away from the others, and keeps her sunglasses on. She swims when it is quiet; early in the morning, and towards the end of the day, when other guests are already making their way to the restaurant, freshly showered and sleek in the scented evening air. At least it is mostly couples here, rather than families; it is tiny really, the hotel, and beyond the pool there is not much in the way of amenities. True, there is one Spanish family with two solemn-eyed boys of four or five, and another couple – Dutch, she thinks, with their very blond hair and excellent English – with a tiny baby, still froglike and wrinkled-new. But for the most part it is middle-aged couples and older, the kind who have been here before and will come again; many of them address the staff by name. She is, she thinks, the only solo guest.

The first two days she had slept a lot, exhausted by the travel and the heat. It is very quiet everywhere; the walls are thick stone and the only noise comes in through the window, which she leaves open always to the breeze. She has brought a book – she has brought a pile of books, in fact, and very little else – but for most of those first few days it lies open and unread on the sheet beside where she rests, her face turned to the window and the sky beyond. She wonders if she is depressed; she thinks not, although she is not sure if it is something she would be aware of herself.

On the third morning she wakes early and feels, for the first time, refreshed. She dresses in shorts and a sleeveless top – here she takes her shower in the evening, before dressing in fresh clothes for dinner – and puts on for the first time socks and her hiking boots. She had bought these years ago, a sudden whim of Tom's that they would become one of those couples who spent weekends tramping the Wicklow Way; they had been worn once, or perhaps twice, and then relegated to the upper shelf on her wardrobe, the one she was constantly meaning to clear out. They are good boots, though, and with the two pairs of socks which she has read are the real secret to avoiding blisters, she feels ready. In the dining room she takes a croissant with her usual fruit and coffee, and when she is finished she goes to the small lobby, cool and rather dim, and finds behind the reception desk the proprietor, a thin woman whose black hair is threaded with grey.

'*Buongiorno*. I wonder—' She hesitates. 'I would like to take a walk, today. A long walk. Is there somewhere nice to walk nearby?' She hears the strange thing her voice is doing, her English broken and singsong, and hopes this is not a gross offence.

'To walk, yes?' The woman mimics the determined gait of a hiker, imaginary walking pole in hand.

Rachel nods enthusiastically. 'Yes, exactly. Yes.'

'Here. See.' The woman takes a map from the pile in the corner of the desk, and licks a finger to unfold it. She points with her pen.

'Here. Now. Hotel.' She gestures around her. 'You walk this way. Not long; twenty minutes only.' She marks a red X on the map. 'There is a gate, and a sign. Trail is maybe five kilometres, or six, and you will come out here.' She marks another X, this one much further along the same road. 'Bus comes there, every twenty minutes. Will bring you back to hotel.'

She folds the map again and hands it to Rachel.

'*Grazie, grazie.*'

'Very hot today. You have the hat?'

'Yes, I do. I'll get it now.'

The woman leans over the desk to inspect Rachel's shoes, and nods approvingly.

'*Grazie,*' Rachel says again, and the woman smiles then, her face transforming into some ancient topography, and the face is rather beautiful.

Rachel goes back to her room to collect a small rucksack and her water bottle, and applies sunscreen rigorously over every exposed inch of her skin. She has the map, and her phone, and still it feels like the expedition is something adventurous, brave even, for which she needs to muster up courage and some degree of grit. She sets off. The road here is treacherous, and though there are few cars on it at this time of day, when they do come they are fast and confident and seem to give little care for the narrowness of the road, or the sheerness of the drop below. She is glad when she reaches the start of the trail. The gate is there, and there too is the red and white sign; in Italian, of course, but that does not matter, it is there, and she pushes the gate open and steps through, being careful to close it behind her. She is at the bottom of a grassy slope, and before and above her a narrow path rises fairly steeply to the crest of the hill, from where it seems to flatten out and lead along a ridge in parallel with the road below. There are no other people around, but far to her left she can see a few goats pulling indolently at the long grass. She begins to climb. Very soon she starts to feel the burn in the backs of her legs, but it is not unpleasant; it feels instead productive and even gratifying. By the time she reaches the top of the hill she is out of breath and sweating. The path is much gentler from there on, and she walks a little way along it before stopping to sit on a large rock half hidden in the grass, and take a long drink from her water bottle. The view is almost ludicrously beautiful; it does not seem real, the blue of the sea and the way the grassy outcroppings of land jut out into the water. A helicopter is hovering just above the waves; she watches, puzzled, as it hangs there for several minutes, dangling a long black pipe down into the water, and then flies up to a distant hillside, where a cloud seems to burst from beneath it. After watching this process repeated, she realises that it is taking up seawater and dumping it on a burning section of the hill. She cannot see the fire from here, but the sudden explosion of the water in the air is mesmerising, and she sits there long after her sweat has dried and her heart rate has returned to normal. It is only when a man passes her, having come from the other direction, and murmurs a greeting in a language that is neither English nor Italian but something low and guttural, that she stirs herself and continues on.

The rest of the walk is fairly flat, but the heat of the day is a slope to climb in itself, and by the time she begins the descent back towards the road her water bottle is long-since empty and she can think of nothing bar the urgent need to find something to slake her thirst. The gate at the end of the path leaves her out at the edge of another village, and she ignores the bus stop which stands directly opposite and walks on into the small street of shops and restaurants. At a convenience store of some sort she buys a bottle of lemonade, still and ice-cold from the fridge, and drinks it down under the awning outside.

She thinks that this has been the best day she has had in months. There is guilt with this thought, of course, as there is always guilt when she realises that she has spent some time in a state other than active misery. The arithmetic of it is not easy; it should be obvious, that any day since the loss of her children is worse than any day spent with them before. And yet. So many of those days were difficult too, whether from worry about Tom or just the vagaries of life with small children; the tiny frustrations, the monotony, the innumerable petty limitations on her own needs and desires. She thinks of the queues at Dublin Airport a few days earlier, the sullen teenagers and the toddlers diving off towards danger in every direction, and she, unencumbered, standing with shoes in hand ready to place them on the belt. Today, too, there has been a calm that is new to her, and, more than that, an enjoyment that seems wholly sensory – the view of the sea from the top of the slope, the smell of the late-blooming flowers at the side of the path, the indescribable relief of the lemonade coursing down her throat. She wonders if this is how animals experience life, as a series of sensations that are simply good or bad, without need for analysis or investigation. It would not, she thinks, be a terrible way to live.

~

Emboldened, the next morning she buys a ticket for a bus tour to Pompeii, and joins the small queue of tourists gathered outside a larger, neighbouring hotel. It is early, but already she can feel the damp patches forming under her arms; she has kept her shoulders covered, remembering from her honeymoon the curiously puritanical rules about dress when entering any tourist site with a hint of the sacred, although she does not know if this will apply today. But at least she is prepared. There are six others waiting, and when the bus arrives, unconcernedly late, they file on, murmuring polite *buongiorno*s to the driver, who nods silently in response. Rachel finds a seat at the back. As the bus moves away from the beauty of the coast the views become less and less scenic, the outskirts of modern-day Pompeii resembling more some sort of dystopian film set than anything fit for a tourist brochure. This the passengers observe with a kind of bemused horror, until eventually an hour later they pull into a large and dusty car park and stumble from the bus. The tour guide is waiting for them, a tall and dark-haired woman who introduces herself as Marta. Her English is briskly competent, her marshalling of the tourists recalling the better type of primary school teacher from Rachel's childhood, all voice projection and smiling insistence.

They are given maps, and troop through the entryway and on inside. Rachel had planned to break away from the group early, but she is reluctant to appear rude, and once the tour starts she finds she is drawn in to Marta's smooth and practised delivery. The guide is slightly dismissive of the usual highlights – the brothel, the dog mosaic with its *Cave Canem* seeming impossibly anachronistic, yet there before their eyes – but becomes almost passionate describing the day-to-day lives of the people here.

After an hour or so they are dismissed, to wander by themselves through the site; in a closing speech that is laden with warnings, the departure time of the bus is repeated by Marta three times. Rachel studies her map and, having no particular yearning for any specific part, sets off in the direction of the amphitheatre; this at least, she tells herself, she should not miss. She climbs the steps, and goes through the arched entrance, and makes her way carefully down towards the front. An ankle sprain would be all too easy here, and an absolute disaster. It is a vast space, wide and shallow, and seems almost to have erupted from the earth through the grass that has overgrown the stone benches in places. She sits on one of these, gazing into the arena. It is impossible to take in that the stone under her legs, cool against her skin despite the heat of the sun, has been here for thousands of years. She looks down at it, this slab of ordinary-looking rock, trying to divine its secrets. Before, this sort of enormity used to scare her – the endlessness of time and space, the realisation of the size of the universe and her own insignificance within it. Now, though – now she finds there is something almost comforting in the knowledge that the world was here, doing much the same things as always, long before she arrived on it, and will continue to turn on its axis aeons after she has gone.

To her left she senses people approaching and when she turns her head slightly, shading her eyes under the pretext of gazing towards the other side of the arena, she sees that it is a couple; at least she presumes they are a couple, the man slim and dark and good-looking, the woman very young and heavy with child. She walks just behind the man, and in the laboured pant of her breathing Rachel is reminded of her own exhaustion near the end of her pregnancies, when every exertion seemed like it must surely shake

135

the baby from her. They walk towards the centre of the stadium. They are arguing; or, he is arguing, his tone unmistakable although his words are unintelligible to Rachel's ears. The girl – woman – she is so young – the girl's voice is pleading, and as Rachel watches she puts a hand on his arm in a supplicating, or perhaps conciliatory, gesture. He shakes it off with a violence that unbalances her already unstable frame, and she stumbles against one of the benches and almost falls. Rachel stands instinctively, her breath catching.

'No, *signora.*'

Rachel turns. A man has come to sit just behind her, and while his eyes too are fixed on the couple, his hand is lifted towards Rachel in a gesture of restraint. She sees that he is quite elderly, his hair sparse and stripped of colour. He wears dark sunglasses, and a shirt that is snow-white and formal, in spite of the heat.

He speaks again. 'Do not, *per favore*. He is dangerous, that one.'

'Yes, but . . .' She trails off. She does not, after all, have any sort of a plan. They both watch as the woman rights herself, her partner watching with a sneer on his face. He says something to her, a single word, and although Rachel is too far away to see, she knows that the woman blushes. The man turns and walks on, the woman again following in his wake. Her hand rests on the swell of her belly.

The older man makes a slight bow. '*Buongiorno.*'

'*Buongiorno.*' Rachel sits down again, and half turns her body towards him, squinting against the sun.

'You are English, yes?'

'Irish.'

'Irish. Forgive me.' He bows his head, bringing his hands together briefly in apology. Though Rachel is still feeling unsettled by the couple, who are now tramping back towards the exit, she cannot help but laugh.

'This is your first time to visit?'

'Yes.' She nods. 'To visit Pompeii, I mean. I've been to Italy before; to Rome, and then Tuscany. But this is my first time down here.'

'You like it?'

'Very much, yes.' She feels eager to share with him just how much she likes it; what a country this is, its generous bounty, its benevolent sun.

He stretches his legs out in front of him; the legs too are smartly clad, in long trousers of pale grey.

'Me, I live in Napoli. I come here often.'

Rachel is surprised by this; she had assumed everyone here to be tourists. It would be like herself spending time regularly in Newgrange, or poking around Christchurch – all things she has meant to do, and has somehow never got around to.

'Why do you come? Come again and again, I mean.'

He shrugs; a slow, expansive gesture, his hands lifting the air.

'I do not know. I like to imagine the people here, before. Some-times I draw.' He dips his head, indicating the sketchpad and pencil on the bench beside him. Then he shrugs again. 'It is a place to come. When you are an old man, like me, there is a lot of time.'

~

On the slow bus journey back Rachel finds herself thinking longingly of the hotel, of her cool and tidy room, of the long shower she will take and the anticipated pleasure of her book with dinner. When she enters the lobby, the younger of the two men at the reception desk – the owner's son, she thinks, but does not have the words to ask – smiles shyly and says '*Buona sera, signora*' and she feels her own smile too wide, too pleased at this tiny recognition of her belonging here.

It is as she is crossing the courtyard with the pool that she hears the shout. A man's shout, and the note of alarm in it makes Rachel's head whip around before it has fully left his throat. It is the little Spanish boy, the younger of the two – younger than she had thought, she sees now; he cannot be more than three. He is dressed, somewhat formally, for dinner, but he is running, running towards the pool which by day he will jump into over and over again, landing in the welcome arms of his father, broad-chested and proud. But it is not day now, it is evening time and the darkness rapidly descending, and he is wearing not the tiny swimming trunks but his clean, pressed shirt and his long shorts, and his father is leagues behind although now he is running too, and it is the father who has shouted, his voice made high by fear. But the excitement of the boy drowns out all other noise. He is laughing as he launches himself off the side, but as he soars Rachel sees his face change with the sudden and terrible knowledge, and then he is in the water, dropping instantly like a stone. Rachel stops only to kick off her shoes, and then she is diving in, the shape of her body clean and arrow-true, and forcing her eyes open against the sting of the water. She sees the shape of him across the pool, upright and struggling, feet below the surface. It feels like minutes until she reaches him, but really it can only be ten seconds, less, for when she pulls him to the surface he is still conscious and gasping, and chokes out great gouts of water in between his cries. He clutches at her neck, her hair, in a desperate way that in deeper water would be a danger to them both; but the pool is not deep, and she finds that she can just about stand on the bottom as she holds his head above the water. His mother, thin and dark and rigid with fright, stands with her hands pressed to her face as her husband kneels by the side of the pool and reaches out to take him from Rachel's arms.

138

'Rápido, rápido! Pásamelo.'

Rachel hoists herself out, a torrent of water falling from her dress, her hair. The red dust of the day has left a thin film, she sees, on the surface of the pool.

'Is he OK?' She steps forward and lays one hand on the shining black head, now still against his mother's breast. But the child, who seconds earlier had clung around her neck as if he would never let go, squirms away from this stranger crossly.

Rachel steps back, suddenly embarrassed.

'You should get him checked over. A doctor,' she clarifies, taking in their blank faces. 'Bring him to a doctor, tonight. To make sure he is OK.'

They nod, and the woman speaks to her husband in rapid Spanish. She stands then, and hoists the child high in her arms. His brother, solemn and silent, presses into her legs.

The man takes Rachel's hand in both of his. There are tears in his eyes, heavy and viscous, threatening at any moment to fall. Rachel does not understand many of the words he is saying, but she does not need to. *It's OK*, she keeps saying, over and over. *It's OK.*

When, finally, they have gone, back towards the reception desk and whatever help can be found for them, Rachel stands for a moment, still dripping, on the blue tiles of the pool terrace. She looks around, but there is nobody else about, although in the distance she can hear the shouts of the waiters as they lay the tables for dinner. It seems unbelievable, that there are no other witnesses to what has just taken place. *Didn't anybody see?* It feels like too great a happening not to have been observed. She closes her eyes for a moment, trying to recapture the desperate clutch of those chubby arms around her neck.

~

She spends a long time in the shower, watching the remaining grime from the day wash off her skin and disappear down the drain. She dries herself and dresses with care, in a blue linen dress and sandals, and pulls her wet hair back in a low knot. In the dining room the smiling waiter leads her to the table on the terrace that she thinks of as her table now, and she places her book carefully beside her wine glass, and tucks her bag under her chair. There is no sign of the Spanish family. As the waiter pours her wine she gazes out to sea. Far, far in the distance there is a flash of light, and then seconds later a low rumble of thunder that seems muffled by the sultry air. All through her dinner she watches the storm roll out at sea, while on the terrace the night remains dry, and fragrant, and still.

She thinks, she could stay here. She could rent, or even buy, one of the tiny derelict cottages that seem to be everywhere, and do it up slowly, hanging long strips of linen at the windows and painting whitewash on the walls. Every day she would sweep dust from the tiled floor and out into the yard, where she would keep a few chickens for eggs and the companionable noise of their clucking. She would need a job of some sort, of course, but that would be easy; she could find work in one of the restaurants, of which there must be hundreds between all the little villages that dot the coastline. She could even clean in one of the hotels; she would not mind. She would eat bread, and cheese, and ripe tomatoes; very simple things, and in the evenings she would drink wine at her open doorway and watch the sun drop over the hills. It would be quiet, always, but here she would not mind. Here, the silence would not be something to fear.

BEFORE

Ten Months

A Flattening-out

'I'm sorry.'

'It's OK.' She doesn't want him to feel embarrassed. Although she is embarrassed herself, her first thought being that it is some failure of her own. Familiarity breeding disinterest, if not outright contempt.

Tom swings his legs over the side of the bed and sits up, rubbing at his scalp with both hands. The door is ajar, as it always is, in case one of the children should wake.

'It's the tablets, I think. I just . . .' He cranes his neck to look at her, dejected. 'It's not that I don't want to.'

'I know.' She rubs his back.

She doesn't believe him, not really. Oh, not that the tablets aren't playing a part; she has read enough to know that this can be a side-effect. They had even made weak jokes about it at the start, back when it seemed like the little white pills really did offer some hope of normal life resuming. But she knows that it is more now than just the medication; he has not seemed to want her in longer than she can truly remember. It is not just physical, that is the thing – not just a refusal of his body to co-operate, which they could attribute to the tablets, to the chaos of family life, even to the relentless march of time, and the first grey threads in Tom's dark hair. But when she holds him close to her now there is a vacancy in his eyes, a blankness where once she had known only desire. The last time they had tried – which was more than a month ago, Rachel thinks now, an interval that would have seemed impossible back in their urgent, greedy early days – it had been the same. Nothing had been said then, there was just an eventual moving apart with an apologetic sigh from Tom, and Rachel had finally dozed off to unsettling dreams. And before that – well, Rachel cannot really remember the last time they had proper sex. She has never had to keep track before. Tonight, she had been the instigator, a role she is not accustomed to; it has rarely been necessary until now.

She studies the whorls of dark hair on Tom's back. They get everywhere, these hairs; curling into the edges of the shower tray, dusting the bed sheet when she goes to change it. It is slightly disgusting, she supposes, if you were to think about it objectively; and yet she has never found it so.

Tom twitches, and Rachel realises her hand is irritating him. She drops it into her lap, aware suddenly of her nakedness, and reaches with the other hand for her T-shirt. She fixes her pillows and lies back.

'Will I turn off the light?'

There is a pause before Tom answers, and when he does he is distracted. 'What? Oh. Yeah. Yeah, sure.'

He stands then, and leaves the room. Rachel hears the bolt slide in the bathroom door, and then water running, and she stretches one arm to switch off the bedside lamp. The darkness of the room is a relief. She wonders how much longer they are both going to pretend that the medication is still working for Tom – if, indeed, it ever worked at all, for certainly there had never been a dramatic improvement in his moods, no surge of wellbeing and enthusiasm for life. At most there was, she supposes, a flattening-out of sorts, a blunting of the ups and downs of his weather; for a time he had stopped crying in the bedroom when he thought she was busy elsewhere, or flying off the handle at the slightest provocation from the kids. And that was some small relief. Except that now he is back crying again; twice in the last few weeks she has caught him at it, and has crept away without saying anything, afraid of reopening that particular can of rotting worms. She has urged him to go back and see the doctor – had hoped, in fact, that the doctor would insist upon it – but he seems to be happy enough to continue to hand out the six-monthly prescriptions without laying eyes on Tom again.

It is not about the sex – God, she would gladly do without sex for the rest of her days if everything else was back to some sort of normality. More than anything she just wishes that he would talk to her. But no, she cannot deceive herself that this distance between them is all Tom's fault, for often now it is she who avoids the opportunity for a conversation, who finds herself suddenly busy with the washing-up or some child-related task when her husband comes into the kitchen. She is afraid of what he might say; because she has used up all the weapons in her arsenal, she feels, and she is out of ideas to fix him.

She lifts her phone, wide awake now, needing distraction. The picture on her home screen is of the four of them on the beach in Kerry last summer, and unbidden the hackneyed phrase jumps to her lips. *In happier times*. God, she needs to crawl out of whatever this maudlin slough is. She unlocks the phone, and her browser opens on one of those women's forums she likes to lurk on, comforting in its anonymity, where people with problems ranging from the horrifying to the utterly inconsequential ask questions to which the answers are usually blindingly obvious. Wandering husbands (*Leave the bastard!*), impertinent friends (*Just say no!*). It is very easy, she has found, to solve the impossible conundrums of other people.

She wonders what she would write herself, were she to open her marriage up to the advice of voyeuristic strangers. *He doesn't. I can't. Help.*

~

She thinks now of their first time, huddled under the thin summer duvet in her flat in Phibsboro, the clank of the dodgy plumbing from the room overhead. Tom's breath hot on her neck. The pull and suck of him, damp skin on damp skin, her hands ravenous, his rough with desire; the awkward clash of limbs, elbow abutting knee, before they found their rhythm. How they had both frozen momentarily, sweaty arms entangled, on hearing Helen come into the flat and crash considerately around the kitchen, and the mingled pride and shame with which she had come out of the bedroom afterwards with Tom's hand clutched sheepishly in hers. The three of them had sat then and eaten huge bowls of pasta around the tiny table with the broken gateleg, and drunk wine, and laughed a lot. She'd never felt so hungry in her life.

And all the other times, other places; Tom's awful flat with Johnny, and the youth hostel in Turkey with the drunk German students passed out in the other bunks. Their first flat together, the one down by the docks, with the cheap laminate floor that bounced when you walked. The honeymoon apartment in Italy, the afternoon sunlight coming through the filmy curtains at the window, and feeling the weight of Tom sleeping afterwards in her arms.

So many places she has known her husband. And now, here in the place they have been the longest, and shared the most, she feels she does not know him at all.

~

144

Sometimes, in her darkest moments – the ones she barely acknowledges to herself, let alone dares to speak of out loud – Rachel allows herself to imagine what life would be like without Tom. It is an indulgence she only rarely permits, fearing that too much repetition will bring a comfort with the idea that might prove impossible to resist. But sometimes, when it has been a particularly bad day, when her reserves of patience have run dry and she bears witness to the uglier sides of her own personality, she has allowed herself the luxury of the *what if?* If Tom lived somewhere else, and came to collect the children on a Saturday morning for a weekend of Fun with Dad. She has fantasised about waving them off after an awkward, stiltedly polite exchange of greetings on the doorstep, and closing the door behind them to the new quiet of the house, and the sadness and the blessed relief of it all.

She can picture it now, the orderly way in which the house would run, the calmness of the evenings after the children have been tucked into bed. But her imagination fails her every time she tries to picture Tom's life without them. Where would he live, for a start? Back with his parents in Wicklow, in the childhood bedroom with the chequered duvet and the football posters on the walls? Unthinkable. And yet the alternative seems worse, somehow – a two-bedroom flat somewhere (and how could they afford this?), bare walls and too little furniture, a fridge full of odd bits of food that could never make up an actual meal. Would he find someone else, someone capable of making him happy in a way that Rachel has for a long time been unable to?

It is not an option, even if the thousand practical and financial considerations could be overcome. Even if none of those things applied, she knows she does not have it in her to do it to Tom. She could bear it for herself, she thinks; she could even, with a bit of persuasion, bear it for the children, for she is confident in her ability to make her children's lives full and warm and happy, even on her own. But she could not bear it for him.

~

The bathroom door opens now, and Rachel puts her phone down quickly and turns towards the wall, stilling her breath into some facsimile of sleep. The mattress dips and creaks as Tom settles into it. She can feel his eyes on her back, and for a moment it seems like he is going to speak. If he does, she tells herself, she will turn to him; she will sit up and switch back on the light, she will reach for him with arms that are open and willing. If he speaks, then she will speak too, and she will listen.

She counts thirty-six of her own breaths before she hears him start to snore.

AFTER

Two Years

Someday She Will Go Home Again

It is done. The whole of Rachel's life – the physical compo-
nents, anyway, the shampoo bottles and dessert forks and
seamless tights, the decorative pillows and charging cables
and the good plates – all this is packed into the forty or so
boxes that stand now in the hall and living room, a Jenga-like
construction that threatens at any moment to topple to the
ground. The money has made its way to wherever it needs
to go, and she waits now only for the moving van to come
and take everything away. Packing up has taken twice as
long as she imagined it would, and she has not slept in over
thirty hours. She should have paid the moving company to do
it, really, but every aspect of this is already costing an eye-
watering amount of money, and there is something distaste-
ful, too, about the idea of strangers' hands sifting and sorting
through the minutiae of her family's life.

The selling itself has been a torture of a different kind, a process that proved both tedious and frequently upsetting. There
had been long legal proceedings first just to be allowed to sell
the house on Tom's behalf – a process with no bad actors, not
really, but one that still seemed fraught with the potential for
hurt and offence at every step. After that the involvement of
estate agents and viewers came as something of a relief, a sign
of progress at least; but Rachel tired quickly of the necessary

147

tidying and primping of the house, the sense that the place was already not fully hers. And now, at last, it is not hers at all, and she finds herself curiously numb.

~

She had thought, at one point, that she would be trapped in this house forever. Because they had bought it, like every other foolish couple their age, in a market that seemed to be rising with unstoppable momentum, and then had watched in horrified disbelief as the whole thing came crashing down around their ears. Though really the house had been the least of their worries, then; they had told each other, in mutually reassuring conversations in front of the nine o'clock news, that it didn't matter what it would theoretically resell for, because they were going to live in it forever. No, back then it was Tom's business that was the real crisis, the recession meaning that everyone's dreams of building one-off cottages and large side-extensions were suddenly wiped out too, and Tom's phone just as suddenly stopped ringing. And even after Tom was gone, although the market had started to improve, the house was still not worth anything like what they had originally paid for it. No matter how late Rachel sat up doing the sums with a growing sense of panic in her gut, she could not work out how, after the bank was paid back – and even supposing they would give her a new mortgage on her own salary – there would be enough to buy her any sort of roof over her head.

Because the truth was, she could not continue to live here. The house had become a tomb, where night after night she lay with her dead children, and what had once been a bitter sort of comfort was now wrapping its tendrils around her and threatening to bury her alive. Some mornings she woke with an inertia that was a blanket of dead air pinning her to the bed, a lumpen weight upon her chest. Twice now she had called in sick to work; she, whose innate conscientiousness had had her struggling to work through pregnancy sickness and flu and, once, a stabbing pain in her abdomen that had landed her in the A&E department halfway through her shift with a simmering appendix. Now, she lay unmoving in her bed with the sounds of the day distant from her ears and the sense that the world was happening elsewhere, while she was trapped in some dimension entirely her own.

It was her parents, eventually, who came to the rescue. She had not told them anything about it, about the urgency of her need to escape – largely from a default position, honed early in adolescence, of never telling them anything unless it was strictly necessary. So when they had turned up, both of them, arriving at her door one wet evening last autumn, she had been taken by surprise. She did not enjoy unexpected visitors; even when they had all lived here together she had luxuriated in the sense of her home as snug and impenetrable, and now she felt an unannounced ring of the doorbell as a positive invasion.

But they were here, anyway, and she tried not to sound ungracious.

'Come in, come in.'

Her father stooped to kiss her; her mother was already at the bannister, draping her wet coat carefully over the post.

'God, it's miserable out there.' She shivered dramatically; she had always taken bad weather as a personal affront.

'Come on inside. I've the fire lit.'

Rachel made tea, listening from the kitchen to the low murmur of their conversation. She wondered what the agenda was here. It was not their normal pattern, this, to turn up together out of the blue. Her mother, yes; her mother would drop in, mid-morning or on her way home from town, although usually even those visits would be presaged with a text message, a cheery exhortation to 'Put the kettle on!' Always she would bring something, a little plant or a box of Danish pastries, a scarf she thought was the right colour for Rachel's eyes. But her father's visits were rare, and never without invitation; usually when she saw him it was in their house, the house she had grown up in, for Sunday dinners with Rebecca and Doug and the rapidly growing twins.

She carried the tea in carefully, wondering if there were any biscuits in the tin. She never bothered with them herself. Her parents sat side by side on the couch, perched too close to the edge in a manner that could surely not be comfortable. Rachel took the armchair by the fire.

Her mother was the first to speak.

'We want to talk to you about something.'

'Am I in trouble?' She said it jokingly, but their faces were unsmiling.

'We want to propose something to you, Rachel.' Margaret went on as if there had been no interruption. 'We know you're unhappy living here. It's not good for you; I've always said it.'

The instinct was always to argue, to deflect. She steeled herself to stay quiet.

'And we know, obviously, it'd be very difficult to buy somewhere on your own, what with everything.' She waved her hand to indicate the vagaries of the economy, a beast she always claimed not to understand at all. 'So we want to help you out a bit.'

Her father spoke then. 'We'd like to give you some money, Rachel. So you can sell this place, and get your own money out of it, and find somewhere new for yourself.'

Whatever Rachel had expected, it was not this. Her first instinct was pique, that they had so accurately read her innermost feelings. Her second, wiser instinct was to choose the less ungracious argument.

'I can't take your money.'

'You can.' Her mother's usual briskness was gone, and this soft determination was somehow more impressive.

'No, really, Mam.' Rachel sat forward in her chair. 'Honestly now. It's very nice of you to offer, and I really appreciate it, but I couldn't do that.'

'Rachel. We want you to have it. Neither of us want you to go on living here; you're not happy, of course you're not, and it's not good for you, going on here. It would put our minds at rest –' here she gripped Frank's hand fiercely – 'to have you somewhere new, a fresh start.'

Rachel put her mug on the shelf behind her, buying time. 'How do you – I'm sorry, it's not my business. But how do you even have that sort of money?'

'Well.' Her mother nodded towards her father, who was growing visibly more and more uncomfortable with this kind of talk. 'Your dad had a very good pension plan, and there was a lump sum from it when he retired. And we have savings, too, over the years. So it's there, we have it, and we'd like to use it now to help you out.'

'I don't know what to say.'

'We did something similar for Rebecca, years ago. When she was having the twins.'

Rachel looked up, startled. 'I never knew that.'

'Well. It was her private business. But we had to help them out; sure she was living in that awful place, remember, and Doug barely had a job. We paid their rent for a year or two, and – anyway. So it's only fair, now, to give you a bit of a hand.'

There was quiet for a minute or two. Just the crackle of the stove and the drip of water from the eaves of the house, and somewhere distant the wail of an ambulance.

Her father, who had been mostly silent throughout, spoke now, and for the first time in her life he looked to Rachel like an old man.

'You can't stay in this place.' He gestured around the room, the benignity of the tastefully painted walls and the polished wooden floors containing for him unseen horrors. And Rachel saw with a terrible shock that he had tears in his eyes, her solid unshakeable father, and after that there was nothing else to discuss.

~

There's the van; a lorry really, long and wide and immediately blocking half the street. The neighbours will give out; but then, they are not her neighbours any more, not after today. She gives a wave from the open front door where she is sitting, and levers herself to her feet. She is impatient, suddenly, to be gone. The new people – she knows little about them, beyond their names and the fact that they have one child – are not arriving until tomorrow, so all she needs to do is drop the key off at the estate agents, and collect the one for the new house. She shows the two men the pile of boxes, the few big bits of furniture she is bringing with her – it is so much smaller, the new house, and she has been ruthless in her culling – and they nod silently, this all being self-evident, and get to work. She does not need to wait. She takes the key and her bag, and gets into her car.

She sees the door across the road open, and is tempted to pretend she has not noticed and to drive away, but Michelle is already halfway down the drive and she is carrying something, a big dish wrapped in tinfoil. Rachel starts to roll down her window and then decides that this is rude – God knows, Michelle has never been anything but good to her – and steps out of the car. Michelle smiles at her as she comes across the road.

'I wanted to catch you, before the big departure.'

'I'm sorry. I should have called, to say goodbye properly. I've had so much on, the last few weeks . . .'

Michelle dismisses this with a wave of her hand. 'Don't be silly. You've plenty to be doing. But I just wanted to wish you all the best, and to give you this.' She hands over the dish, which is heavier than Rachel had expected, and still warm.

'It's a lasagna. I thought it would do you for a few nights, save you cooking. It's only out of the oven; put it straight into the fridge in the new place and it'll be grand.'

Rachel looks at it, feels the weight of such an ordinary, straightforward kindness in her hands.

'That's really so good of you. Thank you, Michelle. I really appreciate it.' She moves to hug her, but cannot manage it with the dish still in her hands, and so she passes it through the window of the car to rest on the driver's seat. Then she does hug Michelle, for longer than seems normal or appropriate, and when she pulls back Rachel sees the other woman is swiping at her eyes with the heel of her hand. Michelle, who is busy with three children herself, and who left food of some sort on Rachel's doorstep every day for those first two weeks at home, and who never shies from saying the names of Rachel's children when she meets her – Michelle is a saint really, and it is only now Rachel is realising it, now that it is too late to tell her. She doesn't have the words. Instead she gets back into the car, settling the lasagna carefully into the passenger seat, and waves from the window, and drives slowly down the road.

～

The new house is in Stoneybatter. It is tiny, tiny being what Rachel can afford; a red-bricked house, a cottage really, in a row of identical red-bricked cottages, and hers has not had the gussying-up that many of the other houses on the road show signs of. But there is something quaintly charming about it, and its two small bedrooms and rudimentary kitchen are more than ample for her needs. It is a house composed entirely of impracticalities – the tiny bathroom off the kitchen, the square of concrete that is the only outside space, the open deathtrap of a staircase ascending from the middle of the living room. It is a house in which she cannot imagine children.

She arrives there before the moving van – she does not know where it is going to park, but that is their problem, she supposes – and lets herself in the front door, and pushes it shut behind her. This is a noisier road than the one she has just left, it is the city really, but even so the house feels quiet, expectant. There is no hall; the entrance lands her straight into the living room, and past it is the tiny kitchen and the bathroom, which has at least been fairly recently refurbished and boasts grab rails and a shower with a seat. Upstairs there is a small back bedroom and a larger front one, and that is all, and it feels like a size that she can manage. There are no carpets anywhere, but the floorboards throughout have been painted in a glossy white paint, and there is a square of not terrible lino in the kitchen.

She should have brought some groceries, she thinks now, milk and tea bags at least; she will have to go out again later. But the village, as people still refer to it, is only a few minutes' walk away. She will go, once the movers have been and gone, once the house is filled again with her boxes and the few pieces of furniture she has kept; she will go, and then she will come home to this house for the first time, and she will discover if this is something she can bear.

~

That first night she wakes repeatedly, each time disoriented and unsure if she has been dreaming. The layout of the room is unfamiliar, the angle of the streetlight through the curtains wrong. Once she goes down to the kitchen for water, and stands for a few minutes in the unaccustomed silence. Somewhere around six o'clock she falls into a deeper sleep, and when she next wakes properly it is just gone ten, and the road outside hums with traffic.

She has taken two weeks annual leave, and she passes those first days in an industrious haze of cleaning and organisation, an occupation that is satisfying in the way that uncomplicated physical work is often satisfying, her progress clear and measurable at the end of each day. Although she is struck sometimes by the unreality of it, of being here. It still feels temporary, like someday she will go home again.

Early on a Saturday morning she dresses in an old pair of tracksuit bottoms and a T-shirt she got at a 5k run one year, back when they were planning the wedding and she was trying to make some feeble effort at developing an exercise habit. She lays thin plastic sheets on the floor of the bedroom – save the bed itself, there is no furniture in here yet – and swings the ends of the curtains over the top rail. At the kitchen sink she fills the reservoir of the new wallpaper steamer, which she has bought in Woodie's for twenty-five per cent off. She plugs it in and listens as it heats up, the scraper ready in her hand, and then she makes a start. It is hot and damp and the noise of it is like a kettle at full boil; at first she tries to listen to an audiobook on her phone while she works, but it is far too noisy for this, and she switches it off temporarily while she digs a pair of earphones out of the bottom of her handbag. There is a second pause while she looks for a pair of gloves, finally finding some in an unopened box of hair dye; the wallpaper, once softened, is sticky with old paste, and it leaves a residue on her hands which is intolerably unpleasant. Once these niceties are taken care of, however, she gets on swimmingly. It is immensely satisfying, to watch the aged paper peel off in long, unbroken strips. There are two layers of it, and underneath the plaster is pink and crumbling in places, but she thinks she will be able to make a reasonable job at patching it up, rather than having to get a plasterer in, which in any case she cannot afford.

It is soothing, to have the whole day to devote to this task, and to see the fruits of it with such immediacy. By lunchtime the wallpaper is gone, three huge sacks of it squeezed into the black bin outside, and she is attacking the remaining bits of paste and scraps of backing paper with a dish scrubber and sugar soap. When this is done she forces herself to stop, and heats up some soup in the microwave, which is at present the only fully functioning part of the kitchen. She sits at the small table – a second-hand find, disassembled and brought home in the boot of her car – and eats; she finds that she is famished, and cuts more and more bread from the loaf until it is all but gone.

The filling of the cracks and the waiting for it to dry, the sanding and the final clean – all of this takes twice as long as she had expected, and by the time she is levering the lid off the first tin of paint the light is starting to fade. She should wait until the next day to begin, she knows that, but she is impatient now to see the results of her labour. The paint – a very pale, muted sort of pink, a colour that she would never have considered before – rolls onto the wall with a creamy ooze that makes her want to dip her finger into the tin and taste it. She gets a first coat onto all four walls, and it is eleven o'clock and she is exhausted and has paint in her hair and the beginnings of a blister on her middle finger, but she does not care. Her sense of satisfaction is almost overwhelming. She runs a bath, hot as she can bear, and sinks under the water, and feels the pleasurable ache in her arms and her lower back.

Lying in bed in the other, smaller room – she is not afraid of the smell of the paint, but had not wanted to go to the bother of taking the dust sheets off her bed – she realises that she has forgotten to eat anything since that rushed lunchtime meal. But she is more tired than hungry now, and the exhaustion wins out. She sleeps, her dreams soft and pastel-coloured for once.

~

Rachel wakes to a ring at the doorbell, the sound clamorous and unfamiliar; she realises it is the first time she has heard its chime. She is tempted to ignore it, to turn over and bury her head under the pillow, but she finds she is too curious. She cannot imagine who it might be. She has slept in an old T-shirt, and pauses only to pull on the pair of jeans draped over the rail on the tiny landing.

There is no pane of glass in the heavy front door, and no peephole either, so it is only when it is already too late to retreat, the door open wide and welcoming, that she can see who is there. Helen, in expensive sunglasses and a long patterned dress, a cardboard tray with two cups of coffee in one carefully manicured hand.

'Hello! I thought you might like breakfast.' She lifts the other hand, which holds a paper bag through which a grease stain is slowly spreading.

Rachel cannot speak. Every cell of her body is resisting this incursion of her old life into the new, ordered one she is working so hard to create.

'I'm sorry.' Helen takes off her sunglasses, and tilts her head. 'Should I have called first?'

Yes. Or not called, ever, and just let me be. Let me start again.

'No. Sorry. Sorry, come on in.' She stands back to let the other woman pass her into the living room. They do not hug. Helen stands in the middle, gazing around her.

'This is lovely. Really.' She turns to look at Rachel, and smiles.

'It's . . .' Rachel shrugs. Helen lives in a new-build in Portmarnock, with three bathrooms and a kitchen that is already done. Her house is always tidy.

'Tea? Or no, you've brought coffees.' Rachel shakes her head, addled. 'This is great, thank you.'

Helen hands her the cup, its lid coming loose in her hand. She proffers the bag.

'Have a Danish, go on.'

'I'll get some plates.'

In the kitchen she squeezes her eyes tight shut, and breathes deeply through her nose.

When she returns Helen has kicked off her shoes, and tucked her feet under her on the couch. Rachel takes the armchair by the window. The curtains are dusty and slightly moth-eaten; they are one of many items on the long list of things Rachel needs to replace.

'So, tell me.' Helen leans forward, the pastry in her hand oozing dark crimson fruit. 'How's it all been? Are you settling in?'

Rachel shrugs. 'I suppose. It needs a bit of work.' She waves a hand vaguely, taking it all in – the room, still mostly bare; the unopened boxes in the corner.

'Still. No rush, is there?'

'No, I suppose not.'

Rachel is acutely aware of the fact that since the accident – 'The Accident' is what she still calls it to herself, in spite of the imprecision of the word, for what else, really, could you call it? – she has not once taken the initiative to call Helen, to send a chatty message or even the most generic of birthday greetings. Always it is Helen who gets in touch, and this which seemed forgivable, expected even, in the first days and months afterwards, now looks less and less so. She has become a bad friend.

'Have you met the neighbours?'

'Just on this side.' Rachel nods towards the wall of the room. 'It's an older lady, she seems very deaf.'

'You can crack on with the wild parties, so.'

Rachel manages a weak smile, and they fall silent again. The two feet of tarnished white floorboards are a gulf between them. Rachel tries to access the depths of her primitive brain, to dredge up the memories that she knows are there. This is, after all, the childhood friend on whose bedroom floor she slept most Friday nights through her early teen years, the pauses in their whispered conversations growing longer as they drifted off to sleep. The girl she lay on a sun-baked Spanish beach with the summer after their Leaving Cert, into whose reddened shoulders she rubbed aloe vera at the end of each day, her own skin still milky white under layers of sun cream. The woman they chose to be her son's godmother, Rachel and Tom's full complement of siblings having been used up when Rebecca and Doug stood for their daughter two years earlier. It is no use. It is like a shutter has come down; the memories are still there, but she finds there is no longer any emotion attached to them. She cannot believe now that they ever had anything in common.

Helen shifts slightly in her seat, and the patterned dress clings briefly to a new curve in her midriff, and then falls away again. It is only for a second, but it is long enough for Rachel to know that the coffee in the paper cup in Helen's hand is for once decaf, and that her visit today is not wholly without purpose. She is seized with a sudden panic, and gets abruptly to her feet.

'Do you want to see the rest of it?'

In silence she leads Helen into the tiny kitchen, lets her poke her head into the bathroom, follows her up the narrow stairs. The wood is cool and, in places, rough under her bare feet. They stand at the window of the front bedroom, looking out at the Sunday-morning street.

'You're properly in the middle of things here. It's like being young again.'

She turns back to the window, and Rachel stares at the back of her glossy head, wondering at this casual cruelty.

~

When they come downstairs again Rachel does not lead Helen back to the sofa, but instead moves towards the front door. Helen eyes her carefully before she follows.

'I'd better get going, so.' It is not quite a question.

'It was good of you to come. Really, thank you.'

Helen bites her lip and for a moment her hand drifts to her middle, but she does not say anything. Instead she puts her arms around Rachel and holds her close for a moment. Rachel can smell her perfume, sweet and floral.

'I'm sorry.' Rachel is not sure if she has said this outside her own head, and if she has then surely not loud enough to be heard. But Helen's face, as she pulls away, is kind, and she presses her lips to Rachel's cheek for a few seconds before she opens the door.

'Call me. Whenever you want to.'

And suddenly there is a brief clutch of hands – Rachel does not know who has initiated it, but she hopes it was herself – and then Helen is gone.

BEFORE

Eight Months

Going Through the Motions

In, in, the key stiff in the lock, she must get Tom to put some WD40 in there, or better yet do it herself, if she wants it to happen this side of Christmas. Straight into the kitchen with the shopping bags, calling out a hurried greeting to Tom and the kids who are slack-jawed on the couch, where she supposes they have been since she left the house. Still, no time to think about that now. She needs to get the freezer stuff out of the bags, the garden peas and fish fingers and alphabet waffles; the fridge bits as well – Tom can do the rest – and then get into the shower. Half six for drinks. She looks at her watch – a quarter to five, she is already pushing it.

It is a mess upstairs, clothes everywhere and all the drawers open, as if the place has been ransacked by burglars with a yen for Peppa Pig T-shirts and sequinned gauze skirts. She would love to get a cleaner; it is something she actively daydreams about, a sort of faceless angelic presence who would hum quietly to herself as she floated from room to room, leaving calm and order in her wake. But Rachel couldn't let anyone into the place the way it is now, and she doesn't have time to do the amount of tidying it would need every week to make actual cleaning feasible or worthwhile. She shoves these thoughts aside to their habitual place at the back of her mind, and pulls off her own clothes, dropping them straight into the laundry hamper with a pointed raise of her eyebrows, which is wasted on an absent audience. The water is deliciously hot and she lingers there longer than she can really afford to, rolling her shoulders in the scalding jets. It had been the first thing they had changed in the house, back when they moved in, putting in the power shower to replace the miserable trickle from the old telephone-style attachment on the taps; Rachel remembers still the luxury of that first blistering deluge. Finally she gropes blindly for the button and turns it off, steeling herself for the sudden chill. She rubs herself dry with a towel that is already damp.

She had at least laid out her clothes before leaving for the supermarket, and she is glad now, looking again at the time. The black dress has not been worn since before she had her children, but it still zips up easily, even if it does not skim her hips in quite the same way as before. The first pair of tights has a ladder which she only discovers once she is doing a final wriggle into the gusset, and there is a brief moment of panic until she finds another pair deep in the recesses of her underwear drawer. She wonders suddenly if people her age really wear tights any more; she has no idea.

Make-up, then, heavier than her usual harried dusting of powder; she gives it the whole works today, leaning in close to the mirror to draw the thin black lines around her eyes. Her hand is still steady; she hasn't lost that, despite being out of practice. She gives her hair another towel, rubbing it briskly in the way she knows you are not supposed to, it breaks the strands or something, but it speeds things up, and then she is flipping her head upside down to dry it furiously, the blast of air at its maximum heat. She runs the straighteners over it quickly, putting a bit of curl in the ends, and stares critically into the mirror. Not bad at all, if she says so herself. They have not deserted her yet, her looks, and she feels suddenly

162

excited about the night ahead, about the opportunity to sit with other women in a noisy restaurant and order cocktails with ridiculous names and pretend to deliberate over the dessert menu.

She adds a spray of perfume, and finds her going-out handbag, the one that fits nothing more than a purse and a phone and lipstick, and heads downstairs.

Tom is coming out of the kitchen, a plastic beaker of water in one hand. Rachel indulges in a little twirl, and a weak smile creases his mouth.

'You look very nice.'

The way his voice rises on the last word. There is a beat, two, and suddenly she knows with a dull, hopeless certainty what he is going to say next.

'Are you going out?'

The sick feeling in her stomach. And yet, she finds she is not even really surprised.

'Tom. Helen's birthday party.'

He frowns, as if both the name and the concept are things which he needs to puzzle out.

'*Tom*. Come on. I told you about it ages ago. It's on the calendar.'

She gestures towards the sheet pinned to the fridge, as if proof is all that is needed. As if being *correct* will force him to concede, with a good grace, and wave her cheerfully off from the door. She does not add *And I told you about it last week*. She does not say *And I reminded you this morning*. She recognises futility when she sees it, when it has taken up residence in her house.

Because it is panic, it is sheer panic, that now crosses Tom's face. That is the worst thing, that she cannot even be angry with him; his reaction is so clearly genuine. But she is angry with him anyway.

163

'It's just dinner, I won't be late back. You just have to give them their tea and put them to bed. Come *on*, Tom.'

'I . . . Rach. I can't. I'm not . . .' His mouth continues to move, wordless now.

'What? What is it?' Her own voice impatient, insisting. None of this will help; it is going through the motions. She knew, as soon as she saw his face, that she would not be going out.

Still, she fights it.

'Tom. This can't happen again. I already missed seeing her at Christmas.' Tom's sudden tummy upset, necessitating hours behind the closed bathroom door, and although Rachel could tell from the unspeakable sounds emanating from within that he was indeed indisposed, still she could not help wondering why these attacks always came on just when there was something pressing to be attended to. On that occasion it had been afternoon tea with Helen, a long-standing pre-Christmas tradition whereby they would get dressed up and meet in the lobby of one of the nicer hotels in town and sit for hours over plates of crustless sandwiches and impossibly baroque mouthfuls of pastry. Instead she had sat at home seething silently by the lights of the Christmas tree while Tom locked himself away upstairs, until he had reappeared around dinner-time sipping in a cautious, convalescent manner from a can of Diet Coke.

Helen had called around late that night with Christmas presents for the kids, and something in her face and her voice – some undercurrent that was not quite pity or concern or hurt, but some distant relative of all three – had made Rachel keep the visit short, professing tiredness, a list of seasonal jobs still to be done.

Now Tom looks at her, and his eyes are pleading.

'I just . . . I don't know what to do with them, Rachel.'

'What do you mean, *do* with them? They're your children, Tom. Jesus Christ.' She turns from him, and stumbles in the unaccustomed heels. Tom's hand shoots out to steady her, and she shakes him off angrily.

'This can't keep happening, Tom. It's not – it's not fair.' Which is true, but this is not what she had started to say; that had been something different, something perhaps irrevocable, and she shies from it at the last moment. She is a coward.

'I know. I know that. I'm sorry.'

'You need to sort yourself out.' Her voice sounds unrecognisably harsh to her, the bitterness like something tangible in her mouth; she finds she does not care. 'I mean it. You have to do something. Go back to the doctor, or something.' It is not, of course, the first time she has said this, and she has no expectation that it will work.

'I know,' he says again. 'I will.'

He cannot possibly think he sounds convincing.

'Are you even taking your tablets still? Are you?' Rachel had policed the medication at first, discreetly, always aware of how many pills should be in the box, and when the prescription was · due to be refilled. But that had dropped away, after the first few months; there was always so much else to do.

'They don't help. They don't – I feel like I'm underwater, when I'm on them. I'm not myself.'

'Well.' She exhales heavily, biting off the myriad unkind, cruel things that jump immediately to her lips. *Not himself.* That would be something, wouldn't it?

~

She hides in the downstairs toilet. Tom is hovering, trying to apologise and explain, and she is truly afraid that she will hit

165

him if she does not get away. She sits on the closed lid of the seat, listening to the babble of the children over the noise of the TV. She will have to tell Helen. She doesn't have it in her to face a phone call, and sends a text instead, and then she sits on in the quiet, staring at the walls. The wallpaper above the door is peeling; it was madness, several people had told her, to put wallpaper in a bathroom, but she had been enchanted by the sprays of peacock feathers, the boldness of the purple and gold. The children love it, and have each picked out a favourite from among the many identical birds. She looks at her nails, which last night she had painted in anticipation of the dinner, laying on the deep burgundy varnish in careful strokes. She has always had good nails, short and broad and square – *all the milk I made you drink*, her mother says, taking credit where none may be due. Rachel cannot abide the stuff now.

Helen's reply comes quickly, but Rachel cannot bear to open it for several minutes. When she does, her cheeks are burning.

Sorry to hear that. We'll miss you.

That is all; there are no forgiving emojis, no pleas for her to reconsider. It feels cold, and Rachel knows that it is no more than she deserves. She sits for ten minutes more, her head in her hands, and then she goes back upstairs, and each step feels as heavy as if she really has spent the night dancing in heels. It takes an age to get all the eyeliner off.

AFTER

Three Years

Taking Pleasure

She is not the oldest there; for some reason she had assumed that she would be, and it is a pleasant surprise to find that in fact it looks like she is one of the younger ones. It's not a big class; nine of them, at first, and then just as the course director is launching into her presentation the door opens again and a tenth person rushes in, a woman of about Rachel's age with very long hair that is an ashy almost-white. She is effusive in her apologies, and the director smiles graciously and waits for the woman to seat herself at the end of the large U-shaped table. But the woman does not stop talking; as she settles herself into the chair and arranges her bags under it and takes out a pair of reading glasses, she talks on and on about the traffic, and the difficulty in finding a parking spot, and the confusing system of numbers and letters used to identify the seminar rooms, and the director's smile becomes a rictus of suppressed frustration and timetabling panic. Rachel shares an amused half-smile with the woman across from her – Niamh something, she thinks it is – and then feels guilty, and wonders if she wants so early to mark herself out as that kind of person. But really, the ash-haired woman is a bit much.

At last she winds down, with a series of contented sighs, and the course director lifts her laser pointer – which, Rachel sees now, has a name-label wrapped around it – and turns resolutely to the screen. Intersecting circles in red and blue highlight the aims and objectives of the programme, which are apparently quite different things. Rachel begins to take half-hearted notes in the large foolscap pad they have all been provided with, but soon she realises that none of this is information she will need to retain, and quietly puts down her pen.

~

When Denise had first raised the idea of the master's degree with her, Rachel had balked. It had been so long since she had done anything approaching academic work – fourteen years, almost, since her graduation from the nursing course, her parents and Becca and streaky glasses of warm white wine in the court-yard outside the examinations hall. She had been excited then, about the new uniform and the salary, the jump in status; and excited too about saying goodbye to the endless logbooks and skills lists, the piles of folders now languishing somewhere in her parents' attic. She had not foreseen a return to the classroom. And yet here she was, having been beguiled by Denise's offer of funding, her suggestion of routes to promotion. The prospect of a change.

It is a two-year programme; part-time, of course, and Rachel probably could have continued on her old roster and fitted it all in around work. But instead she has decided to reduce her hours for the duration – when you figure in the tax, the difference is not huge – and the extra couple of free days in the week already feel like a luxury. She imagines herself getting up early and settling at the kitchen table to write essays and assignments; doing a Pilates class, maybe, or learning to knit. The serenity of these images appeals to her, although the reality is that, in her free mornings since the new roster kicked in last week, she has stayed late in bed watching episodes of an Australian comedy series on Netflix. She finds the accents soothing, reminding her of the soaps her mother watched all through her childhood, and presumably still does.

~

The morning is largely taken up with learning each other's names. Despite its self-importantly long and unwieldy title, the degree is a management course, basically, a qualification in leadership for people working in health. It is open to all disciplines, and so they are a mixed bag, her classmates; there are two other nurses, a couple of physiotherapists, a handful of GPs. Seven women, three men; about par for the course for this type of undertaking. Rachel has found that men, a tiny minority in most of the less glamorous healthcare jobs, are generally overrepresented at the academic end of things.

At half past twelve they break for lunch, and move as a large, self-conscious group towards the canteen on the floor below. They lose a couple of members en route – the girl Niamh, who slips into a bathroom and doesn't rejoin them until they are back in the classroom again, and a suited man who waves his phone vaguely as he stalks away down the other end of the corridor. But the remaining eight sit down together, decanting plates of salad and undercooked chips from wooden trays which they pile in a tidy stack at one end of the table. Rachel finds herself between the ash-haired woman, who is called Carla, and one of the two remaining men in the group – a young and sandy-haired, very tall man named Lewis. She remembers that he is a physiotherapist, and from Wales.

'Well. What did you think of all that?' He tucks into his panini with a relish that seems undeserved; the bread is overtoasted at each end, and sagging in the middle.

'It was – grand, I suppose?' Rachel shrugs. 'It's what you expect from the first day, isn't it? Hopefully it'll get a bit more interesting as it goes along.'

'Have you done anything like this before?'

'No, never. I haven't studied anything since my degree, really. Have you?'

He shakes his head. 'I've always wanted to do the management side of things, though. My family are all teachers – school teachers, I mean. Must be in the blood, bossing people about.'

She cannot help returning his smile; he is lovely, but so young, the enthusiasm is bursting out of every acne-scarred pore of his ruddy face. It is just a bit exhausting.

The last session ends just after four o'clock, and so Rachel gets home earlier than she would on an ordinary work day. The house is warm, bathed in early autumn sunlight. She has grown to love it, her little home, which she has arranged in just the way she likes it; there is an order now to her evenings, a predictability that pleases her. After dinner she pours a single glass of wine, which she measures scrupulously to the halfway point of the glass, and she does the crossword, filling in the block letters with a pen she keeps especially for the task. Occasionally she impresses herself by coming up with words she didn't realise she knew, and others that are familiar but which she would have said she could not define; *oriel, husbandry*. At ten o'clock she makes a final cup of tea, and with it she eats something she will have bought particularly for this time – an unusual French cheese, sliced and placed carefully on a plain cracker, or half of a chocolate eclair. She eats slowly, taking pleasure in nourishing herself.

170

~

This first part of the course is a week-long 'intensive' module, and on the Thursday evening someone starts a vague murmuring about going for a drink after the last session on the Friday. Rachel's first instinct is to decline. It is hard work, she has come to feel, immersing herself in a group of strangers day after day; the exhaustion she feels when she arrives home each evening has little to do with the rigours of the course, which has not so far proved taxing by any yardstick. But the others seem enthusiastic, and so she silences the pleading voice inside her and joins in the discussion about where would be suitable, although it has been so long since she has had anything resembling a night-time social life that she cannot add much. They settle eventually on a well-known bar on Baggot Street, one where they will be able to get something to eat. The next day she dresses a little more carefully, in a long patterned dress and her green jacket, and she leaves the car at home and takes two buses across town instead.

This last day of the module turns out to be more meaty than the preceding ones, and they receive their first assignments, which will be due four weeks later. Over lunch they discuss the plans for the evening, which all ten of them turn out to be attending – surely a record for this kind of thing. After the end of the last session, which the programme director herself delivers with a congratulatory flourish which seems to Rachel a little premature, they gather up coats and bags and loose sheets of paper destined never to be looked at again, and there is a slight giddiness in the air, the mild hysteria of adults for whom after-work drinks are something of a novelty.

She is crossing the car park, making for the bus stop, when somebody calls her name.

'Rachel. Are you on foot? I've space for one more in here.'

It is the pharmacist named Peter, a tall, slightly balding man with a low, mellifluous voice that Rachel has already noted. He is standing by a Toyota, reassuringly old and scratched in places. Through the rear window Rachel can see two of the other women from the course buckling their seat belts; Joyce waves at her enthusiastically.

'Hop in.'

She is forced to stop. 'I'm grand. I'm going to get the bus. Thank you, though.'

'It's no trouble. Really.'

The passenger seat is empty, awaiting her. She stands yet, wondering if he can see the trembling in her legs, the way the blood feels like it has drained from her face. She has successfully avoided this scenario for more than three years, and yet now, when any number of reasonable excuses should be jumping to her lips, her mind is curiously blank.

'I . . . OK, so. Thank you.' She breathes deeply through her nose, opens the door, sits into the car. He smiles, and closes his own door; the heavy, metallic clunk of it is surely only in Rachel's mind. She forces herself to speak.

'Will you not be having a drink yourself?' She regrets immediately this line of questioning, so boringly Irish, but Peter is unperturbed.

'Ah, I will of course. I'm going to leave the car in town, I can park in Trinity. Perk of the job.' He flashes her a brief smile as he looks over his shoulder, reversing carefully out of the spot. The car park is already half empty; the weekend has begun.

'You teach there, isn't that right? I've lost track of everyone's CVs from the first day, there was a lot to remember.'

'I do. Just two days a week, at the moment. But there might be a permanent job coming up in a couple of years and, well, I thought no harm in being prepared.'

Rachel cannot think of anything else to say. In the back seat Niamh and Joyce are whispering quietly to each other. Outside there are cars everywhere, though mostly heading out of the city, to homes in commuter towns and weekend breaks in the country. Visits to ageing parents in rural villages, where they will instantly regress to teenage dissatisfaction and petty complaints. The late summer sun is warm on her face through the car window. She closes her eyes.

Peter parks near the back of the college, a part Rachel does not know well, her occasional walks through the campus tending to keep to the more picturesque squares towards the front. They walk, the four of them, up Pearse Street and around by the Alexander, and so along Merrion Square. Rachel keeps her gaze ahead, aware dimly of the spectre of the National Maternity Hospital to her left, its brick facade and heavy sash windows. She has fallen into step beside Joyce, who is also a nurse, and so there is an easy route into conversation, a comparing of training, of current roles; the inevitable colleagues they both know, and avoid giving opinions of until they have established that the other feels the same way. When they reach the bar they find that two of the others have already secured a table, and within half an hour the whole ten of them have arrived, and the table is filling up with tiny dishes of calamari and *patatas alioli*.

She waits for the question; it is inevitable, in any gathering of new acquaintances, and so her uneasiness is not so much about if but when, and who it will come from. When it does, the first time, it is Sheila, the older of the nurses, whose eldest child is about to start college.

173

'And have you children yourself?' She is refilling her wine glass from the little bottle as she speaks, and so Rachel does not have to meet her eyes.

'No. No, I don't.' She had not known what she was going to say, but this answer, when it comes, is curiously simple and satisfying. She does not feel it a betrayal.

'Ah well. Plenty of time!'

And that is it, as it turns out, and suddenly she can breathe again.

~

By the time the second module comes around, it is deep into autumn. This one is only two days, and halfway through the Thursday session they are split into pairs to complete a role-play task, the sort of thing Rachel dreads – that surely everyone dreads, it is pure sadism, this. She is paired with Peter, and he raises his eyebrows mournfully at her as he pulls his chair over beside hers.

'Do you enjoy these things as much as I do, or even more?'

'Oh God, I live for them. It was this or a drama course at the Abbey. I clearly chose correctly.'

Peter laughs at this, which is gratifying. He peers down at the pages they have been given.

'Do you want to be the department head, or the terrible student?'

'Student, please.'

He is gracious, she decides, in allowing her without argument to take the easier role, and they begin. He turns out to be very funny, Peter, he has a dry, unembarrassed wit about him that she has had no opportunity to witness before now. Rachel finds herself breaking out of her role constantly to laugh, and once or twice she feels the stern eye of the module facilitator turning in their direction. She doesn't care. It is very nice to laugh with someone.

174

~

She spends Christmas at her parents' house. It is a grown-up Christmas – Rebecca and Doug have taken the boys to New Zealand, a surprise gift of a trip from Doug's parents – and so the three of them sleep late, and exchange a few presents slowly in front of the fire, and spend most of the rest of the day eating smoked salmon and pigs in blankets in front of the TV. That evening she is back to work for a week of nights, and she finds herself grateful for the brevity of the celebration.

~

They are in the corridor, in the short break between morning sessions, which they have taken to spending here rather than in the big canteen. She has insisted on buying the coffees this time; although today, a cold January day, it is a hot chocolate Peter has requested, which Rachel finds at odds with his age and general air of maturity, and therefore somehow delightful. The corridor is wide and carpeted, and here and there are red plastic chairs dotted in cosy clumps of two and three, as if inviting people to sit, to relax. But they have been standing, the two of them, she leaning against the wall with one foot flat against it, her knee pointed towards him. They have been talking about work, and then there is a pause, a little, happy pause, and then his face changes and when he speaks again his voice is different too.

'I wanted to ask. Will you have dinner with me some night? This weekend, maybe, if you're free.'

Rachel pulls away from the wall, and steadies herself. She is surprised at her own reaction to him, the small excitement and the much larger, overarching sense of panic. Although she knows she has been flirting with him – for what is the foot against the wall, really, but flirtation? – she still does not feel ready for this.

He reads her face, and offers retreat.

'I'm sorry. If I'm out of order, please tell me. Maybe you have – maybe you're not available? I wasn't sure.'

'No, I'm – I'm single. If that's what you're asking.'

He smiles. 'It was, sort of. There's no subtle way to find out, really.'

'No.' She finds herself smiling back.

'But if you're not interested . . . That's fine, you know. I won't make things awkward.' This is an impossible promise, but she appreciates his making it.

'No. it's not that. It's just – it's been a while. Since – any of that, really.'

'For me, too.'

'OK.' She takes a breath. 'Let's do it, then.'

'Really?'

'Yes.' And his smile is compensation enough, she thinks, for the part of her that suddenly feels like it is falling.

~

They meet at the restaurant. He has offered to pick her up, but she does not want him to come to the house, not yet, nor to set up the expectation that he will then drop her home. Instead she walks into town, enjoying the chill of the air on her face. The shops are already exploding with cards and other tat for Valentine's Day, a holiday she has never really understood.

He is there when she arrives, reading a paper through wire-rimmed glasses which he removes when he sees her. He stands up, and kisses her cheek across the table.

'Did you walk in?'

'I did. It was lovely.' She unwinds her scarf and pushes it through the sleeve of her coat. 'Bracing.'

A waiter brings bread, and fills their glasses with water, and they study the menu – a little longer than necessary, perhaps, because there is some awkwardness there, it is true; but she thinks it is an awkwardness born out of nerves and expectation, rather than any real distance. And once the wine has been poured and they are tearing the bread and using it to mop up the olive oil and the dark, sticky vinegar, she finds the conversation flows easily. They do not talk about anything very serious; the course, a bit, and then holidays they have been on, books, family. He is from Mayo, which she knew already, and has two older sisters, which she didn't. He describes himself, when pressed, as an adequate sort of uncle.

When the dessert plates are cleared she sits back, pleasantly sated, but he leans towards her, his face suddenly serious.

'Listen. Can I say something?'

Rachel has never known any good conversation to open with these words, and she feels an emptiness suddenly in the unreliable middle of her.

'It's nothing bad, I just – I felt I should tell you.' A pause, and his face looks pained, and sorry, and sad. 'I know about what happened. I know who you are.'

She can feel the colour leave her face; actually feel it, like a plug has been pulled somewhere and all the blood in her body is suddenly circling some drain. She grasps the edge of the table, afraid that she is going to pass out, and he reaches for her hand.

'It's OK. I'm sorry. I didn't mean to – I just wanted you to know, so you wouldn't feel it's something you had to tell me. Or keep from me, or whatever. I didn't want to be lying to you, pretending I didn't know.'

'How do you know? Did somebody tell you?' She has, for the course, gone back to using her maiden name; the loss of the name that is etched into her children's gravestones a constant source of guilt, but her need for anonymity in this new environment eventually winning out.

'No, no. I just—' He shrugs. 'I'm good with faces, I don't forget them. I remembered yours from the news. The funeral.'

Yes; there had been cameras at her children's funeral, an intrusion at the time both monstrous and irrelevant, although she hates the idea that somewhere there exists now footage of her slow trembling walk up the steps of the church, her wild and unseeing eyes.

'Jesus.' She sits back in the chair again.

'I'm sorry.' He looks wretched now. 'Maybe I shouldn't have said anything.'

'No. No. That would be worse.' Though she does not know if this is true.

She cannot sit any more. She stands, her legs threatening at any moment to betray her.

'I'm going to go home. I'm sorry. I can't stay.'

'Please. Rachel, *please*.' He sounds truly desolate now. 'At least let me drop you home.'

But that is unthinkable, to sit in a taxi with him. She shakes her head mutely. He is on his feet too, now, but she stays him with an outstretched hand.

'It's OK. I'm OK. I just have to go. Please, please don't follow me. Please, Peter.'

She does not care who sees her. She looks only straight ahead of her, and runs.

~

Early the next day he phones. It is the first time he has called her, his nameless number flashing up on the screen, but she knows it is him. She watches the phone until the noise stops and the light dies away, and she waits for the soft beep that will tell her he has left a message. When it comes, she listens to it at once. The words are what you would expect – he sounds truly abject – but she hardly hears them. Instead, she listens over and over to his voice, until she finally falls asleep.

He will call again, she thinks.

~

But he does not call again. Rachel is at first surprised, then offended, and then gradually comes to the realisation that he will not phone, because he is not the sort of man who phones again and again a woman who has made it clear she does not want to hear from him. He does not think himself entitled to her time, or her forgiveness. He will not try to wear her down.

She sits with this new knowledge for a few days. She will have to see him again, of course, but not for a month or two; or maybe she will drop out of the course, she is not really enjoying it anyway, and she does not need letters after her name. She can put him behind her, and one day his face will fade from her mind and she will have to search the deepest crevices of her memory to recall the particular sound of his voice. She thinks all this, night after sleepless night on the couch in her icy living room, and a strange feeling starts to gnaw at her, and she realises it is panic at the thought that this new and nebulous thing may be slipping away before it has even started.

She plays the voicemail again.

She composes many messages, and types them out, and then hits delete and watches the letters disappear one by one.

She sits looking at her phone, long into the night.

On the following Saturday she calls him. She listens to the ring and imagines him staring at the phone, wondering whether to pick up. If it is all too late. *Come on.*

'Rachel.' His voice is hesitant.

'Hi.'

'I'm so glad you called. I didn't want to keep bothering you, but I – I was hoping you would. I wanted to – to check that you were OK, and to apologise. Sincerely. It was completely wrong of me to ambush you like that. I'm very embarrassed.'

'You don't need to be. I shouldn't have run off like that.'

'No, I don't blame you at all. It was really unthinking of me – in a public place like that. I don't know what came over me.' She feels, from his voice, that he is walking up and down as he speaks, and she wonders about the type of room he might be pacing in. 'I just – the more we talked, and the more I found myself liking your company, it felt wrong to secretly have this knowledge about you that you weren't aware of. Do you know what I mean? It felt unfair that you didn't know I knew.'

'Yeah. I get that. I do, Peter. I'm not sorry now that you told me.'

She has been standing, staring unseeing out of the window, and now she lies on her bed and stretches out until she feels that pleasurable ache in her calves and feet.

'I would have hated to find out later. That you knew, I mean. I would have felt silly.'

'I didn't want that. But I'm sorry I didn't pick my moment better.'

She knows, in a way that he doesn't, that there is never a good way to have that conversation.

'Do the others know? On the course, I mean.'

'I've no idea. I don't think so; we've never spoken about it.'

'OK.'

He clears his throat. 'I'm so sorry, Rachel. For what happened to you. I wanted to say that, too, the other night. How sorry I am.'

She is lying flat, too low down the bed for the pillows, and so the tears roll down the sides of her face and are lost in the duvet.

'Thank you.'

There is silence for a bit, and she thinks that she could fall asleep. That would be nice, to fall asleep here with him on the other end of the phone.

Then she thinks of something else.

'That's why I was so strange about your car, by the way. That time you gave me a lift into town. I never travel in anyone else's car, really; I haven't been able to, since it happened.'

'God. I never even thought. I'm so sorry.'

'No, it's fine. I'm just sorry if I came across a bit – unbalanced, or whatever.'

'You didn't. I thought you were lovely.'

She feels herself blushing, in this empty room.

'Would you have any interest in trying again?' The words are diffident, but she is not fooled. She finds she is smiling, although he cannot see her face.

'Yes, I would. I'd like that.'

The relief in his voice is almost a tangible thing. 'Would you come to my flat, next Saturday maybe? I'll cook.'

~

His flat is in a part of Dublin she does not know well; a mid-seventies, Brutalist block, outwardly stark and unappealing.

But once inside the rooms are large and light, generously windowed, and the view, across a park to the city beyond, is impossible to ignore.

'Oh. Wow!' She turns to look at him in disbelief.

'I know. It's the main reason I bought the place.' He slips the coat from her shoulders.

'I don't blame you. That's fabulous.' She stares at it for a long time, trying to orient herself, before turning to take in the room itself. It is sparsely furnished, but in a deliberate, thoughtful way; there is nothing studenty or bachelor-like about it. A long, deep sofa in a slubby blue; a low coffee table. At the other end of the room is the small kitchen, which is cluttered and steamy with whatever is bubbling away on the cooker, and rich with good smells.

'This is nice.' She smiles at him, trying to relax. She has not been in this situation in such a long time.

'I'm really glad you came.' For a moment she thinks he is going to kiss her, but instead he nods once, his cheeks reddening slightly, and turns to hang her coat on a hook by the door.

Rachel sits on a high stool at the kitchen counter as he prepares the meal, drinking slowly the wine he has poured for her. He is an accomplished cook, it seems, although in a deliberate rather than an instinctive way; he stops frequently to check the recipe book open on the counter. She is touched by his efforts.

They eat at the small table in the middle of the long room; a salad first, of butternut squash and tomatoes and peppery leaves, and then tuna steak, which she has not had before and finds she likes enormously. There is an apple tart afterwards – 'Bought, I'm afraid, but they do a very good one' – and cream, and then coffee that is far stronger than she is used to.

Peter pushes back from the table.

'Was that enough for you?'

'Enough?!' She laughs at his face, his earnestness. 'I haven't eaten like that in years. It was fabulous.'

'Good.'

'Let me clear up.'

'Leave it. Come and sit.'

He brings the wine, and refills their glasses, and they sit on the blue couch which is low and deep and faces out towards that view, melted now into night, and the lights of the city. Peter pulls her towards him, and lays a hand on her hair.

'It's very nice to have you here. Thank you for coming.'

'Thank you for asking. That first time, I mean; the coffee. I'd been hoping you would.'

'I was sweating like a teenager. I bottled it twice before I managed it.'

'Really? I'd never have known.'

'Oh, believe it. This cool exterior is . . .' He draws a hand down himself with a flourish. 'A mere facade.'

'Did you think I'd say no?'

'I thought it was very likely you were just humouring the old guy by talking to me.'

'Oh, now.' She swats at his leg reprovingly, then leaves her hand there.

'I'm years older than you, by the way. Just in case you hadn't realised.'

She tries to suppress her smile. 'Yes, I'm aware.'

'Seriously, though.' He turns to look at her. 'It's a big gap.'

'It doesn't feel like a big gap.'

'No, it doesn't, does it?' But his face is serious still.

Rachel sits up a little. 'Are you – you've never been married, or anything?'

'No.' He frowns, gently; everything about his face is gentle, she realises, it is hard to imagine him looking harsh or steely.

'No, I've never been married. I was with someone for – a good while, I suppose. The best part of a decade. That ended about three years ago.'

'What happened?'

'Nothing dramatic. Just – fell out of love, I suppose.'

'Did you live together?'

'Yes.'

She looks around her.

'Here?'

'Yes.'

'Any children?'

'No.' His gaze is frank and open, and she feels herself redden.

'I'm sorry. All the questions. I just – you know everything about me already. Or a lot of it, anyway.'

'It's fine. You can ask anything you like.'

And so she does, and he answers every question patiently, and when she has run out of steam she leans into him again on the couch and they are both quiet for a bit. It is not just the imbalance, the fact that she was, for a short time, a newsworthy figure, her life laid bare for public consumption. There is also a need in her to vet him, to dissect his personality and his past for signs of strangeness, of disorder. It is an impossible task, and she knows this, but she is compelled to do it anyway.

And that night, and over the days and weeks that follow, he seems, improbably, to understand.

BEFORE

Five Months

Someone Else Entirely

Her face is a mask of concentration, the tiny pink tongue held firmly between pearl-like teeth. She places her card down carefully, looks at it once and then again, unable to believe the evidence of her own eyes. She looks up at her mother.

'I got a Snap.' Her voice is a whisper; a prayer.

Rachel nods earnestly, trying not to laugh. 'Go on, so. Say it.' She finds she is whispering too.

The tiny hand slaps down on the pile of cards. 'Snap!'

Rachel hears her phone ring in some other room. Tom, probably, having forgotten the shopping list and now wandering directionless in the aisles. She goes to find it, buzzing frantically on top of the microwave. It is not Tom's name on the screen, though; no name at all, but a string of unfamiliar digits.

'Hello?'

There is a pause of a few seconds, and then a voice; a man's voice, and not one she knows.

'Hello.' Another pause. 'Is that – would this be the wife of a Tom Callaghan, by any chance?'

Jesus. *Jesus*. He is dead, the car gone under the wheels of a lorry or through the railings on the flyover.

'Yes.' Even she cannot hear her own voice, and she tries again. 'Yes, this is she. This is Rachel.'

'Rachel. Yes. Thank you. My name is Fergal Barrett.' He identifies himself as the manager of the supermarket at the round-about, and her mind immediately races to other possibilities – not a car accident, but a collapse in the freezer aisle. A gunshot from would-be thieves, strung-out and trigger-happy. Absurdities.

'What is it? Is Tom all right?'

'He's had some sort of a – an episode, I don't know. I don't know.' He clears his throat, his discomfort thrumming audibly down the line. 'He's very distressed. I'll need someone to come down and get him immediately, I'm afraid. Otherwise I'm going to have to call the Guards.'

'No. No, don't do that, please. I'm on my way.' Shoes, keys, purse – nothing is where she has left it. 'I'll be ten minutes. Less. Please.'

Already she is picking up her daughter and flying out the front door.

~

Frantic, she is frantic now, and she has to tell herself to slow down, not to run her own car into the nearest tree, as that would help nobody. It is her own fault, she should never have let him go; he has been bad lately, terrible really, his mood, but it is only the local supermarket and she does it herself every bloody week and she just wanted him to do it for once. And she had made him a list and put the shopping bags into his hands before he went out the door, she had really made it as easy as possible for him. But still, she should have known.

He has not been able for this sort of thing, this stupid task of ordinary life, for a long time. And it is no life, really, walking on eggshells around the man she is supposed to love and be loved by, afraid that every little thing will bring down one of the black moods that descends on them all like a cloud. She has tried to protect the kids from it, as much as she can, and this too she resents, this extra work. Except that she is not allowed to resent any of it, because he is ill, and she is supposed to love him. She does love him. And then she is turning into the supermarket car park and she wants with every fibre of her being not to have to go through those doors.

~

It is only as she is unbuckling the straps of the car seat that she realises she has forgotten to put shoes on her daughter. No help for it now, and so she carries her, squirming on her hip, across the car park and in through the automatic doors. The place is quiet, with only a handful of shoppers moving ponderously through the fruit and veg section, which is heavy on the pumpkins at this time of year; overhead a row of Hallowe'en skeletons sway cheerfully in the draught from the air conditioning. Rachel stops for a moment, looking around for Tom, or for someone who is in charge. But nobody appears, and so she starts searching the aisles.

She sees them almost immediately, the little tableau of people all standing separately and unsure, a cast waiting for the house lights to fall. The manager, the one who rang her it must be, shifting his weight from foot to foot impatiently; beyond him a tall security guard tapping his walkie-talkie rhythmically against his leg. A woman with a basket who hovers at the end of the aisle, staring openly. And Tom. He is sitting in front of the breakfast cereals; sitting, on one of those rubber stools the staff stand on to pack the shelves. His face is in his hands, his fingertips buried deep in his hair. In front of him, in the trolley which contains otherwise only grapes and

187

a bunch of green bananas, sits their son, his dribbling babble unstanched by any drama.

It is to him that Rachel goes first, bending to look into his brown eyes, to check that he is unworried and unhurt. He is fine. She looks around, seeing no other options for her daughter's unshod feet, and lowers her carefully into the body of the trolley. Then she turns to her husband.

'Tom.' She squats in front of him, resting her hands on his knees. 'Tom, it's me.'

It is a moment before he lifts his head, and then the eyes that gaze into hers are dull and unfocused. She had intended to be stern with him, to punish him for the horror and humiliation of all this, but she finds that she cannot. She finds, instead, that her own eyes are filling with tears.

'Jesus, Tom. What is it, love? What's going on?'

He shakes his head at her, closes his eyes again as if he cannot bear the world.

'Did something happen? What—' She casts around, as if the answer will somehow reveal itself: an aggressive fellow shopper, a belligerent staff member. An essential item out of stock, perhaps.

The manager, the Fergal fellow who had spoken to her on the phone, steps forward now with another clearing of his throat. He looks as if he would rather be anywhere else.

'I believe another customer found him here.' He gestures to the woman at the end of the aisle with the basket. 'He seemed – upset.' It is clear that this word does not do justice to the reality of the situation, but he is not a man given to hyperbole.

'He was kneeling on the floor.' The woman says it in a whisper, as if Tom will not be able to hear her. She has come to stand just behind Rachel, who rises from her crouched position and turns around. Her legs are starting to ache. 'I was worried about the baby. I tried to speak to him, but I couldn't get anything out of him. He was just crying, on and on.'

It is true, Tom has taken to crying in the oddest of places. It is a testament to how bad things have become that it is not the fact of his crying that is strange to Rachel, but only where and when he chooses to do it.

'I'm so sorry. Thank you. Thank you for calling me.' She turns her head to include all of them in this – the woman, the manager, the silent security guard who stands poised and unperturbed. She can feel the manager's yearning for them all to leave, it is something almost tangible in the air. She turns to Tom again.

'Tom, love. We're going to go now, OK? We're going to walk out to the car and go home. We'll get all this sorted.' She tries to keep her voice calm and authoritative, although to her own ears she sounds like someone else entirely.

Tom's eyes are still blank, but he rises at least and stands there limply, his arms hanging useless by his side. Rachel looks at the two children in the trolley, at the lack of shopping that she will somehow have to remedy later. At some other supermarket, of course; she knows she will never come back here.

The woman nudges her gently.

'You go on with him. I'll follow you with the kids.' She places her own basket on the floor and pushes it towards the side with one sensibly shod foot. Then she takes the handle of the trolley and unleashes a beaming smile on the children.

'Now. Will we go for a ride in this yoke?' And she is off, making for the doors, and so it is Rachel who follows, one arm around Tom's waist and the other holding tentatively to his sleeve. She wonders with a sudden panic what she will do if he simply refuses to come with her, but he does not resist. The manager follows them at a distance.

At the main door the woman is waiting with the trolley for directions, and Rachel has to think for a moment where she has left her car. The setting sun is in her eyes. Eventually she orientates herself, and presses on towards the relative sanctuary it offers. Tom's car, of course, is somewhere here too, and will have to be rescued later; forget that for now. She opens the passenger door and pushes Tom inside, and pulls the seat belt securely around him. She is aware that her movements would be less gentle if she did not have an audience.

Her son's high-pitched giggle rises into the air. Rachel closes the door with something like a sigh and turns again to the woman, who is playing peekaboo, her curly-haired spectator rapt. His little feet kick back and forth in unsuppressed excitement. Her daughter is more watchful, aware perhaps that something is terribly wrong. But then, she is always the more serious of the two.

'I really – I can't thank you enough.' Rachel lifts her son from the seat of the trolley and holds him to her.

The woman shakes her head.

'I did nothing. But is he – will he be all right? Has he done this before?' Her voice contains more concern than curiosity, but there is curiosity there too, which is understandable.

Rachel does not know how to answer. No, not this specific thing, this very public and humiliating breakdown; no, he has not done this.

But yes, yes. Yes.

'We'll be all right.' She shrugs, defeated. 'I'm going to get him some help.'

The woman does not look quite satisfied with this, and Rachel does not blame her, but it is the best she can offer. She straps her son into his car seat, lifts her silent daughter into hers. The woman watches. Rachel wishes that she would leave now;

190

she has been so helpful but there is a line, and Rachel is barely holding on.

She straightens and tries to smile.

'Thank you again. We're going to go now. I need to get them home.' She waves towards the car.

'Of course. You go on. I hope – I hope everything goes well for you.'

Rachel finds she cannot speak, and presses her lips tightly together as she nods.

The woman starts to move away, then turns back again. 'I never got your name.'

'No.' And some bit of her does not want to give it, some bit of her wants to remain anonymous, as if this will make the whole thing deniable. But the politeness is bred deep.

'Rachel.' She holds out her hand, reaching around her son.

'Rachel. I'm Rita.' They shake hands briefly. 'Good luck to you, Rachel.'

And then she is gone.

~

She calls Tom's boss. She calls her mother. The next morning she calls the doctor's surgery, and then that afternoon there is a long call with the clerk from the psychiatric hospital, mostly involving detailed questions about their health insurance coverage. And then there are three interminable days, and then Tom is gone, and she finds that she can breathe again.

AFTER

Four Years

A Whisper Below the Surface

It feels, bizarrely, a bit like a blind date, and Rachel fidgets with
her hair as she waits. She has taken the corner table, her back
pressed against the upholstered cushion of the bench seat, so
that she can see everyone who comes in and out of the café.
The waitress brings her freshly squeezed orange juice, the pulp
floating lazily in some invisible current. It's busy in here, and
she thinks that maybe it would have been better to choose some
other time of day, mid-morning perhaps or the late-afternoon
lull; but, then, she had reasoned to herself that at least if conversation ran dry, the choosing and consumption of lunch might
provide some sort of scaffolding.

The other woman, when she arrives slightly late and flustered
from the rain, is taller than Rachel had imagined, and older too,
and her long dark hair carries a halo of frizz from the drizzle
outside. Rachel knows at once that it is her, and yet she hesitates,
thinking wildly of escape for a last long second before she half
rises from her seat and lifts her hand. The woman's face lights
with relief, or perhaps only recognition, and she weaves through
the chair backs and buggies and bags of shopping littering the
floor.

'Rachel?' Her voice is slightly deep.

'Yes. Hi.' Rachel stands properly this time, and they shake
hands, and sit down again with much adjusting of seats and

straightening of clothes. The woman – Julia Caffrey, her name is, and Rachel thinks for a moment of Mrs Caffrey at school, who taught music, and whose hands were huge and gnarled and could no longer stretch the octave on the tuneless piano in the assembly hall – takes a pair of glasses from her handbag and puts them on the table before pushing the bag under her seat. She has long, slim fingers herself, and Rachel wonders if she too plays the piano, if she used to pick out the familiar tunes of nursery rhymes while her children shouted out the words.

Julia Caffrey had been living an anonymous and, to all appearances, contented life until the fifteenth of July two years before, when her husband Graham, a prison officer at the high-security place in the Midlands, packed their twin daughters into the back of the family Citroën and drove to the pebbled shore of the lake, only two miles from their home. Rachel imagines the girls' delight about this unexpected late-evening jaunt, the way they would have kicked their matching three-year-old feet excitedly as they chattered in the back of the car. 'I always dressed them the same,' their mother said later in one of those long interviews on the Sunday-morning radio, a piece Rachel listened to over and over again. 'I would have had to stop at some point, I'm sure they would have started giving out to me about it as they got bigger. But I just loved dressing them, and doing their hair. All the little things.'

At the lake, Graham lifted a child in each arm – he was a big man, muscled, and this was as nothing to him – and strode into the water. A woman walking her dogs spotted them perhaps twenty minutes later, a large, irregular, floating mass, like refuse that had become snared and tangled together. When they were pulled out, the stony beach rough against their milk-white faces, each little girl had one of her father's large hands tangled in her hair.

All this Rachel knew, because the story had been huge, it was everywhere, and for a few days there had been a wearying hesitance again in people's eyes when they spoke to her, as if they feared the echoes in this new tragedy might dig up something she had now largely put to rest. She wanted to tell them how ludicrous this was, how laughable the very idea that her own memories were ever more than a whisper below the surface.

But she had been fascinated by Julia Caffrey and her daughters, and had read article after article about them, long into the night. And then had tried to put the story out of her mind, and it was nearly two years later when there was the radio interview, and on the station's website a picture of the mother again, the same woman but different too.

Now there is a period of studious silence as they both gaze at the menu, and then Rachel orders a sandwich and the other woman a salad, with the bacon please, and a coffee that she drinks black and unsweetened. Then they look at each other, and Rachel knows that this was a mistake, that she has nothing in common with this woman, really, bar their communal bad fortune – and surely this is grotesque, this ham-fisted attempt to forge some kind of bond? But they are here now, it is too late, and so she plunges in.

'Thank you for coming. I know it probably seems a bit . . . odd, all of this.' She waves her hand vaguely – the café, incongruously bright and cheerful; the hordes of shoppers.

Julia shakes her head. 'It's fine. It's a straight run in from Lucan.'

This isn't really what Rachel meant, but she takes the lifeline anyway.

'How are you finding it there? Must be a big change from – from where you were.'

194

'It is, I suppose. But I lived in Dublin as a student, I had digs in Drumcondra. I loved it there. Only moved back home when I got married, so.' She is a teacher, Rachel knows, at secondary level; science and maths. She wonders how it feels to be surrounded all day by other people's children, hale and vital and still growing. Still living.

In any case, this was how Rachel had tracked her down; the interview had mentioned the Dublin suburb she had moved to, and it had been then only the work of an hour or two – the silent, secret hours before dawn, on a sleepless night – to check the websites of the schools in the area, until she found her name. She had written to her care of the school, enclosing her own email address – a halting, formal letter, and dropped it into the post box already half regretting it and with very little hope of a reply. Peter, she could tell, had thought it a mistake, although he never said so.

There had been nothing for weeks, and Rachel had tried to put it out of her mind, embarrassed by her own display of need. And then late one night her phone buzzed with that low essential sound, and turning over sleepily in bed she looked at the notification and felt her stomach lurch. It was twenty minutes before she could bring herself to open the email. That initial response was brief, as awkward as her own, but it was not dismissive, as Rachel had feared it would be, and it seemed to invite an answer. Rachel had waited until the next day to respond, and after a few more slightly terse exchanges – neither of them, it seemed, was the confessional type – they had agreed to meet.

'I moved as well, two years ago. I'm in Stoneybatter now,' Rachel offers. 'It was too hard, staying in the house.'

'Oh, I would have burned ours to the ground, if I thought I'd get away with it.' Her tone is casual; amused, even. 'I nearly did it, too, one day; I think I went a bit mad for a while. I never slept another night in the house after it happened.'

Then she reaches down into her bag.

'I brought some pictures of the kids. If you want – you said you'd like to see them?' The words are offhand almost, but beneath them there is an ache, and Rachel finds herself liking the woman a little more.

'Yes, of course. I'd love to see them. Love to.' Although it feels too soon, really, in their relationship; this feels like something that should come later, once they have learned to trust each other – it is very precious, really, what she is holding across the table in the long laminated envelope. But Rachel senses the need in her, and so they look through the pictures together, a thin stack of actual printed photographs, and the children are of course beautiful. Rachel cannot tell them apart, the girls, from picture to picture, and she wonders at Julia's ability to know one from the other instantly. It was her biggest anxiety, about ever having twins – that at some stage she would mix them up, and fail to realise. Tom had laughed, once upon a time, at her gift for catastrophising about something that was never even on the cards.

When she has handed the stack back to Julia, who replaces them carefully in her handbag, Rachel feels she ought to reciprocate, and so she passes her phone to the other woman, and watches as she scrolls slowly through the album. Julia lingers for a long time on each shot, sometimes asking questions which are specific and, to Rachel's ear, flavoured with genuine curiosity – what was the name of the ragged bunny her son held in most of the pictures? Did her daughter like having her hair washed, or did she screech as Julia's little girls had done? It is an unexpected joy, Rachel finds, to talk about them like this, and she is almost disappointed when the food comes, and they put the pictures away.

While they eat they talk of other things. Julia tells her that she is thinking of moving again; that she had thought the city would be a welcome distraction, but she cannot get used to the traffic, the noise everywhere. Rachel is surprised to hear herself telling the other woman that she finds the masters course singularly uninspiring and is having doubts about even finishing it, something she has not yet admitted even to Peter.

'But you like your job? The nursing, I mean.'

'Ah yes, I do of course. I suppose I just wanted to push myself a bit more.' She shrugs. 'I don't know. I hate the thought of not finishing something I've started.'

They finish their food, and the table is cleared, and they look at each other. Rachel has a flash of panicked frustration; it has achieved nothing really, their meeting here, although if pressed she could not say what it was she had hoped to get out of it.

She makes one final effort.

'Do you want to walk for a bit, maybe? I think the rain's stopped.'

'Yeah, OK.' They gather up brollies and bags, and Rachel goes to the till to pay – she insists on this, the whole thing having been her idea, and the other woman does not demur – and then steps outside, to where a weak sun is playing on puddles and there is a steady drip of water from shop canopies and unswept gutters. Julia is waiting, pressed in against the window of the next-door shop to keep out of the way, her chin tucked apologetically to her chest. When Rachel touches her arm she lifts her head and smiles, and it is the first time she has smiled, Rachel realises, and her face is quite different then.

'Thanks for that.' She nods back towards the café.

'Not at all.' Rachel looks around. 'Will we go this way, maybe? It looks quieter.'

They walk in silence at first, and this is a relief. Once they reach the canal there are fewer people about, and the path, barely visible under the piles of fallen leaves, is wide enough to walk side by side.

Julia is the first to speak.

'They kept asking me, after it happened, if he was violent. And I'd say no, he wasn't, because he never hit me. But he'd do other things. He used to pin me up against the wall, his two hands either side of me, and talk right into my face. Terrible stuff, just insult after insult, all sorts of names, and I'd have to stand there and listen to it all. And one time, he locked me in the bathroom while I was in the shower. Which wouldn't have been too bad, but he turned off the heating and I only had the towel I'd used to dry myself. I didn't want to shout, it would have woken the girls. He left me in there all night.'

Her voice is very calm, musing almost, as if she is describing things that have happened to someone else. But her face, when she turns to look at Rachel, is pale.

'What about your Tom?'

It is a long time since anyone has called him that.

'No.' Rachel hears the hesitation in her own voice. 'He wasn't violent, or – or cruel, like that. He never did anything to me. He was just – just sad, and then strange, towards the end; he would get fixated on things, little things only but it was like they became huge in his mind. We got a second notice for the TV licence and it was like he'd been caught embezzling funds or something like that, he was tearing his hair out. And our little boy –' she has to concentrate here, and the view of the canal is obscured by a sudden mist – 'he was a bit slow to talk, it was nothing really, he was already starting to catch up, but Tom – Tom was convinced he had brain damage. That I must have eaten the wrong thing when I was pregnant, or something like that.'

198

'He blamed you for it?'

'No, not exactly – or, at least, I didn't think so at the time. He was just so worried about every little thing. It felt like I spent my life trying to soothe him, trying to talk him down. And then resenting him for needing all that from me.'

Julia stops to pick up a leaf, a particularly unblemished specimen of a deep, rich red. She turns it in her hands.

'Some people thought it was my fault. What Graham did. One of his friends said – he wasn't a nice man, Paddy Kennedy was his name, I'd never liked him anyway – but he said that I must have made things very difficult for Graham at home. To have driven a good man to do what he did.'

Rachel is sickened, yet not surprised. She already knows the world to be full of terrible people.

'I think some of his family felt the same, although they never said. His brother wouldn't look at me afterwards. At least his parents were already dead, they never had to know what he did. I was glad of that. I'd always liked his mother.'

She turns to look at Rachel; she has kind eyes.

'It must have been harder for you, that your husband didn't die. That you still had to deal with him, afterwards. I was spared that, at least.'

This is so blunt, and at the same time such an accurate description of a thought that Rachel has had many, many times, that she is momentarily stunned. To think of Tom, dead and gone. No hospitals, no lawyers, no need for that terrible day in court which, despite the kindness of everyone involved, still haunts her in those confused moments between sleep and wakefulness. No years of stonewalling correspondence with the bank. The blessed release of it.

'I've never said that to anyone,' she says when she can speak again. 'I felt too guilty. But it's like – because he's still alive,

I still have to have feelings about him. Opinions. People expect it. Most people expect me to hate him. And I do, because look, look what he did to me. What he took from me. But he was sick, and I still can't believe that the part of him that did that was the real Tom.'

'Are you still married to him?'

Rachel starts to shake her head, then stops, correcting herself. 'Well, yes, officially. It's been – complicated, to sort out. But no, we'll be divorced soon. Very soon.'

Julia nods. 'That's good. I mean, I'm sure it is? To feel you can move on from him.'

Rachel nods; her own feelings about this are so confused and ever-changing that she has not been able to articulate them, even to herself.

'I've been seeing someone new.' She blurts it out suddenly, and is immediately regretful. She has told very few people about Peter.

Julia smiles again, and this time it is an open, radiant beam.

'That's wonderful.' She gives Rachel's arm the briefest of pats. 'I'm glad for you.'

'It's early days.'

'Still.'

'Yeah. Yes. Thank you.' She bites back the reciprocal question on her lips, the automatic *And how about you?* It is none of her business.

Julia looks at the leaf in her hand, and runs her fingers over its veined surface.

'I'm going to keep this one.'

She places it carefully inside her big, shapeless handbag, and they walk on into the cooling day.

BEFORE

Four Months

The Long Way Around

It is not a prison. Rachel keeps reminding herself of that, because the fact is that it feels very much like a prison, or at least how she imagines a prison to be. All the doors – and there are many of them – are locked tight, each one requiring a buzzer to be pressed and a wait for swiftly moving feet before she is admitted, although then it is always with an understanding smile and words of quiet welcome. She is asked, with an apologetic explanation that yet invites no argument, to open her handbag at the desk, and the few things she is bringing to Tom – chocolate, puzzle books, magazines she knows he will never read – are carefully scrutinised before being passed. She is brought finally into a large and airy room, and invited to sit, and then the nurse – she presumes he is a nurse, although he wears no uniform – leaves, and she sits uneasy in the plastic-covered chair and looks around her. There is not much to see. A table in the corner with some board games on it, the boxes torn and splaying at the corners; a small bookshelf filled with paperbacks. On the walls, washed in that shiny yellow paint that is easy to clean, are photographic prints of tranquil scenes – a lake shore at sunset, a rainbow over mountains; at the bottom of each is an inspirational quote, laid out in a white-on-black typeface that looks curiously dated. The whole thing has a quasi-religious feel that reminds her of school corridors. She is not unused to hospitals, of course, but this one has a very different feel; she would not have thought it possible to miss the relentless bustle, the unhappy mixture of smells – bleach and illness and roast dinners served up before the Angelus bell has rung – to which her nose has become almost inured.

The door opens again and she turns, suddenly flustered, as Tom comes in. Her first thought is of relief; he looks the same, really, and then she admonishes herself for thinking otherwise, for it has only been a week. It has felt long, though, that week, as had the preceding one when Tom was still on the admissions unit; the normal household routine upset, the children fractious and unsettled for reasons they didn't understand. Rachel had been able to take only a few days *force majeure* leave from work, and in fact it was a relief to drop them off with the childminder, that first day back, and to drive in the new silence to the hospital. She had taken the long way around.

Now he smiles at her, her husband, and she feels the reflexive smile on her own face. He comes towards her, his face open and welcoming, and she is unsure, suddenly, whether she should hug him – whether it is OK to do this, in this place in which neither of them is in charge. Then she shakes herself mentally, and stands up, and reaches for him.

~

The first time she came to visit Tom, seven long days ago now, they had not hugged. Then she was directed to a different room, this one on the secure unit, where he had spent the first five days. She had come empty-handed that time, unsure what would be allowed, and sat prim and upright in the same sort of plastic chair, her hands desperate for something with which to fidget.

The Tom who was brought to her then was slow and childlike in pyjamas and soft chequered slippers, and on sight of him she had embarrassed herself by bursting into loud, inelegant sobs. Tom had remained unmoved, and it was only when she had recovered herself enough to push the hair back from her face and to fish a stained tissue from the depths of her pocket that he spoke.

'Don't be upset. I'm all right.' His voice slow, effortful.

'I'm sorry.' She wiped her nose viciously, already past the first rush of emotions, and angry at herself for allowing it. 'I just – I hate seeing you in here.'

He looked around vaguely. 'It's not that bad.'

'No, I know that.' She made an effort to inject something into her voice, some note of hope. 'They seem very nice.' She was aware of the proximity of the nurse, just outside the open doorway.

Tom nodded, uninterested. Then, 'I'm sorry about all of this.' He sounded tired.

Rachel looked at him. 'It's not your fault.' She was not sure if she believed this, not completely, although she knew it to be the truth.

She tried to focus on more prosaic things. 'Are you able to sleep all right in here? Are you eating?'

He shrugged. 'I'm sleeping OK. They have me on a lot of stuff, I think.'

'And what's the food like?' This was desperate, this attempt at small talk, but she was floundering.

The shrug again. 'It's all right. I don't have much of an appetite.'

'Well. It'll come back.'

And then she couldn't think of anything else to say, and so she just took his hand in hers, and they sat like that in silence until it was time to go.

~

Now there is new life in Tom's eyes, and perhaps even a trace of the old one. He pulls his chair close to hers, and slips his hand around her back as they talk. It feels like a long time since he has held her like this.

'How have you been?'

'Fine.' She finds herself smiling; a sensation she has to get used to again. 'Fine, Tom. I'm grand. How are you?'

'I feel better.' He has not said anything so declarative in years, she thinks.

'Do you? Do you really, now?' She hears herself, sounding like her mother. 'Be honest with me.'

He laughs. He is rubbing her back in a way that feels slightly frantic.

'Honestly. Not back to normal, maybe. Not yet. But I feel like I have some energy again, at least. I've stopped crying all the time.' He rolls his eyes, and this sort of self-deprecation is so unlike the person he has been for years that she finds herself laughing incredulously.

'That's great, isn't it?'

He nods, and he leans in and presses his forehead into hers. It hurts, a little, in a way that feels good. She closes her eyes, and they stay like that for a bit.

When he pulls back finally he looks around the room, his left foot tapping restlessly.

'I thought you might bring the kids.'

Rachel sits up again, abrupt.

'The kids?' She almost laughs again. She has never even considered bringing the children here. She cannot stomach the idea of exposing them to this place, as benign as it all seems, with its whispers of madness in unseen corners; and really she cannot stomach them seeing Tom here, that is the true reason. If she could, she would have them forget about their father entirely until he reemerges into their little lives the same man as before. She is not interested in anything in between.

She cannot, of course, say any of that.

'I think it's probably better if they wait until you're home, Tom.' She injects all the right things into her voice – softness, understanding, concern. 'It'd confuse them, coming in here.'

She tries not to see the disappointment on his face.

'What have you told them? Where do they think I am?'

'I just said – I said it was work, you know.' She waves her hand incoherently. They are so easy to trick, the pair of them, satisfied with the vaguest references to Daddy's job. It breaks her heart a bit.

'It won't be long, Tom.' She lays a hand on his arm; she tries to hearten her voice, to give him an assurance she does not strictly feel.

'I know. I know.' He nods once, twice, three times; but the light has drained out of him, just a little.

Rachel casts around for a new topic.

'I talked to Roger yesterday. He rang, wanted to see how you were.' Tom's boss in the City Council offices; a large, mild man whom Rachel liked instantly the first and only time they had met. He has been understanding beyond Rachel's imaginings, through all of this; as if, somewhere in the past, he too has held the hand of someone he loved, while they broke and were made whole again.

Tom raises his eyebrows. 'Will I still have a job to go back to?'

'Of course you will.' Her voice is scolding; God, this wretched mother-and-child dynamic, it seems impossible to avoid slipping into it. 'He was very keen to stress that, that you're to take as much time as you need, before going back. He doesn't want to lose you.'

'He's a good guy, Roger. I'll give him a ring myself, in a few days.'

'Has your mam been in?'

'Yesterday. Doing her usual bit, trying to work out what everyone is in here for.' Now Rachel's laugh is real. She can imagine it perfectly, Bernie peering curiously at everyone she sees, and asking pertinent questions in a stage whisper. She is almost childlike sometimes, Bernie.

'She was very upset, when you first came in.' She has not really meant to tell him this, although God knows it can hardly be news.

Tom looks pained. 'Yeah, I know. I know. God, I'm sorry about everything.'

Rachel thinks suddenly of Bernie's revelation, more than two years ago now, of Tom's undisclosed hospital stay as a teenager. She has never mentioned it to her husband. It seems ludicrous now, to consider this still a secret between them – presumably Tom's doctors know all about it, presumably he or somebody else has told them? She almost starts to open her mouth, to ask Tom about it, but something stops her; it feels like a disloyalty to Bernie, who in turn had been disloyal to Tom.

'But listen.' Brisk again. 'It was the right decision, and you look so much better, Tom. Really, so much better.'

He does smile then, with half his mouth. 'You're not fed up with me, so? I wouldn't blame you.'

On an impulse she presses her lips to his, suddenly bold. 'Not even close.'

She does not stay much longer. He walks her to the door of the ward, in his tracksuit bottoms and socked feet, and they hug again, and he kisses the side of her head, the secret place just above her ear. She tells him that she will see him soon; that she loves him; that it will not be long now. Then he calls to the nurse at the desk, who looks up and nods in recognition and leans in to press some hidden switch, and the door unlocks with a soft click. As it whispers shut behind her again she turns on impulse and presses her hand to the glass pane high in the door. She has to stand on tiptoe to reach it, but Tom is there already, his head filling the frame, blocking out the light.

AFTER

Five Years

Merely an Island

On the morning after the third day that Peter has come home to find Rachel still in bed, the room dim and smelling faintly sour, he phones the departmental secretary and tells her he'll be working from home. Rachel hears his voice from the living room, that calm, easy tone that belies nothing; a mild tummy upset, the postgrad student who will cover his lecture. It is twenty minutes more before he knocks on the bedroom door and comes carefully in, her coffee mug in hand.

'Here.' He sets it down on the bedside table, and sits on the edge of the mattress, which sags gently beneath him. Rachel stares at the weave of his trousers, which she can see from this close vantage is not the uniform grey it appears to be, but a matrix of black and white threads. She pushes the hair from her face.

'You're not going in today?'

'No. I thought I might stick around.' His voice is mild. 'You don't seem very well.'

'Hah.' It is a sharp exhalation of breath only, there is no voice behind it, but it sounds even to her own ears cruel and scathing. She pushes herself up on one elbow and takes a sip of the coffee, as if in atonement. Peter's face is unmoved.

'Won't you talk to me, love? I want to help you.'

Even the effort of the half-sitting position is too much, and she lies down again. She wishes he would leave; it is too much, to have to make even this pathetic attempt at conversation with him. It is all too much.

$$\sim$$

He lives here now, Peter; lives here officially, after months of living here unofficially, his clothes and books and piles of academic notes making only occasional forays back across town to be recycled or replaced. But now the big airy flat is rented out, and Peter's clothes fill the wardrobe in the spare room, and Peter's bike has taken up permanent residence in the tiny courtyard. She had not wanted to live in his flat herself, as nice as it was; she has become attached to this poky little house, to its terrible water pressure and uneven floors. She had worried about breaking this news to Peter, who after all had had the flat for far longer than she had been in the house. But then he had suggested it himself, this move, telling her that it made more sense for work, really, and he liked the proximity to the Phoenix Park. And so here they were, tripping over each other sometimes on the tiny landing and in the narrow kitchen, but both seemingly content.

The master's degree is over; they have both finished the course and done well, never comparing exact marks, although Rachel suspects that Peter has outshone most of the class. Now their theses stand side by side in their identical bindings on the bookshelf in the second bedroom, destined never to be opened again. Rachel has attained her promotion, and has found it far more challenging than she expected, but is enjoying it nonetheless. Was enjoying it, or at least she thinks so; it is hard to remember, now, the feeling of going into work each day with a sense of purpose.

She cannot explain what has happened; there has been no event, no trigger for this heaviness that has swept over her. Its coming has been long and slow, a wave seen at first from a distance as something far away and unthreatening. And then its slow, inexorable approach, gradually getting bigger and bigger until she realised with fright that it was going to overwhelm her, and there was nowhere to run. Sometimes she is struck with an image of herself as seen from afar, a tiny figure on a speck of land that has turned out not to be a continental mass but merely an island, barely protruding above sea level. Now she is under the water, and she cannot breathe.

Peter rests a hand on the pillow, as if sensing that she does not want to be touched.

'Are you sick, do you think? Do you feel unwell?'

She shakes her head. 'It's not that. I'm not – I'm fine.'

Peter does not bother refuting this blatant untruth.

'Rachel. Love. I want to help you. I need you to talk to me.'

And so she tries to tell him about the wave, but before she gets past the first *I feel* she is overtaken by something that bubbles up out of her, a hot steaming rush of noise and breath and fear, and then she is crying and he takes her finally in his arms.

~

Days pass like this, each one only a little better or worse than the one before. She forces herself to get dressed, to wash herself and make some attempt at meals, and most of the time she succeeds. Peter phones work for her, and is on the phone for a long time, and when he comes back to her he says that they seem pretty supportive, although in time they will need doctor's notes and certificates and other things. She cannot think about any of that now. Most of the time she sits, on her bed or on the narrow couch in the living room; sometimes she puts the TV on, the background hum a comfort, although she finds it impossible to follow a storyline. Nor is she able to lose herself in a book, a loss which seems devastating at times, and at other times irrelevant. She does not feel sad, exactly; she does not feel at all.

~

She had not seen it coming, that is true; and yet there was one day, two or three months earlier, it was the Easter weekend and they had all gone for a picnic in the grounds of Malahide Castle, her parents and Rebecca and her gang. The day was bright but breezy and her mother brought a thermos of tea and Peter walked over to the café for coffees, and they sat in fleeces and turned their faces up to the brave sun. As her mother was doling out bacon sandwiches and slices of quiche, Rachel looked towards the other side of the park and saw two children there, a small tousle-headed boy and a girl a little older, and for just a moment she was so sure that they were her children that she almost lifted her arm in a cheery wave. Then she blinked and they were strangers again, and she was embarrassed, but she did not think that anyone had noticed, although once or twice later in the day she caught her mother gazing at her with a concerned frown.

But that – really, that was nothing at all.

~

And then there was the time only last month when she and Peter had been talking about the house – they were always talking about the house, and what could be done with it, where the limits of its possibilities must be drawn. And they were half-jokingly wondering whether it might be best to cut their losses and just turn the second bedroom into a giant wardrobe, and Peter had said almost casually that they might need it one day for a bedroom again, and she had felt it like a physical blow, a sudden devastating punch to her gut. Because it couldn't be casual, could it? No one could ask that of her without realising what it would mean. And since then she has had flashes of rage, molten and dangerous, about the most innocuous of things – Peter's shoes placed haphazardly against the wall, a smear of toothpaste in the bathroom sink. Even being in bed with him, a place that was once a refuge and a balm, has become something she tries to avoid, and twice now in recent weeks she has had to disguise a sudden wave of irritation as passion, and clutch him closer to her in a show of ardour that rings false even to her own ears.

But none of that could mean much. Surely. Surely not.

~

One morning she finds herself standing barefoot in the courtyard garden, the uneven paving slabs damp beneath her feet. It is early enough that it is not yet fully light, despite the time of year, and there are no sounds beyond an occasional bird, shrill and clear in the stillness. Her legs are stiff, as if she has been standing there a long time, and she has no memory of waking up or coming outside; and the thought of this, the thought that she may have been standing here alone for minutes or hours frightens her so much that she starts to cry – to wail, in truth, until Peter comes running, wiping the sleep from his startled mouth. When he takes her in his arms she cannot explain what has happened, or why it has terrified her so.

~

212

The thought hits her one sleepless night, that she could end up in the same place as Tom. This she knows to be impossible, and yet she has to press her face into the pillow to stifle a sudden, horrified scream.

~

Rebecca comes. Rachel hears her voice downstairs one morning, a warm early-summer's day. She has been awake for a while at this stage, since before Peter heaved himself out of bed and went down to the bathroom to run water and mutter incoherently at the radio. When he came up the stairs again she kept her eyes closed, but could sense him pausing at times as he dressed in the silence, waiting to see if she would stir. At last she heard him go back down the stairs, boil the kettle, open and close the fridge. When the doorbell rings, she can tell from his tread in the living room that he has been expecting it.

'Thank you for this.' His voice low, and worried, and kind.

She cannot make out what her sister replies, but Peter laughs once in response, and then she hears him take his bag from the hook at the bottom of the stairs and close the door softly behind him. There is silence for a few minutes, and then Rebecca's light footsteps are on the stairs. She comes in without knocking. She does not say anything, but sits on the end of the bed until eventually Rachel turns from the window and meets her eyes.

'The big guns.'

Rebecca smiles. 'There you go, you haven't lost it.'

'Fuck off.' She turns back to the window which shows, with a disloyal lack of pathetic fallacy, a flawless patch of blue sky.

'Move over.' Rebecca pulls herself up the bed and sits up against the headboard, dropping her yellow ballet shoes one by one to the floor. She gives a sigh of apparent contentment.

'This is a great bed. You've a much better mattress than ours.'

'Well, Peter's old. If you skimp on the mattress at this stage of life, you're done for.' It is a little forced, but Rebecca has come all this way.

They are quiet for a few moments. Somewhere on the street, a child lets out a sharp, aggrieved cry.

Rebecca speaks finally. 'So. What's going on?'

'I don't know.'

'Peter says you seem very down. You haven't been getting up much, or going to work.'

Rachel pulls herself a little up the bed.

'It feels like – like getting up, or seeing anyone, would just take so much more energy than I have. Like, the thoughts of having to go to Mam and Dad's for dinner, and make normal conversation for an hour – I couldn't physically do it. I would fall down.'

'Mam's worried. Obviously.'

'I know. I'm sorry. She calls me, I just – I can't talk to her.'

'It's all right. She knows I'm coming here today, I'll keep her at bay.'

Rachel reaches for her hand, which is cold and slightly clammy as it always is, and squeezes it. They are quiet for a minute before Rebecca speaks again.

'Are you just sad?'

'I don't know. I've been sad for so long. I don't know what it feels like not to be.'

She remembers suddenly the teenage Rebecca's rages, about food or exercise or something less concrete, less explicable, and how she would thrash around her bedroom like something possessed. None of them could go near her when she was like that, but later, when the screams had been replaced by a silence that was both a terror and a relief, when their father had brought

214

their broken mother down to the kitchen and shut them inside, Rachel would push open the door and sit beside her sister on the floor and touch her, very lightly, on some place that wasn't too intimate – a shoulder, a foot, the back of her wrist. And gradually the long silent jags of crying would diminish, and sometimes Rebecca would even fall asleep there, on the worn blue carpet with its patina of mascara stains.

Now Rebecca presses her thumb deep into the space between Rachel's thumb and her index finger. It hurts, in a way that feels real and anchoring.

'I don't want to be asking you what's wrong, as if you don't have good reason to be depressed.'

'It's OK.'

'But why now? Has something happened?'

'No. Nothing's happened.' Rachel shakes her head slowly, bemused. 'Everything is – everything's better than it has been in ages.'

'Is it Peter?'

She shakes her head again.

'No. Not in that way. Peter's great, he's very good to me.'

She takes a heavy breath, reaching for the words.

'I just. I don't think this is the life I was supposed to have.'

Rebecca lies beside her, and strokes her hair while she cries for a long time.

It is not the explanation, but it is as close to it as she can get. The feeling that nothing is right. This house, which is not the home she had been promised she would grow old in. The wrong man in her bed. Her job, which she loves, but resents too, because part of her will always wonder whether, if her teenage years had not been so consumed with her sister's pursuit of thinness, she might have had more options when she stared down the barrel of her university application forms. She will never tell

Rebecca this – she loves her too much for that – but she will hold it forever, close to her heart, ready to be taken out and stoked back into life any time they have a falling out.

And everything else that has been stolen from her: birthday presents and Christmas mornings and the tooth fairy. Breakfast cereal and ballet lessons, tears over homework, going upstairs on the bus. Tonsillitis and pocket money, parent–teacher meetings, night terrors, conversations about bad touches and period pants. The feel of a child's hand in hers. Cinema trips and swearing and broken hearts, entrance tests and vomiting bugs, unsavoury friends, football practice, *you're not going out like that*. Disney films and dirty jokes and mobile phones and missed curfews and summer camps and teenage acne and *just one more bite, go on*.

She has found – to her great surprise, at times – that it is still possible to build a life without all of this richness. But so often, even when she tries, she just cannot see the point.

~

Rachel hasn't been to a GP in years, preferring the anonymity of the women's health place when she has needed a smear test, or to have her contraception changed. She is still registered with the old practice, she supposes, but she knows that her own doctor there has since retired, and in any case she does not want to sit again in the waiting room with its familiar wooden toys, the immunisation posters on the wall. There is a surgery on the main street near the house, she could walk there in minutes, but this too seems too intimate, too much of a risk of bumping into somebody she knows, and now she wonders if these are all just excuses, and whether she has any real intention of going at all. Finally Peter suggests a new, purpose-built practice in Drumcondra, and after three days of looking at the phone she makes the call. The receptionist sounds reluctant but eventually agrees that they can take her on, and after giving her details and promising twice that she will call and cancel if she is not going to keep her appointment, she puts the phone down. She is exhausted.

It has been a long time since she has had to tell her story to someone new, to tell it from the start, and on the way in the car – Peter drives her, she has not driven anywhere herself now in weeks – she finds herself rehearsing how she will tell it, putting a series of simple, unemotional sentences in order. She feels as if she is going to a job interview. She has showered, and dressed with unaccustomed care, although drying her hair proved a task too far, and she has pulled it back wet into a low knot. Peter pulls up at the entrance to the practice.

'Do you want me to come in with you?'

She looks at him; his dear, kind face.

'No. Thank you, but no. I'll be all right.'

He leans in as if to kiss her, but instead she presses a hand to his cheek and turns to get out of the car.

Inside, the place is all chrome handles and vinyl floors, a TV high up in the corner playing an afternoon chat show. She gives her name, and the receptionist – who seems much friendlier in person, although maybe it is a different woman altogether – gives her a form to fill and directs her to a chair in the waiting room. The questions on the sheet seem harder than they should be, and she does not feel she has got them all right, but after she has spent what she thinks is long enough poring over it, she hands it back to the girl at the desk, and sits again. People on either side of her are called – it is a big place, there seem to be several doctors working at once – and she sits on, not impatient. She tries to slow her breathing – in for seven, out for ten.

The doctor who finally calls her name looks very young. Rachel has no reverence for doctors, she has seen too many of them stumble straight out of college and onto her ward, ill-prepared and blinking in the light. Still, most of them do all right in the end, and the ones who don't tend not to be the ones suffering from a lack of confidence, but the ones with rather too much of it. This girl – it is impossible to think of her as anything else, she cannot be thirty yet – does not seem like one of those. She brings Rachel into a small room, hot in the bright sunlight that pours in the window, and offers her a chair.

'Now. What can I do for you, Rachel?'

The words that come out of Rachel's mouth are not what she had planned to say, and, once out and irretrievable, she cannot believe she has said them.

'Do you know who I am?'

~

She is kind; she is so kind really, this doctor, and with more of a grasp of the world than her dewy skin and wide, fawn-like eyes would suggest. Once she understands – she had not, in fact, known who Rachel was, but once Rachel starts to explain she remembers the story, and while her eyes do not quite fill with tears, there is such compassion in her face that Rachel ends up telling her far more than the bald summary of her past she had planned. She is kind, and calm, and she manages to avoid looking at the clock on her computer screen more than once or twice, although at one point, as they are close to wrapping up, the phone on her desk rings and Rachel knows from the few words of conversation that it is the receptionist offering her an escape from what is surely a torturous consultation. She herself has had occasion to make one or two of these calls

218

over the years. The doctor, though, does not rush her, and nor, when they get on to speaking about medication, does she proffer it like a magic bullet. She tells Rachel that she thinks it will help, that she may feel unwell for the first week or two she takes it, that she will need to stay on it for a minimum of six months to avoid relapse, and probably longer. She gives her also the names of two private counsellors, both of whom she says are expensive, and very good.

'Will you come back and see me, in a month?' They are standing now, Rachel's hand already reaching for the door.

'Yes, if you want me to.' She realises that this young woman is worried about her, about her safety, and she is touched, and slightly embarrassed. It feels like weakness, this position, however much she tells herself it is not.

Peter is in the car, his seat pushed back and his eyes closed. She watches him for a moment, and then taps on the window. He is instantly awake.

'Well. How did you get on?'

She buckles her seat belt.

'OK, I think.' She holds up the prescription and he takes it from her, and looks at her steadily. He is the only person whose sympathy she does not find excruciating.

'Will we go and get this now, so?'

Rachel nods, and turns back to look out the window.

The traffic is heavy now, and it takes them a while to make their way back to Stoneybatter, and to find a spot to pull in near the old-fashioned pharmacy with its glass cabinets and its deep mahogany counter. She makes Peter go in with the prescription; she does not want to feel the eyes of the staff on her. While he is inside she sits still in the car and tries to work out whether she feels any different; the lifting of a weight. She cannot tell.

Back at home she takes the small packet of white pills out of the bag, and places one on the little coffee table. Peter brings her a glass of water from the kitchen, and sits beside her on the couch. It feels stupidly ceremonial, this moment, and more to bring it to an end than because of any real confidence in the outcome, she pushes the tablet to the back of her mouth and flushes it down. She leans against Peter, his warm, comforting bulk.

'I don't feel any better.'

He sighs heavily, but she can hear the smile in his voice.

'Let's just give it a minute, will we?'

She closes her eyes, and burrows farther into the shadow of his arm.

BEFORE

Two Weeks

Tidying Up

There's Tom's car in the driveway, bang on time as always now. Rachel knows the new job does not excite him in the way that having his own enterprise did, but as far as she is concerned there is something to be said for having him home at a reasonable hour, for being able to share the tedium of the dinner clean-up and the wrangling of the children towards bed. She stands now at the window of the living room, watching as he switches the engine off and sits motionless behind the wheel. She feels a sudden rush of impatience, which she tries to still. He is entitled to these few moments.

When there is no sign of him after five minutes, however, she goes to the foot of the stairs and raises her voice, bright and excited.

'Daddy's home.'

It is a betrayal, really, but only a small one. They are on their feet immediately, the pair of them, thundering down the stairs towards the front door which she opens wide, and then they stand jumping on the threshold, and Tom has no choice but to come inside.

Rachel kisses his cheek; she is not cross, not really. 'How was your day?'

Tom shrugs, his smile tired, and she does not ask any more. She leaves him to the children while she puts on the rice, checks the chicken in the oven, chops the head of broccoli into smaller pieces. From the living room she hears the babble of high-pitched voices, each fighting for primacy; hears her daughter trying to tell Tom a joke she has heard at playschool, and Rachel can tell that Tom is not paying attention, and has to quell the urge to swoop in from the kitchen and interfere. *Resist, resist.* But when they are all sitting down at the table together it is all right, there is chat and even laughter, the children giddy for some inscrutable reason, and Tom tolerant of their nonsense in a way that he is not always, not every day. Their son is, for some reason, wearing a Hallowe'en mask pushed up on his forehead.

Rachel puts his plate in front of him and sits down herself. 'Who are you today?'

He looks at her suspiciously. 'Spiderman.'

'Ah, I see.'

He gives a sudden hiss and flings out his left hand, an invisible web shooting from his tiny wrist. Rachel recoils in feigned shock, and he grins with delight.

His sister, at four, has already mastered a world-weary expression. 'Can I have some ketchup?'

'Yes, of course.' Rachel goes to the fridge to get it, and squeezes a satisfying mound of it onto her daughter's plate. The bottle makes a loud and flatulent sound as she releases it, and the children laugh in uncontrolled delight. As soon as Rachel has picked up her fork again her son asks for another cup of water, and Rachel resists the urge to argue with him, to challenge with 'Why didn't you ask for it before I sat down?' Because he is not yet three, and there is no point.

The chicken is slightly dry – Rachel has inherited her mother's fear of undercooking it, and it always ends up going the other way – but she is hungry, and once she has finished her own she picks the leftovers from the children's plates. It is dark outside – it is only the end of February, the clocks will not go forward for another month yet – and in the black abyss of the kitchen window she can see the reflection of the pendant light swaying gently, her children's faces caught in its protective glow.

~

After dinner Tom starts to load the dishwasher without prompting, and the children loll sated and sleepy in front of the television. Rachel goes upstairs and starts sorting the clean laundry, a job she always enjoys; it is a legitimate excuse to escape from the children, and there is something soothing in the folding of tiny T-shirts, in reuniting lonely socks. She dumps everything out on the big double bed and separates it into piles before she begins – Tom, herself, their daughter, their son. The children's clothes are already largely segregated by colour and design, however much she has tried to avoid this; the world will not let little girls escape long from the clutches of purple unicorns and sequinned slogans exhorting them to 'Smile!' Although her son's current favourite pyjamas are a bright yellow set with pictures of kittens, retrieved from his sister's cast-offs, so maybe all is not lost. Her own clothes strike her suddenly as tired, faded; some of them, she thinks, she has had since before she was married, and she tries to work out when she last shopped for anything for herself beyond plain cotton T-shirts that would wash well.

Rachel hears the slow trudge of a child's tired footsteps coming up the stairs, and knows that it is her daughter, her unique tread as different from her brother's as a fingerprint. She will not use the downstairs bathroom after dark, as she cannot reach the light switch there, and she would rather come upstairs than ask someone else for help. Rachel hears her carefully lower the toilet seat and sit down. She sings to herself, some tune from

223

playschool unfamiliar to Rachel's ears. Rachel had found it strange, unsettling even, the first time her daughter had come home with knowledge that she had gleaned somewhere other than at her mother's feet, with evidence of a life outside the family circle. It had felt – stupidly, she recognises, but still, let her be stupid – like the end of something.

Now Rachel calls out. 'Do you need any help?'

There is no answer for a moment, and Rachel thinks she has not heard. Then her voice comes in reply, high and fluting.

'No, thanks.'

The singing resumes, and Rachel goes back to sorting the clothes. The piles grow larger – him, her, her, him.

Tom, Rachel, their daughter, their son.

~

Later, the children asleep, she brings her book to the living room, resisting the urge to turn on the TV for the comfort of its background noise. Tom is at the computer, engrossed in something – a map, it looks like, one of those satellite ones people use to spy on their neighbours' extensions and whether they've got the right planning permission.

He has always liked maps, Tom, of course, and scientific documents of all sorts – nautical charts, the periodic table, diagrams of the internal combustion engine. So many passions, her husband used to have; still has, she presumes, although they have been buried somewhere under the layers of everything else that their lives have become. Rachel used to marvel at his ability to get genuinely excited about so many and disparate things, even as she dreaded at times the long, tangential disquisitions on railway gauges or the decoy operations of the Second World War. She is happy, she finds to her own surprise, to see the map.

'All quiet up there, anyway.' She lays a hand on his shoulder. He turns, startled; he has not heard her come in.

'What are you up to?' She smiles, to remove any accusation from her voice.

'Oh, nothing.' He switches to another tab; his email inbox, which Rachel sees with some surprise is almost empty. Usually it is full of unread messages, a mass of unsolved crises or potential missed opportunities which sets her teeth on edge. But today there are a handful of emails, six at most, and all are opened and read. Tom, tidying up; wonders will never cease.

He looks up at her. 'Sorry, did you need me to do something?'

'Not at all, they're both asleep. I'm going to read.' She takes a blanket from the basket by the fireplace – it is a cold night, despite the red glow of the stove – and collapses heavily onto the couch. 'Make me go to bed at a reasonable hour, will you? I'm wrecked.'

Tom frowns. 'Sorry. You were up early again.'

'It's all right. I'm used to it.' She shrugs; she feels chronically unrested, and yet on the rare morning when Tom does wake without prodding and brings the children downstairs so she can lie on, she finds it difficult to fall back to sleep.

She puts her feet up on the couch and opens her book, which is about a woman travelling alone in Africa. She loves the heat that comes through it into this gloomy evening, the way she can feel the glare of the noonday sun reflecting from its pages. It has been a long time since she has felt that sort of heat herself; not since that Italian honeymoon, evenings full of red wine and the scent of gardenia. Maybe they will have a holiday abroad this year; not Africa, obviously, or even Italy – it would mean a flight, and with two small children the baggage limits fill her with terror – but somewhere close and attainable. A campsite in France, maybe. They can't really afford it, but maybe it would be worth the stretch, to be transported somewhere dry and sunny where the food is good and plentiful. The children have never been abroad, and it is about time. Tom has always loved the heat; he seems to come alive in weather that would have most reasonable people languishing on their beds in the middle of the day. Maybe they can teach their daughter to swim. Rachel decides she will do some research first, before she talks to him about it; it is always much harder to say no to a definite plan.

From upstairs comes a wail, and Rachel swears silently at the ceiling, even as she moves to hoist herself off the couch. But Tom is on his feet already.

'I'll go. You stay there.'

She is already opening the book again. 'You're a saint.'

'I'm not, you know.' He says it almost seriously, and she is for a moment taken aback, but then he smiles, and it is the old smile, the one that made her love him.

He disappears up the stairs, already calling out the soothing words that will settle their fretful son. Rachel decides she will have a glass of wine. It has been a while; recently she has not felt like it, but tonight it seems like the thing. As she passes the computer she glances at the map, which is open again; she sees now that it is of the area around Tom's parents' home in Wicklow. Maybe he is going to propose they move the family down there, build a glass monstrosity of a house on some plot of land with terrible drainage but a great view, a stone's throw from her mother-in-law. *Over my dead body*. Still, it is something to see him getting interested in things again.

She can feel him coming back to her, against the tide.

AFTER

Seven Years

However Slightly

'Bernie? It's me. It's Rachel.'

'Rachel.'

Her voice is the same, and yet not; older, frailer, with a quaver to it that was not there before. Although maybe the quaver is just because of who is calling; this ghost from the past.

'I'm sorry. If it's a bit of a shock, I mean. Calling out of the blue.'

'No, no. I'd been thinking about you, love. Wondering if you would ring.' It is a cold day, but Rachel can hear from the particular echo of her voice that Bernie has come outside to take the call. She pictures her standing in her garden, among her winter flowers.

'I heard about Tom. That he's out, I mean. That he's home.'

'Yes. Yes. He's here with us, now.'

'That must be . . . God, Bernie. God.'

~

Rachel had seen her once, more than a year ago now. The shops had not long reopened after lockdown, and it was a novelty to be wandering around town again, a freedom that still felt slightly uneasy. She herself had been coming out of Hodges Figgis, weighed down with two paper bags of books, Peter's birthday haul. The sky was light still, although it was early evening, and she turned left, towards the college, and the multi-storey where she had left her car, and home. And there was Bernie crossing the bottom of Dawson Street, her mask dangling below her chin, her steps slow and slightly hesitant. Rachel stopped. She could have called out; she was near enough, she could have run after her and laid a hand on her arm and halted her already halting progress. But she could picture it too well – Bernie's initial confusion, fright even, as she navigated the infinite void between the face in front of her and her memories. And then – what? No easy conversation, Rachel knew; that was unthinkable, even now.

And so she had stood there, her arms aching and her hair starting to mist around her face in the light summer rain, and watched until Bernie's stooped figure had disappeared down Nassau Street. She felt like a coward.

~

Now, Bernie clears her throat.

'And how are you, love? I think about you a lot.'

'I'm fine, Bernie. I'm well.' This is the truth, she thinks, or most of the truth.

'I heard you're getting married.'

Rachel squeezes her eyes closed tight.

'Yes. Yes. Next month.'

'A Christmas wedding. That'll be lovely.' Her voice is warm. 'I was delighted for you, when I heard.'

'It'll be a small do, you know. Just family, really.' Hearing the note of defensiveness in her own voice, but Bernie seems not to notice.

'Of course. I'll be thinking about you, on the day.'

~

It is to be in City Hall, the wedding, the building turning out not to be the grey Orwellian wasteland of Rachel's imagination, but instead a sumptuous, ornamented temple, its ceilings high and filigreed. Rachel had actually gasped aloud when they walked into it together, covering her mouth immediately as the sound reverberated through the cavernous space. It is perfect; they could walk there from home, if they wanted to. Rachel will wear her hair in a low knot, and carry a sheaf of long-stemmed Vanda orchids; Helen's daughter Iris, who at barely five maintains an air of calm self-possession that Rachel secretly envies, will carry a basket of rose petals down the short aisle.

Rachel's mother keeps asking her what the wedding will be like, with a bemused, sceptical air; to her mind it cannot be a real wedding, Rachel knows, missing the essential elements of the priest and the church, and burdened furthermore with the inescapable fact of a previous husband. But, regardless, Margaret's love for her future son-in-law remains as steadfast as ever. Though perhaps she would have loved anyone, really, willing to take on The Problem of Rachel.

On Peter's side there will be no new parents-in-law to navigate, anyway, both of his having died early; tragically early, really, of heart disease that was sudden and unexpected and catastrophic. So there is that legacy coming down the line for Peter, although Rachel refuses to think of that now. Instead she thinks of the silk sheath dress, its grey so light as to be almost white, that hangs expectantly in the wardrobe in the second bedroom of the house in Stoneybatter. The house she and Peter share, although they are still not sure if it will be their home forever. It is starting to feel, however slightly, small.

~

There is something else Rachel needs to say.

'I had meant to get in touch with you before now, Bernie, I feel bad. You sent a card to my mother. When Daddy died.'

'Oh. Yes. Yes, I did.' Bernie's voice is slightly fearful. 'I hope she didn't mind. Or that you – that you weren't offended, love.'

'No. God, no, not at all. I was so grateful, Bernie, that you would think of him. I should have got in touch, to thank you. It's just – it's been a tough time.'

'Of course. I was very fond of your dad, Rachel. He was always such a gentleman. You'll miss him now, when you get married.' And Rachel nods into the phone, unable to speak.

~

Yes, it is her mother who will walk her down the aisle, resplendent in pale pink satin and a new hat. Her father's health had been failing for a year or two, in a gradual, almost imperceptible way – imperceptible at the time, anyway, although looking back now Rachel finds she can track the stepwise changes in him. The invisible space billowing beneath the same thinning shirts he had had for decades; the way he would have to pause for breath halfway up the stairs. The slowness of speech that was partly his hearing and partly something else, some delay in the synapses that connected the things he wanted to say with his ability to form the words. But really there was nothing, nothing concrete, until the early summer day in the house, the last time they had all been together.

They were celebrating. Rebecca had graduated from her degree course – she is a teacher now, Rachel's flighty, troubled sister – and after the ceremony they had all driven back in convoy to their parents' house, where their mother had the usual excessive spread she always brought out on these occasions. Rachel felt she had been eating this same meal for decades – the chicken pieces, marinated overnight in giant dishes of sticky black sauce that would get on everyone's clothes; the rice salad, the trays of garlic bread. Rachel and Rebecca were children again, rolling eyes silently behind their mother's back as she fussed over the folding of napkins, and whether the beers for the men had been sufficiently chilled. Rebecca's boys, lumbering giants now of twelve, barrelled around the kitchen getting in everyone's way until they were able to escape into the garden, where with the addition of a football they were transformed somehow into balletic creatures, nimble of foot and hand. Peter and Doug, who seemed to like each other well enough despite a total dearth of common ground between them, clinked bottles awkwardly and stood watching the kids in a silence that was, Rachel hoped, a comfortable one. It was a good day.

After dinner, and a cake, and the briefest of valedictory speeches extruded from Rebecca under great duress, Rachel helped Doug to load the dishwasher, and they sat with the doors to the garden open, watching the children play. Her father, who had been quiet all day – but he was always quiet, there was nothing different this time, there was nothing – her father gave a yawn and rubbed his breastbone with one great gnarled hand.

'I'm just going to sort out a few bits in the front room. If you don't need me for anything?' He looked to his wife, who was sitting finally; her labours ended, the homage she felt due to her satisfactorily paid.

'Go on, so.' Her smile was kinder than her tone.

'He'll doze off, now,' she said when the door had shut behind him. 'Wait 'til you see.' Nodding sagely, as if this gave her some indefinable upper hand.

It was Rebecca who found him an hour later, going into the front room with his cup of tea. She did not scream, or even call out – that would not be her way, even without the instinct to avoid frightening the boys. Instead she came out quietly, closing the door behind her. She went straight to their mother. Margaret was sitting in the armchair at the end of the kitchen, her own tea long grown cold in her hand, her face weary and contented. Rebecca knelt at her feet.

'Mammy.'

She never called her this; neither of them did, not since they were very small children. Rachel had always hated the word, its mewling bleat.

'Mam.'

Only on the second utterance did her mother turn to look at her, and Rachel remembered this later and wondered if she knew, even then. If she was choosing to delay this news by the few seconds her slowness would buy her. God knows, she would not have blamed her.

'It's bad news, Mam. It's Dad.'

Rachel, standing by the counter where she was boiling the kettle for the umpteenth time that day, felt her legs suddenly lose their grip on the floor. Peter's hand moved instinctively to steady her, even while his body was turning to the closed door of the front room, as if expecting their father to come out and explain himself.

'I think Daddy has died, Mam.'

There was a noise in the room, a sort of general, muted gasp. Rachel heard it from behind her; she was already moving to the door of the front room. Perhaps he was not dead. Perhaps he was sleeping, only, the heavy, hard-won sleep of the old and frail. Or if he was dead, perhaps it was not too late, and his feeble heart could be brought back to life with the judicious application of mouth to mouth, of fingers to flesh.

She opened the door. He was sitting by the empty fireplace, his head resting against the high back of the armchair, his mouth slightly open. There was no colour in his face, and when she touched his cheek with the back of one trembling hand, it was cold and dry. He was dead; indisputably, definitively so. Rachel made a soft, strangled noise, an animal in distress, and turned to bury her face in Peter's chest.

~

She steels herself, finally, to ask. 'How is Tom?'

There is a pause before Bernie answers, and when she speaks her voice is very measured.

'He's all right. Much better, overall, than – than what he was.'

She pauses again, and Rachel forces herself not to interject.

'He's very quiet. He lives quietly, I mean. He doesn't really go out.'

'It's still early days, I suppose.' It has been seven years; she does not need to count.

'True, true.' Bernie sighs, unconvinced. 'And he seems happy enough, really. Joe likes having him around, they watch the matches together.'

'That sounds good.'

'Did you want to talk to him, love?' There is fear in her voice; she will acquiesce, if that is what Rachel wants, but she does not think it is wise.

'No. No. Just tell him – tell him I wish him well.'

'I'll do that, pet. You take care of yourself, now. And I hope everything goes well for you.'

And Rachel is so touched by this unsought benediction that her eyes sting with tears, and she forces a bright smile onto her face as she says goodbye, so that Bernie will be able to hear it in her voice.

BEFORE

Four Hours

Not Long Now

The drive to Bernie and Joe's is long enough as it is, but there is a lay-by with a tiny play area just over the Wicklow border that they made the mistake of stopping at once, and now the kids clamour to pull in every time they make the trip. Rachel doesn't mind; it is a bright day, though cold even for March, and for once they are not running late. When she turns in and switches off the engine, theirs is the only car there. They tend to share the driving, herself and Tom, on these trips – Rachel likes to do the outward leg, and then have the option of a snooze on the way back.

The children fall out of the car, coats streeling open, already running before they hit the ground. They race for the wooden slide; their son trails behind his older sister, but every day the gap is closing. It is only in the last month or so that Rachel has become able to stand at a distance while they play, that the need to hover over her youngest has dissipated; he has in recent weeks gained a sturdiness that allows her to sit on a playground bench with a coffee and supervise from a distance while he follows his big sister around. It feels like a milestone of sorts.

Today there is no coffee, and no bench either, so instead she and Tom hunker on one of the piles of artfully placed logs that are dotted around, each just a shade too low for comfort. She huddles into him, hoping for an arm around her shoulders.

234

He looks down at her. 'You cold?'

'A bit.'

But almost immediately he is distracted.

'Is he all right on that? Look.' He points to the top of the slide, where their son is pulling himself laboriously up to stand.

'He's fine. Look at him, he's being so careful.' She hears the unrestrained fondness in her voice, and wonders if to other people it sounds cloying. She does not really care if it does.

Tom is worried still. 'It's very high.'

'It's good for them, apparently. A bit of risk.'

'Right so.' He looks at her then, with the faintest of smiles, and she rolls her eyes.

'Indulge me. And my new-age ideas.'

'Don't I always?'

For a minute it is like it used to be.

Then the children's voices lift in some sudden and furious altercation, and immediately Tom is on his feet.

'Tom.' She says it softly, but he understands, and stops where he is. They watch for a moment; the argument is brief, if heartfelt, and within a minute or two they are co-operating on the seesaw again. Tom stays standing, though, his eyes unreadable. Really it is too cold to squat on the ground; Rachel stands too, and stamps her feet, and pushes the cuff of her jacket back to peer at her watch. Two more minutes, that will have to be enough for them. Bernie gets querulous if they are late, which they frequently are, and will refer to it all afternoon in what she thinks is an oblique manner.

Her son calls her to lift him into the swing, and she hoists him above the seat and down again, pushing his unco-operative feet through the gaps. He is almost too large for this contraption, designed really for wobbly toddlers who have not quite found their legs. She pushes him higher and higher, his delighted laugh breaking the air. She remembers the joy of it, the sensation of flight; how, older of course than her children are now, she would push herself off at the height of its arc and soar for a moment before plunging to the ground. All of that is ahead of them.

Two minutes on the swing is enough for her son, and he clamours to be let out again. She lifts him down, and he runs back to the slide, where his sister has set up camp at the top. Rachel trudges back to where Tom is still standing. There is a sudden breeze, and the bark underfoot stirs and settles again. It is quiet here, the only noise the low hum of cars out on the dual carriageway. Tom shifts his weight from foot to foot, and she wonders if he is impatient to be on the road again. He is still his mother's son.

'We'll make a move in a minute.'

'Yes. Yes.' His voice is slow, ponderous, and he does not turn.

'You all right?' She places a hand on his arm.

He looks around then, lifting his own hand briefly towards her, and then letting it drop away.

'Fine.' There is a pause, and then he speaks again. 'It's all going to work out, isn't it?' It is a question, and yet he does not say it like a question.

'What do you mean?'

But he does not answer, and so she gives the only response that seems possible.

'Yes. Tom. Yes, of course. Everything's going to be fine.' She smiles, wondering a bit; but oh, the relief at this new calmness that has come over him. She can be patient.

She looks at her watch again.

'We'd better . . .' She raises her voice. 'Come on, guys.'

They do not respond, of course; she had not really expected them to, but when she lifts her son from the seesaw his protest is brief and perfunctory, and her daughter takes Tom's hand as she prances along beside him to the car. Tom buckles her in, taking his time with the seat belt, testing the strength of it with his large, capable hand. She gives a wriggle of childish delight, and leans forward to Rachel, who is settling back into the driver's seat.

'How much farther to Granny's?'

Rachel looks pointlessly at her watch. 'Not long now,' she says, rounding down. 'Twenty minutes.'

Her daughter gives a satisfied nod and settles back into her seat, looking out the window. Rachel clicks her seat belt in and turns the car slowly to nose back onto the main road. Tom has his eyes closed already; his head is tilted back in the seat, as if he plans to sleep. She pauses, waiting for an opening in the traffic, and looks in the rear-view mirror, finding her son's eyes waiting for hers. Rachel lifts her left thumb firmly in his direction, their private shorthand since he was old enough to raise his own pudgy fist in response, and is rewarded with the slow honey of his smile.

AFTER

Ten Years

A Solace

It is still cold; it is only March, after all, but there's a hint of something balmier in the air, a promise of spring. Rachel parks the car just beyond the tall black gates and sits for a minute. It's quiet here. A weekday morning; not, she supposes, a typical time for lots of visitors, unless it is a day with particular significance.

The baby stirs in the back, a tiny whinny of some infant dream, and Rachel holds her breath until he is quiet again. There is a mirror above his car seat, in which she can see his sleeping face reflected; his neck tilted back, the snub of his little nose pointed to the window and the sky beyond.

∽

The baby has been hard-won. Rachel thinks now of her calm assumption that things would happen smoothly for her, that what had been simple and uncomplicated before would prove so again. But she had reckoned without the intervening decade, the changes wrought by time and the impact of Peter's greater age – although on this last point there had been an unsatisfying lack of clarity, a general shrug from the doctors who seemed to assume it was much more likely to be a problem with her. And in the end it had happened naturally, just as they were about to

238

embark on the expensive raft of tests and procedures that they were both dreading; they were at least spared that.

But still, it had been a long twelve months of trying, rewarded with a pregnancy that was full of tiny complications – none of them, ultimately, leading to any real problems for the baby, but just an accumulation of little stresses that seemed to suck the joy and anticipation out of the whole period. Or maybe it would have been like that anyway, even if everything had been straight-forward; maybe that was just what it was like, to have a baby in your forties. 'Geriatric pregnancy' was the official term, the consultant had told her with an apologetic laugh, though Rachel had not really found it funny.

Still. He is here now, and he is perfect. Some days she still cannot believe it.

To the surprise of no one, Peter has turned out to be an excellent father. Everything is a delight to him, every noise and movement and emission of this tiny human he has helped to create is a source of daily wonder and joy. Rachel is trying to train herself out of the impulse she has to apologise when Peter is the one to get up with the baby in the morning, or when she hands him over as soon as her husband comes through the door at the end of a long day. Because she is realising that Peter truly does not mind, that he finds real privilege in the ability to tend to his infant son's simple, unrelenting needs. She does not know if this will last – probably not, it will surely all become workaday to Peter at some stage; it is not possible to live life indefinitely in this heightened state of emotion. But for now, for as long as it lasts, she will take it.

There are other things, that linger on. Rachel still does all the driving, when they go out as a family; Peter accepts this, and does not ask. Sometimes she wishes he would challenge her on it; it might make it easier, to be forced to defend this unreasonable policy of hers, to be made to articulate the things he already understands. She knows she needs to work on this; her counsellor has led her to the conclusion without ever seeming to say anything concrete. If this is to be Peter's only experience of fatherhood – and she senses it will be, without them having really discussed it – it would not be fair of her to let it be diminished for him.

~

She lets herself out of the car, and goes to the rear door, and removes the baby's car seat from its cradle, the tilt and lift automatic to her again now. He is getting heavy; a few more weeks and it will no longer be comfortable to carry him like this. She will dig out her old baby sling again; it is there, somewhere, in the attic of the new house, in one of the few boxes of such things she has kept. The new house; it is still the new house to her, nearly two years on. It is a big suburban semi, the new place; much more like her first home, her home with Tom, than the terrace in Stoneybatter, although not like enough that she is seized with unwelcome bouts of *déjà vu*. And it has a big garden where the sun shines most of the day, and neighbours who are friendly and incurious. Rachel is happy there. Although sometimes she finds herself missing the old sash windows of the Stoneybatter house, the small, low-ceilinged rooms.

The sun is bright, and she pulls up the cover to block its rays from the baby's sleeping eyes, and goes through the gate and along the central path. The graves here are the older ones, although none are very ancient; it is a newish cemetery, this, and even the earliest inscriptions date only from her grandparents' generation.

At the end of the first section she turns off the path and walks along a narrower one to the drystone wall, and turns again. There are big, shady trees here, much older than the bodies they watch over, and she thinks of when this must have been some farmer's field, with cattle lowing mournfully under a darkening sky. Back when this was not Dublin at all, but countryside, and the bright lights of a much smaller city still a distant beacon.

The plot is on the end of a row; the last row, when Rachel picked it, but now there are others beyond, stretching almost to the next cross-cutting pathway, and there is some curious comfort in this, the evidence of life and death churning ceaselessly on. She sets down the car seat – he is still sleeping; it is an enviable gift, the uncomplicated sleep of very tiny babies – and turns his face away from the sun. The flowers she has brought are in the crook of her other arm. She lays them down, now, at the foot of the light grey marble, and settles herself cross-legged to one side. She had started doing yoga again, before the baby, and she takes pride in her ability to sit like this still, although getting up again often involves a click of some indignant joint, or an involuntary grunt of effort.

'Hello.' She keeps her voice low, although there is nobody around; she does not find it quite natural, to talk to them like this, although not to speak seems wrong too. She stills herself and listens, but there is only the breeze, which is light against her face.

Rachel notices for the first time the other flowers; not the ones she brought the last time, dry and faded now, but a fresh bunch of tulips, a flare of red deepening to purple at the tips. Her mother, perhaps; or more likely Bernie, who still comes, she knows, although the drive is long and her eyesight is not what it used to be. She finds herself touched that someone else has remembered the day.

She feels a soft vibration, deep in her pocket, and a moment later her phone starts to ring. She fishes it out and glances at the screen before silencing it. She will call him back. The baby has stirred with the noise of the phone, and she watches as he gives three slow, deliberate blinks before opening eyes that are very blue. He looks about him, and finds her face, and smiles.

'Hello there.'

Rachel leans forward and places the back of one finger against his silken cheek. It is an impossibility, the softness of that skin.

A bird calls, long and low, somewhere overhead. Rachel looks at her watch. He is quiet for now, the baby, staring intently at a single cloud that drifts slowly across the watery sky, but she knows that soon he will become restless and start to kick, his unending needs never more than a moment away. She turns back to the grave. She sees that there are the beginnings of one or two weeds, brought into life by the longer days and the weak heat of the sun, and she grips these now and tugs them from the earth, roots and all, in one satisfying pull. She tosses them to the side. Rachel kneels then, and with one slow forefinger traces the letters of her children's names on the headstone; the firm downstrokes, the smooth and undulating curves.

They are not here, her children, not any more. She finds them elsewhere, sometimes; in the first smiles of her baby son, and the way his hair curls after a bath. They are in the high teen-age voices of other children, girls the age her daughter would be now, with their gossamer clothing and their eyes lined in black uncertain rings. Her son she finds sometimes in the gangs passing home from the primary school at the end of the road, the shove and snigger of them, the new unchildlike smell. And sometimes she sees them in her own face, as she stares into the mirror after a night of broken, milk-damp sleep, and counts the new lines around her eyes.

And, she supposes, they are with Tom too. And she hopes that this is a solace, and not a haunting. She would not wish that for him.

~

As she leaves the cemetery her phone rings again, and this time she answers it, cradling it between her cheek and her shoulder as she fits the car seat back into its base. The baby looks up at her with his big, solemn eyes, and she kisses his nose before she shuts the door.

'Peter.'

'Hi. I just wanted to see how you're getting on.'

'I'm fine. Just getting back into the car now.' She waits for a tractor to rumble slowly past, its driver lifting three fingers in a lazy wave, and steps around to the car door.

'Sorry, I don't mean to be disturbing you. Stay as long as you need.'

'No, it's fine.' The noise of the tractor fades as she closes her door. 'I'm finished here now.'

'Are you all right?'

'I am, I think.' She clicks her seat belt into its socket, and reaches to adjust her mirror.

'OK. I love you.'

'And you. Will you be late home?'

'No, with a bit of luck. Might even be early.'

'Great.' It is a Friday; tonight they will order a takeaway for dinner, and watch eight or nine trailers for different things before settling on an episode of an old American sitcom they have both seen several times before. The baby will doze all evening on one or other of their chests, and go to bed when they do.

'How's himself?'

And she looks back at her son, at the mirror framing his little face, the honeyed cheeks and the precious bud of his mouth, and the fear that will always be a part of her jostles noisily with the joy of him, the wonder of his very existence, and it is getting closer to being a fair fight.

'He's perfect.'

Peter laughs. 'Isn't he just.'

She puts the phone into its cradle, and starts the car.

'You're driving. I'll let you go.'

'Talk to me for a bit. If you've time?'

'I do.' She hears the low rumble of wheels on a wooden floor, and knows that he has pushed his chair back from his desk, and is propping his feet among the piles of paper strewn across it. She pictures his smile.

'Go on, so. I like the sound of your voice.' She indicates, and makes a careful turn into the sun.

ACKNOWLEDGEMENTS

An email from Julia Silk, in the early summer of 2023, changed my life. Her immediate and unflagging enthusiasm for this story was a literal dream come true, and was mirrored by her colleagues Sam Edenborough and Maria Brannan at Greyhound Literary Agency. I feel very lucky to have them all in my corner.

Thank you to Ansa Khan Khattak, my editor, whose quiet confidence in the book at every stage of the process has been incredibly heartening. Thanks also to Nico Parfitt, Juliette Winter, Louise Court, Olivia French, Rose Cook, Helen Parham, Richard Rosenfeld and everyone else at Sceptre and Hodder & Stoughton who brought this project safely down the long and winding road to publication. Huge thanks to Elaine Egan and the whole team at Hachette Ireland for their boundless energy and enthusiasm. Thank you particularly to Natalie Chen for a cover that I love more and more every time I see it, and to Niall McDiarmid for the use of his beautiful and arresting photograph.

Although the internet is a godsend to a lazy researcher like me, there are times when there is simply no substitute for being able to run something by an expert in their particular field. Thank you to Kieran O'Loughlin for the psychiatry, to Marion Berry for the law, and to Adraian Tonito for the Spanish. Any errors or inaccuracies are, of course, my own.

Ireland has a well-deserved reputation for its support of the arts, and one of the biggest boosts to my writing came in 2021, when I was awarded a Words Ireland literary mentorship with the wonderful writer Henrietta McKervey. This novel is undoubtedly stronger for her keen eye and her considered advice in its early stages. Being chosen as a runner-up in the Irish Writers' Centre Novel Fair in 2023 was another huge encouragement as I prepared to send the book out into the world.

They say you should never ask family or friends for advice on your writing, as they'll be too nice about it and won't give you anything helpful. In Paul Gleeson and Sarah Baxter I have been blessed with siblings who – although obviously very nice – are also keen readers, and have the gift of offering criticism in a way that is both encouraging and very useful. Laura Henderson and Alita Byrd also provided valuable feedback on earlier work, for which I am very grateful. My parents have been unfailingly supportive in this endeavour, as they have been throughout my life, and I can never thank them enough.

To Kate, Luke and Henry, for the boundless joy they have brought to my life, and all they have taught me. And for sleeping just enough to allow me to get a novel written (and not a second more).

Finally, to John, who brings me more true happiness than I could ever find the words to do justice to, and who told me once, on the deck of a boat on our honeymoon, that he knew I'd do it someday. This, as everything else, is for you.